Sword Beach

Book 6 in the

Combined Operations Series

By

Griff Hosker

Published by Sword Books Ltd 2016
Copyright © Griff Hosker

The author has asserted their moral right under the Copyright, Designs, and Patents Act, 1988, to be identified as the author of this work.
All Rights reserved. No part of this publication may be reproduced, copied, stored in a retrieval system, or transmitted, in any form or by any means, without the prior written consent of the copyright holder, nor be otherwise circulated in any form of binding or cover other than that in which it is published and without a similar condition being imposed on the subsequent purchaser.
A CIP catalogue record for this title is available from the British Library.
Cover by Design for Writers

Contents

Sword Beach i
Prologue 2
Chapter 1 6
Chapter 2 17
Chapter 3 32
Chapter 4 50
Chapter 5 56
Chapter 6 68
Chapter 7 84
Chapter 8 96
Chapter 9 104
Chapter 10 111
Chapter 11 121
Chapter 12 132
Chapter 13 146
Chapter 14 164
Chapter 15 172
Chapter 16 184
Chapter 17 195
Chapter 18 205
Chapter 19 216
Chapter 20 226
Epilogue 237
Glossary 239
Maps 241
Historical note 242
Other books by Griff Hosker 247

Dedicated to my little sister, Barb, and in memory of my dad who served in Combined Operations from 1941-1945

Prologue

October 1943

This was my first leave in a long time. I could not remember the last one. The journey north from Southampton had given me time to reflect on the war in Sicily and Italy. We had lost men in the landings, especially the crew of our captured E-boat, *'Lucky Lady'*. I doubted that I would see her crew any time soon and that was sad. The war meant that goodbyes were a luxury. I was just grateful that I had kept my section together and largely intact. I knew that had been more luck than anything else. machine-gun fire was indiscriminate; it killed the brave as well as those who hid in the sand.

The Company Sergeant Major Dean had intimated, when he picked us up from the Sunderland aircraft, that there was another operation in the offing. Lieutenant Colonel Dawson, the commanding officer of Number 4 Commando, had insisted that my section be given leave. That was always an ominous sign. Leave was a perk doled out when danger was imminent. I would use the ten days I had been given wisely. I would appreciate this land for which I fought. It might be autumn but I would walk the lanes and enjoy the flurry of leaves whirling around. I would go to the pub and listen to the *Old Contemptibles* as they complained about the way the young generation were fighting this war. Most of all I would spend time with Mum. Mum was the rock in our home. While Dad had been here there and everywhere it was Mum who had been our constant companion while growing up. She was doing the same still. Mary was now a ferry pilot and doing her bit for the war. While Dad and I fought our wars Mum looked after the home and waited for us to return. She was delighted to see me as Dad was still in the

Mediterranean. It seemed they couldn't win the war in the air without him. It left Mum at home, on her own worrying about all of us. The hug she gave me standing in the hallway with an October gale slamming doors shut, was held longer than ever. I felt her pressing her face into my chest.

"I am so glad you are safe!" When she stepped back to look me over I saw the hint of a tear in her eye. She smiled and shook her head. "I must be getting soft in my old age."

"You are not old, Mum."

She shook her head, "I feel old. Now come on in. Leave your bag there. We'll go and have a drink to celebrate." She took my arm to lead me to the lounge and then stopped, suddenly, "How long?"

We both knew what she meant. I smiled, "They have given me ten days!"

"That is good but we both know that you will be back in the thick of it soon enough." As she plonked me in Dad's armchair, she suddenly noticed my new rank. "Captain Harsker now! Well done, you!"

I nodded, "Not bad for a ranker!"

As she handed me my whisky, she admonished me, "You were down for Officer Training and you chose that route."

"I know. I am just saying I never expected to be promoted."

"You are just like your dad. He was always too modest. The pair of you are like peas in a pod. So, where have you been?"

"You know I can't tell you the details, Mum."

"I don't need the details. You are brown as a berry so I am guessing somewhere hot."

I sighed. Mum would have made a great inquisitor! "North Africa, Sicily and Italy, and that is all I can tell you." In truth, I was not telling her anything that she couldn't learn from the newspapers.

"And now you are home. If you give me your ration book we will nip to the village and get the shelves filled. There isn't much in the pantry at the moment. Still, we have the veg from the garden and Old Jack brought me a couple of bunnies yesterday. We will have them for dinner."

The thought of one of Mum's homemade rabbit stews with vegetables from the garden made me feel like I was home. I helped her prepare the vegetables and we chatted in the kitchen. I enjoyed her tales of village life and the garden. She pointed to birds as though they were old friends and addressed them by name. That was Mum.

When we came to eat she opened one of the precious bottles of wine we had left from before the war. Not having had a good drink for a while meant that Mum had to help me to bed. I was transported back twenty odd years. It felt good.

The leave flew by. It always did. Mum and I went for long walks down leaf-filled country lanes. I helped her to tidy the garden. We sorted out things from my room; with a war on others could make good use of what we might have put in the dustbin before. I read newspapers and their propaganda. If you believed all that you read it was a wonder we were not in Berlin already. Still, it gave me a view of the war from a civilian's perspective. One day we even travelled up to town to look in the shops. We enjoyed the fish and chips. It was one of the few things not rationed and as such a treat to be enjoyed. As we stood in the queue a couple of teenage girls giggled and gossiped. Mum smiled. As we walked down the cold streets, steam rising from our vinegar-soaked chips, she said, "Those two girls were talking about you."

"Mum! They were not!"

"Tom, you and your dad know war and fighting but you have not the first idea about women. How I got your father to marry me I will never know! He just couldn't take a hint! You are a good-looking young man; they found you handsome. You have a smartly cut uniform. If you had a moustache you could pass for Errol Flynn or David Niven."

"Now you are being ridiculous!"

She sighed, "I just hope one comes along soon!"

"One what?"

"A girl of course! Someone to grab you by the scruff of the neck and sort you out. I have done all that I can!"

Two days before I was due back Mum had a letter from Dad. I went for a walk in the garden to allow her some privacy while she read it but she came hurtling out after me. "Why didn't you tell me?"

"Tell you what, Mum?"

"That you had been put up for the Victoria Cross!"

"It slipped my mind and besides I might not get it."

She hugged me and said, thickly, in my ear, "I am so proud of you and yet so annoyed at the same time." She stepped back with tears coursing down her cheeks. "Proud because you are a hero and annoyed because being a hero means you might get killed. I don't want to lose you, Tom. I want to bounce your babies on my knee and help your wife to make cakes!"

"But I haven't even got a girlfriend!"

"Exactly! You were too serious as a boy. Too concerned with studying. If we had known the war was coming then we might have encouraged you to have a girlfriend or something. Remember your aunt. She had the love of her life taken from her. You have not even met a girl yet. Be less of a hero, please, for me! Come out of this madness alive. When this is over no one will remember what you did in Italy or Sicily or wherever it was. Survive!"

**Part 1
Pas de Calais**

Chapter 1

"Morning, Sir! Good to see you back. I'll have your bags taken down to the digs for you."

"Thanks, Sergeant Major Dean. Is anyone else back yet?"

"No Sir. It is just the skeleton staff: cooks, Quartermasters, armourers. The Brigade won't be back until November. It is just your section. You have the run of the camp to yourselves."

"Who is in command here now then?" The Colonel would be with the Brigade.

"The adjutant is Major Rose. He isn't here yet." He went over to the door. "Do you want a cuppa, sir?"

"That will be perfect, Reg!"

"Larkin, a cup of tea for the captain. Drop of milk and no sugar!"

I sat in the spare seat. "How is Mrs Bailey, sorry, Mrs Dean, Reg?"

He beamed, "Happier now that I made an honest woman of her. She has missed you and the lads. She will be like a mother hen again now that you are all back."

I noticed a map of the Channel pinned to the wall. Pointing to it I said, "Invasion?"

He shrugged, "The papers are full of it and every man and his dog in the pub has an opinion. We have heard nowt sir but the Major has to go to London once a week for a briefing. He put a map in here and one in his office. I daresay he will tell you when he arrives."

Private Larkin came in with the tea. Reg growled, "And where is mine?"

"Sorry Sarn't Major, you didn't say and... I'll get one now."

The young private fled and Reg shook his head. "God help us when sprogs like that have to go against Jerry!"

I laughed, "We were all like that once, Reg. He'll do all right. The bad apples are few and far between. They soon realise that the Commandos isn't somewhere you can hide." I sipped the hot tea which was almost black. It was reassuringly strong. Standing I went to the map and ran my finger down the coastline. "Hitler has built a strong line of defences here. It isn't the same place we raided in forty-one."

"You are right there sir." Larkin came back and put the tea down. Reg sipped it. "What was it like in Sicily and Italy?"

"Not as bad as it will be here." I tapped France. "The Italians gave up soon enough and that caught Jerry with his pants down. France is occupied and that famous Atlantic Wall is made of concrete. The hardest thing we had to face in Italy was wire and a few mines."

The door behind me opened and Major Rose stood there. He was a short, neat man and at least ten years older than I was. "Thought I heard voices." He held out his hand, "You must be Captain Harsker. Heard a lot about you." He shook my hand, " Harry Rose, adjutant for my sins." He tapped his right leg. "No more active duty for me; a bad landing. Hate parachutes! Still, at least I am still part of this war. Come next door. Tom isn't it?" I nodded, "A cup of tea for me eh Sergeant Major."

"Yes sir."

He took me through to his office. I carried my tea with me. As he sat down he took a pipe from a rack and began to clean it out with a penknife. "Your name is well known in Whitehall you know. Winnie himself mentioned you in one meeting. Said you were the sort of chap we needed. High praise indeed and now I hear you are in for a Victoria Cross. Well done old chap, well done!" Larkin brought the Major's tea. "Thanks, Larkin." He began to fill his pipe. "Can't start the day without a pipe full of Baby's Bottom and a cup of the Sergeant Major's tea." He proffered the pouch of tobacco.

"No thank you, sir, I don't. But I know the tobacco. Made by Dunhill, isn't it? My granddad liked it."

"A very restful habit. Cigarette then?"

"No sir, I don't have that habit either."

"Dear me. You aren't a monk, are you? You do drink."

Laughing I said, "Yes sir. I enjoy a good red wine and whisky too."

"Thank the lord for that I was beginning to worry. Then tell me how do you control your nerves if you don't smoke?"

"I'm not sure I suffer from nerves, sir. I don't see the point in worrying. If you have a problem you deal with it. Worrying never gets you anywhere. When they send my section in we know that there will be problems. We just deal with them."

He had his pipe going and he leaned back in his seat. "I think I understand you a little better now. It is no wonder you get to go behind the lines so often. Between the two of us, I think the brass have a little trip behind German lines planned soon."

"Pas de Calais sir?"

His mouth dropped open, "How in God's name did you know that?" I gave him what I thought of as my enigmatic smile. "It is hush, hush. Even I was only told two days ago and I haven't told a soul."

"Call it an educated guess. Before we were sent to Italy and Africa it was where we did most of our work. It is the closest part of the Atlantic Wall to England."

"Good guess. Yes, well, that's all I know but as soon as your chaps arrive you and I will pop up to London for a briefing. I would make the most of these little jaunts if you enjoy them. I think that the powers that be would like to use Commandos as regular soldiers now. An elite unit but used in larger numbers."

"Yes sir, we saw that in Sicily and Italy. They did a damned fine job."

He looked relieved at my comments. "Good, good. And the other new units will use Bren Guns and Lee Enfields."

I said nothing for I remembered Dad breaking the rules in the Great War by using weapons he found useful. I would still use my Luger, Colt and Thompson even if I was issued with standard weapons. I knew that using weapons we were familiar with could only increase our efficiency.

He looked up from his pipe, "Is that to your liking, Tom?"

"If that is what we are issued then we will use them. I think the Colt and the Thompsons were damned fine weapons and they never let me down. The rate of fire came in very handy more than once. The Lee Enfield is a good weapon but it has a slow rate of fire."

"But we can't issue them to every Commando."

"How about captured Werke Maschinenpistole? They are just as good as the Thompson."

"German weapons! Have you gone mad?"

"They don't jam and they have a good rate of fire. I would have one in a flash."

"You are a rum bugger! I look forward to watching you in action. Anyway, the issue of new weapons is some time off. Get yourself sorted and when your men arrive set up a training programme and we will pop up to London."

I sought out Daddy Grant. He was the Quartermaster and had been my sergeant when I had been corporal. "Daddy, what do you think about the new weapons?"

He smiled, "I knew you would be in sir. Don't worry. I have stashed away some gear for you and the lads. It is just that we can't issue it in the open. I will see your sergeants when they land. The rest of the Brigade are coming back soon. I would make sure you have what you need before then."

"Thanks, I will see the chaps as soon as they arrive."

He handed me one of the assault vests I had seen in Sicily. "You might as well have this one now sir. They have been used for some time to replace the webbing. A bit easier to use I am told. You can hang grenades from it easier and it affords a bit more protection." He pointed to my Captain's pips. "Save your battle dress being damaged too much. Congratulations on the promotion sir. Well deserved."

"Thanks, Daddy."

I had paperwork to do before the section was due back from leave. When that was over I sketched out a training programme. As I had expected Sergeant Poulson and Sergeant Barker arrived back by noon and I explained to them what we would need to do to keep hold of our acquired weapons and equipment. They were both old hands. "I'll have a word with Reg Dean. There must be somewhere safe we could keep it at Mrs Bailey's."

"I am not certain, Gordy. He wouldn't want her in any danger."

"She won't be. I was thinking of something secure in the bottom of the garden." He shrugged, "You know the lads. They will keep their ammo in their bedrooms at the digs, sir."

I nodded, "Just make sure the other sections don't know about this." I handed them the sheet of paper on which I had scribbled my training programme. "I will be off to London with Major Rose. When I return I will have a better idea of our next operation."

"It is getting on to winter sir. Do you think we will be doing much?"

"If the whole Brigade is coming back then something big is in the air. Besides, we appear to have turned the tide a bit. We have North Africa and Sicily now. Half of Italy is in our hands. I reckon that the second front the newspapers are banging on about might actually be closer than we think. I know the U-boats are making life hard but on land and in the air we are winning. "

Sergeant Poulson said, "You are right there, sir. There was nowt to be had in the shops. I felt awful. I mean we don't go short, do we? Yet they have to scrimp and save. Make do and mend. When we need a new uniform we just get one. They don't. It doesn't seem right somehow."

"And it isn't. That's why I am happy for them to send us overseas anytime they like. If it brings the war to an end that bit closer then I am happy."

Sergeant Major Dean arranged for our travel warrants to London. I was now more accustomed with the journey from Falmouth to London. The Major was equally familiar. As soon as we boarded the London Express he headed for the restaurant carriage. "Might as well have a drink eh, Tom?"

I was beginning to realise that Major Rose enjoyed a drink. The carriage was filled with uniforms. They were all taking advantage of the bar. Before the war, this would have been packed with holidaymakers. Those days were a distant memory. Holidays by the seaside would have to wait until Europe was back in the hands of those who had a right to be there.

Despite the quantity of drink Major Rose consumed he appeared to be able to handle it. The only sign of the alcohol was a slight reddening of the cheeks. I made two drinks last all the way. We took a taxi to Whitehall. The meeting was in a nondescript, rather shabby building, tucked away from the main streets. The windows were covered with tape to stop bomb blast damage. Security was tight and the two military policemen examined our faces and passes carefully as we entered.

"If you gentlemen would wait in the lobby someone will be down to take you upstairs." They watched us like hawks while we waited.

It was a dingy lobby. The bulb that hung forlornly down was little better than a candle. The room had a musty damp smell.

Major Rose saw me wrinkle my nose, "You will get used to it old chap. They use any buildings which are still standing. The German bombers have destroyed many fine buildings. London will not be the same when this is all over. The war and all that."

"Captain Harsker! Good to see you again!"

I looked up to see Lieutenant Hugo Ferguson. I had last seen him in Sicily where he had been our liaison officer.

"What are you doing here?" My face fell, "Don't tell me, Major Fleming is here too?" My heart sank. I did not get on well with the ambitious and cavalier officer.

"Colonel Fleming, remember? Yes, he is here. We will be giving the briefing today. He is part of this operation. He is one of the planners." He led us towards a stairway. "How are the chaps? How are Alan and the crew of the *'Lady Luck'*?" When we had been in Malta and Sicily Hugo had got to know the crew well. It was as close as he ever got to action.

"*'Lady Luck'* was badly damaged. They are trying to rebuild her again. They lost the chief and some of the other crew, it was a rough operation. But my lads are fine. You are happy here?"

"Oh yes; this operation is big. Huge!"

The shabby door through which we entered did not prepare me for the enormous room which lay beyond. I guess they had knocked rooms through when they had taken over the building. Colonel Fleming sat at the head of the table, smoking. No one else was present. Hugo nodded to two spare seats and we sat. I saw a large map on the wall. It showed the coast from Holland down to Normandy. From the arrows, I could see I guessed that the invasion would take place in Normandy. That would be a long crossing!

The Colonel's voice made me start, "I trust, Captain, that you will keep this knowledge to yourself."

"Of course, sir."

"We are expecting a couple of guests this morning but I see no reason why we should not begin the briefing." He lit another cigarette. The smoke from that, allied to Major Rose's pipe, made it feel as though I was in a London fog.

"The Major knows the background to your mission but not the detail. We were still working on the plan last week." He stood, using a pointer to illustrate his comments." We will be invading Normandy, here. It will be next year. You're one of several teams sent over to make the enemy think that the Pas de Calais," he tapped the area across the Channel from Dover, "will be the intended target. " He stubbed his cigarette on the floor and lit a third. "Any questions so far, Captain?"

"We have been in that area a number of times, Colonel. Every time there are more defences. I am not certain of the value of such raids. We will need the skills of our Commandos when we invade."

"Since you were there last they have quadrupled!" He seemed almost pleased. "The strategy is working!"

It begged the question of how we were to achieve our aims given the size of the enemy forces.

"Now we have been clever about this. Although we are softening up the guns on the coast with the bombers we intend you and the other teams to attack the hinterland. It would be a logical strategy if we were intending to invade the Pas de Calais. Your team will be dropped behind enemy lines. Your targets will be bridges, roads and railway lines." He tapped four places some thirty miles from the coast.

"Sir, what about the French resistance? Surely they would be better placed for such operations."

"In theory, yes, Major Rose, however, some have been infiltrated and our radio transmissions intercepted. This is a method guaranteed to bring success." Colonel Fleming was driven by the need to succeed. His glory came at the expense of others. "Captain Harsker and his team will go in by Dakota and be picked up by sea."

I saw an immediate problem. "Sir, how do we coordinate the pick up? If radio transmissions are being intercepted, we can't use that method."

"Quite right, Captain. You were chosen because, even amongst commandos, you have shown great skill at evading the enemy. We will be giving you a time and a place with a secondary one twenty hours later."

Major Rose turned and stared at me. I saw questions in his eyes. I shrugged, "We have used this method before. I am still here." The way the Colonel had said it made it sound as though it was easy. It was anything but.

The door behind me opened. Colonel Fleming glanced over as a hand gripped my shoulder, "Tom, I heard you in the building. Thought I'd pop in and say hello."

I turned and saw Major Foster standing there. It had been the Major, then a Captain, who had got me into the Commandos. He had been seconded to the War Office before we were sent to Africa. I stood and shook his hand, "Haven't seen you in ages, sir. Things still going well?"

He nodded, "I am kept busy. Planning all this." Colonel Fleming coughed. "Anyway, I'm intruding. Perhaps I will see you later eh?"

" I hope so."

He nodded to Fleming who waved an irritated hand. After the door had closed the Colonel continued, "Your first mission will be in ten days. You and three of your team will be dropped behind enemy lines." He went to the map on the wall. "Here. Before you leave I will give you the maps and details. There is a railway which crosses the road. We wanted it destroyed. As it is only twenty miles from Calais and the coast you should be able to get back to the rendezvous with time to spare." He had never been behind enemy lines; he had no idea of the problems posed by such an escape. At least there would be only three of us I had to think about.

"Major Rose, you will ensure the rest of the Captain's team is kept in readiness for his return. There will be a second mission a week after the first."

I began to realise the importance of his plans.

"This is not a one-off then, sir?"

"No, Harsker. We have four such raids planned before the New Year. After that, you will get a respite." Ominously he left it at that. I deduced we would be doing something similar in the New Year.

The door opened and the Colonel sprang to his feet. Major Rose and I couldn't see who it was but if they were senior to the Colonel that meant they were senior to us. We stood to attention too.

The cloud of cigar smoke gave me an idea of the identity of one of the men. It was confirmed when the Prime Minister, Winston Churchill, appeared followed by the commanding, six-foot-tall figure of Lord Lovat. He was in charge of the 1st Special Service Brigade and as such the most senior officer.

The Prime Minister said, "Just a flying visit. I wanted to meet this young man I had heard so much about. Introduce us, Simon."

Lord Lovat, whom I'd met before, said, "Prime Minister, this is Captain Harsker. He's recently returned from Italy."

The Prime Minister put out a podgy hand, "Knew your father; commanded him after the Great War. A splendid fellow. I can see from your medals that you are a chip off the old block."

"Thank you, sir."

"Captain Harsker has been put forward for the Victoria Cross, Prime Minister."

"Just like your father. I have read reports about you. You are a killer. That's good; the Nazis are ruthless." When he said '*Nazi's*' the '*a*' seemed to go on forever. "We have to be as tough as they are. We can't play the game like gentlemen any longer. We are fighting thugs and we have to be as tough as they are." I nodded. "What do you and your chaps think of this Hitler Order?"

"They don't like it, sir. But we make sure we don't get caught. The Germans made a mistake with that order. It makes the men fight even harder. If you are going to be shot anyway then why surrender?"

"Precisely!"

Lord Lovat said, "You realise, Captain, that the role of the commandos is changing? Those who are in a position of power have deemed that we will become like regular troops soon."

I pointed to the map, "Surely sir, you will always need small groups to go behind enemy lines and cause havoc? Lawrence in the Great War showed how effective that could be. Remember the Spanish fighting Napoleon? They tied up much greater numbers of French troops with a handful of dedicated fighters." I took confidence from the Prime Minister's nods. "Do not throw the baby out with the bathwater, sir!"

That made the Prime Minister roar with laughter. "I have not heard that in a long time. Don't worry, Captain Harsker, you and Colonel Fleming think alike. Well, we must be off. Say hello from me to your father the next time you see him, eh?"

And then they were gone. I saw that Colonel Fleming had a wide grin on his face. It seemed we were to be bedfellows for some time to come. If the Prime Minister thought well of me then the Colonel would continue to use me as he climbed the greasy pole to General.

On the overnight train, travelling back to Falmouth, I could not sleep. Major Rose had consumed enough drink before we went to our compartment to be able to sleep sitting up. My mind, on the other hand, was filled with the problems and challenges of the mission. I studied the maps for the first operation. I was grateful that this first one, extraction apart, looked to be fairly easy. The railway bridge over the road was far enough from houses to suit us down to the ground.

It seemed I was to be on every raid while I would rotate my men. I already pencilled in the three whom I would take on the first raid: Sergeant Poulson, Corporal Fletcher and Private Beaumont. Whilst being the newest member of my section, Roger Beaumont was very clever and understood explosives. Scouse and Polly had shown themselves to be resourceful. Neither panicked no matter what problems manifested themselves.

Then I examined the maps. Getting to the target would be easy. A stick of four men could not drift far off course. The demolition of the bridge and railway line looked to present no problems. It was the extraction I did not relish.

The pick-up by a motor launch would be to the west of the Cap Gris Nez. There were cliffs there. We needed to abseil down them. That was difficult but not a problem. It was the journey there that would present difficulties. I realised we would need to use all the darkness which would be available once the demolitions went off. The manhunt would be on and we would be in danger. The fastest time we could make would be four hours. I doubted that we would have that luxury. I guessed we would be five miles short by dawn. I scanned the map and aerial photograph for a sign of cover. I found one; there was a copse at the edge of a field close to the cliff. I put the papers and maps back into the locked briefcase I'd been given. It was handcuffed to my wrist.

I listened to Major Rose snore as I planned the rest of the task I had been given. I would put Gordy Barker in charge of preparations for the other raids. He was experienced and would ensure that everyone knew what they were doing. The second raid was to be on a large railway junction to the north of the line. The RAF had hit it repeatedly but despite heavy losses, it continued to function. We would be more precise. We would destroy the points themselves; they would be harder to repair.

The third and fourth targets were going to be the most difficult as they were communication centres. They were just five miles from the coast. Our extractions there would be simpler but we would have more Germans to contend with. They could be messy operations.

I briefed the whole of the section on the first two operations. I did not tell them of their purpose. I knew I was being cold and calculating but if they were captured and tortured they could not give the details of the invasion away. I explained who I would be taking on the first two missions. Disappointment was on the faces of the others but that could not be helped. We spent the short time available to us working out how to make the most use of the explosives we would take. Private Beaumont had been going to go to University to study Engineering. Knowing how to make things made it even easier to work out how to destroy them.

Chapter 2

Our Dakota pilot, Flight Lieutenant Johnson, was new to this kind of clandestine venture. He had been part of the flight which took in the ill-fated paratroopers in the Sicily invasion. The losses there had shaken him. That showed on his face and the way he nervously puffed on his cigarettes. I wondered why he had been selected for this hazardous mission. Flying alone over occupied France was never easy. The airfield, not far from Southampton, was covered in Dakotas. They were all heavily camouflaged. I worked out what they would be needed for. Driving to the airfield we had seen vast camps being erected. I had guessed that they were for the troops who would be participating in the invasion. The Dakotas, I had no doubt, would take in the paratroopers who would drop behind enemy lines.

The Lieutenant ground out his cigarette. "Sir, I have never done this sort of thing before. We go in alone, is that right?" I nodded. "Drop you then we tootle off home?"

"Yes, Flight Lieutenant. So the closer to the target we drop the better for us."

He looked nervous as he puffed on another cigarette. "Thing is, sir, normally we have lots of other birds in the air. Finding the target is easy, we just follow my leader. This sounds a lot trickier."

Nodding I said, "We are twenty miles due east of Calais. You can use a compass and airspeed indicator. I think the flak from the guns will be a good indicator of our position. Have you a good flight sergeant?"

"Oh yes. Flight Sergeant Wilson was in the service before the war."

"Good. He will have a better handle on things. Don't worry. The others will get easier after this."

"Others, sir?"

"I'm guessing that having been given this one you will have other drops to make."

I smiled, my words had not been reassuring for the young pilot. As we went to get our chutes Scouse Fletcher shook his head. "Doesn't fill you with confidence does he sir?"

Polly shook his head, "Not everyone is a cocky Scouser who thinks he can get by with a cheeky smile and a bit of cheerful banter."

" If the army was made of lads from the Pool Sarge, the war would have been over long ago." He spread his arms, "I am one man! What can I do?" The other two laughed. Scouse was a one off. I was glad I had him with me.

Our Bergens were filled with explosives, detonators, and camouflage netting. Daddy Grant had advised us to hang onto them. They were being replaced by standard issue. We liked our Bergens. When the order came to exchange them my section had feigned innocence. Scouser had said, "Left them in Salerno, sir. I bet some thieving Pongo had them away, eh sir?"

The same thing had happened with the Thompsons and the Colts. Major Rose had shaken his head in disbelief." You chaps have been unlucky, most unlucky with your equipment."

Scouser had chirped, "Yes sir, it was all I could do to hang onto me skivvies!"

We climbed aboard at dusk. With just four of us and Flight Sergeant Wilson in the main cabin, it seemed like a huge empty space. While the aircrew ran through their pre-flight check the Flight Sergeant handed me my Bergen and said, "Excuse me, sir, would you be related to Group Captain Harsker?"

It was his old rank and I nodded," I am his son."

His face lit up. "A good pilot, sir. I served briefly under him but his name is a legend. I'll make sure we hit the drop zone." He spoke quietly "The Flight Lieutenant is a good pilot too sir. He just lost his way a bit when his brother brought it over Sicily. He is the best pilot in the squadron. Squadron Leader Markwell knows that. Between you and me, sir, I think this is a way to build his confidence."

That explained a great deal."Thanks, Flight. I appreciate your confidence."

He nodded, "It is like you are one of the family, sir. You grew up in the service. You understand." I did indeed. Even in peacetime, there was a bond in a squadron. Everyone relied on everyone else. The pilots couldn't do what they did without the aircraftmen. Everyone understood that.

When the doors closed the Dakota became a tomb. With just his own aircraft to worry about the pilot soon had us in the air. We blacked up as we headed east. We had checked our weapons and equipment more times than enough. We sat in silence. My men knew their business. I had no new ones to worry about. That would only happen when we lost men. It was my job to ensure that we lost no more Commandos. I ran through the plan in my mind. The door to the cockpit opened as Flight Sergeant Wilson emerged. He said nothing, he did not need to.

I rose and my men rose with me. I clicked my parachute on the rail in the centre and followed the Flight Sergeant to the door. As it began to open Polly checked my parachute and then tapped me on the shoulder. I turned and made sure that he was hooked on securely too. The red light came on when the door was opened. There was a rush of roaring air. Speech would be impossible. Flight Sergeant Wilson waved us forward. As I reached the door the red light changed to green and I stepped out into space!

No matter how many times I did this it was always a relief when the parachute blossomed open above me. I looked down to darkness. The flak which had assaulted us before Calais had now stopped and the skies were eerily silent. I opened my legs to look down at the ground. I was hoping for something which would give me a clue as to my position. I caught sight of the shiny rail which showed me that we were close to the railway. I headed for it by tugging on the cords.

As I drew closer to the ground I spied some open land. It looked like bombs had flattened a building of some description. I steered my parachute for it. I braced myself for the landing, flexing my knees and springing up to make an upright landing. I began to gather in my parachute. Taking out my dagger I slashed the cords. They would come in handy. I rolled up the parachute.

After taking off the webbing I jammed the chute into the Bergen. I discarded the webbing. That was a deliberate act. It would protect the local populace and show that we were the enemy and the saboteurs had come by air.

By the time I stored the canopy, the others had landed. I took out my Colt and fitted my silencer. They also tried to rid us of them. I took out the map and my compass. We were three-quarters of a mile from our target. With Sergeant Poulson bringing up the rear we set off.

One worry we had was traffic on the railway line. We had rubber-soled shoes on and I kept touching the rail to my right. The vibration from any train on the tracks would be transmitted to me. As soon as I heard traffic ahead I stopped. It meant we were close to the road. I edged towards the bridge which crossed the road. I had hoped it would be quiet enough so that we could have walked down without observation. The one car which passed appeared to be the only one and the road looked to be empty in both directions.

" Fletcher, Beaumont, lay the charges. The Sergeant and I will keep watch. Listen for a whistle."

Poulson and I slid down the embankment. The railway line ran north to south and the road east to west. I took the west while Sergeant Poulson took the east. Five minutes passed and then I caught the sound of an engine. I whistled and pressed myself into the shadows of the bridge. There was a curve in the road and the masked lights did not pick me up as it sped around the corner. It was a Kubelwagen. There was a curfew and any vehicles we saw were likely to be German army vehicles. When it had passed I whistled the all-clear. Ten minutes later Beaumont and Fletcher appeared and gave me the thumbs up. I went under the bridge to whistle Sergeant Poulson.

We now had to hurry. Private Beaumont had used fifteen-minute fuses. We ran along the road to the west. If we saw or heard anything we would dive into the ditches which bordered the road. We had only to use this main thoroughfare for six hundred yards and then we would take the small side road which led north. We were lucky. We managed to run down the main road unseen and we dived into the narrow side road. Five hundred yards up the side road the night was lit up by the explosion. We could not help but turn back to look. The bridge had been blown. Equally important was the fact that the road was also blocked

No one said a word although we all knew there would be a hue and cry as the Germans sought the saboteurs. We had to leave the road as soon as we could. I spied a field to the left. When the hedge became thin enough I led us through it. It was muddier than I would have liked. Our footprints would be easily seen. It could not be helped. We ran along the scrubby bushes which lined it. It was not a perfect cover but it would have to do. The going was much slower than we might have hoped. Suddenly I caught a flash of light ahead. I dived into the ground knowing the others would copy me. A German truck and an armoured car appeared just moments later. I waited until the sound of the vehicles receded then stood. We had to hurry and I risked the road. We ran as only commandos know how. We had to take cover in the ditch and the field which bordered the road twice but by my estimate, we made six miles in just over an hour. We had been lucky.

We stopped just half a mile from the darkened village which lay ahead of us. The way around it involved a long detour. I waved Scouse forward. He could scout better than anyone I knew. We gave him a start of thirty yards and then followed. I took my Colt out once more. I knew it was less than three hours to dawn. We had to be close to the coast by daylight. I hoped to be safely sheltered in the woods I had spied by dawn. Private Beaumont tapped my arm and pointed. Scouse was sheltering behind a corner. He turned and, putting his finger beneath his nose like a Hitler moustache, he held out three fingers; Germans.

Sergeant Poulson also had a silenced Colt. I pointed to Beaumont and signed him to watch our rear. When we reached Scouse I risked a look around the corner. There were three Germans and they had a Kubelwagen parked across the street. It was at a crossroads. The only way through the village was past this roadblock. The range was forty yards. At night that was marginal. Every moment we delayed increased the chance that we would be captured. I tapped Polly. He came forward. I aimed at the one to the left, and he was the one on the right. I hissed, "Fire!"

I squeezed twice and did not wait for the man to fall. I fired another two shots at the last man. All three were dead.

"Move!"

We ran to the Kubelwagen. Two of the Germans had two bullet holes, the last one three. The Colt was as reliable as ever.

"Put the bodies in the back. We head north. I'll drive."

The sound of the Kubelwagen starting seemed like an explosion yet it might be expected for it had been driven into the village by the Germans. I gave the others my amended plan as I drove through twisting and narrow side roads. "We will drive north of Boulogne and abandon the Kubelwagen. It will be missed. Then we head back to the woods. I want them looking north." We now had an advantage and I wanted to deceive the Germans and their search.

"Makes sense sir."

"What do we do with the bodies, sir?"

"Leave them in the vehicle."

Ironically driving the vehicle was safer than running. In the dark, our woollen hats looked like German field caps. We passed one vehicle heading south as we neared Boulogne. I raised my hand to wave to the driver as we passed.

"Next side road we take it!"

"There sir!"

I almost rolled the vehicle as I threw it to the left. It was a farm track. As soon as we stopped I jumped out. "Get your bags and let's go."

"Are we gonna booby-trap it, sir?"

"No Scouse. Too many civilians." We were skilled at laying booby traps.

We headed back down the track. Crossing the main road was nerve-wracking. It was just one and a half hours before dawn but we only had two miles left to run. Once we made the narrow side road I breathed easier. When I saw the woods looming up I knew that half of the danger was past. We still had to lay up during the day but we had done the most difficult part of it. All we had to do now was make the rendezvous with the launch.

We kept running on the hard roadway for as long as we could. When we entered the woods I looked for stones on which to stand. We wanted as little sign of our passing remaining. Forty steps in we found the tumble of rocks and used those. Finally, after four hundred more steps we found a clearing. When I dropped my Bergen my men knew we had reached our camp. We each took out our camouflage nets and spread them above the clearing. There was no sign of water, we would have to husband what remained. We had a long day and half a night to go.

"I will take the first watch. Three hours on. Scouse you'll be up next."

"Righto, sir. So far so good eh sir?"

Polly cuffed him on the back of the head." Don't jinx it! When you see Falmouth harbour then you can be a cocky little bugger again!"

"Sorry, Sarge, forgot!" My men were superstitious about such things. They knew that fate had a way of intervening just when you thought you had everything in hand.

They rolled up in their parachute canopies. They were almost as warm as a blanket and much lighter to carry. Soon they were all asleep and I rose to scout the perimeter. As I went I gathered dead dried wood. I made piles across the main path into the camp. The noise of their breaking would warn us of an enemy. Once I had scoured the outside I returned to the camp and ate some dried rations and washed them down with a little water. I spied a handful of blackberries which remained on the bushes. I picked and ate a handful. They were overripe and the juice spurted out. After dried rations the taste was exquisite.

Scouse had been right. Apart from the German checkpoint, the operation had gone as well as we could possibly have expected. We still had the extraction. I checked the maps. We had five miles yet to cover. The cliffs were just eighty feet high and we would be descending to rocks below. We knew they could not be mined. Getting out to the launch might be tricky. We might have to get our feet wet. However, I thought that the journey along the coast road would be the only serious obstacle

It was fifty minutes before the end of the watch when I heard the aeroplane. The sound of the engine told me that it was a spotter. They had found the Kubelwagen. I remained still and trusted to the netting. A pilot would be looking for men moving. They would see trees and foliage. I resisted the urge to look up as its engine drew closer. I would learn nothing. It receded and disappeared to scout further south.

I woke Scouse, "Your watch. A spotter just came over. I've laid dead wood on the paths in. They will warn you of any footfall."

"You get your head down, sir. I'll keep a good watch."

I went to a tree and relieved myself. Taking out my canopy I rolled into it and I was soon asleep.

I woke halfway through Sergeant Poulson's shift. Scouse was still asleep although Beaumont was awake. "Anything?"

"The spotter was back an hour ago."

I looked at my watch." Two hours until dark. We will give Scouse another hour and then we'll be ready to move. We will use the dusk to negotiate the woods. If we get to the cliffs early it won't hurt."

While we waited we reloaded our weapons. Now that we no longer had support for the Colt we would have to be creative. I managed to get fifty rounds for my Luger from the dead Germans. Although it had no silencer it was a good weapon. I packed the Colt and silencer in the Bergen and along with the Thomson. I would use a Luger if we had a firefight. Beaumont and Fletcher had two machine pistols with two magazines taken from dead Germans. We were adept scavengers.

Scouse had been up no more than ten minutes when we heard the sound of the engine. It was not far from where we had entered the woods. We grabbed our bags and cocked our weapons. Sergeant Poulson still had a silenced Colt. When we heard the sound of dogs followed by German voices we knew they had found us. I waved Scouse to the west. Sergeant Poulson would bring up the rear.

When they found the camp they would have confirmation that we had stayed there. There would be too much evidence to ignore and the dogs would have our scent. Then the net would begin to tighten. We ran but we avoided making any noise. The sound of the dogs told us that they had our scent. I knew, without turning, that they were closing with us. I turned and took out my dagger. Fletcher and Beaumont did the same. We saw the dogs hurtling towards us. There were four of them and they were huge Alsatians. Sergeant Poulson shot two with his silenced Colt but one leapt at me. I held out my left hand as it lunged. As I pulled my hand back, I drove my dagger through its brain. it made no sound as it fell. Scouse had managed to kill the fourth dog but his hand was bleeding; he had been bitten. German voices sounded in the distance. I saw Beaumont booby-trapping the trail leading to the dead dogs. We ran.

When we reached the edge of the woods we just ran across the road and into the field on the other side. It had animals in it. There was no cover. I spied, up the gentle slope, a low hedgerow; it was a boundary marker. We were halfway to it when the booby trap went off. It was followed by a fusillade of shots. They had suspected an ambush. Once we reached the hedgerow we lay down.

There was no more cover for half a mile. We would have to wait until dark. We watched as the grey uniforms burst from the woods and spread out with guns at the ready. Twelve Germans appeared and were led by a Feldwebel. He pointed left and right. His men hurried down the road. He and his two remaining men came to the hedge and used their bayonets to cut their way in. They examined the ground. The sun was setting in the west.

I heard another vehicle and the three men returned to the road. Two vehicles arrived, a German truck and an ambulance. I prayed for the sun to set faster. We dared not move while there was any light. The other three were lying in the dell below the hedgerow. I said quietly, "Couple of booby traps!"

Sergeant Poulson nodded. He and the others used the German hand grenades to make booby traps. It was unlikely that civilians would trip them here. The coast would be a restricted area. Already the Germans were spreading out across the field and heading for our position. I checked my watch in the fading light. The motor launch would be below the cliffs from eleven o'clock onwards. It was now five-thirty. We had time, perhaps too much time. The Germans were close enough now to smell; pickled cabbage and the smell of German cigarettes drifted over to us. As the light faded to black they were less than sixty yards from us. I risked moving. I slid down to the dell and waved the others to follow me. The ground was rising rapidly towards the cliff. It was also becoming much rougher; there were stones and uneven pieces of ground. I did not head directly for the clifftop. I wanted them to follow us. I saw a cowpat and I stepped in it deliberately so that they would be able to follow. I had seen them using torches to search for us. They were German soldiers and as such very methodical.

Suddenly the first booby-trap at the hedgerow went off and I heard shouting. There was a pop and night became day as a flare was launched. We had moved far enough from the hedgerow to be beyond its light and I hurried south. A second explosion brought machine-gun fire as they fired at shadows. When we reached the clifftop path I headed down it for twenty paces. By that time I had cleaned my shoe of the cowpat and left evidence on the trail.

"Walk backwards in your footsteps and leave the path. We will find somewhere below the clifftop to hide."

We moved backwards leaving as little sign of our passing as possible. I saw lights moving down the field. They were only shining their torches a short way ahead of themselves. They were looking for us and for booby traps. Scouse found some stones leading down to the cliff. It was almost a path but there was a sheer drop to one side. He waved me forward. This was a decision for an officer. A mountain goat would have found it easy and in daylight, with pitons and time it would not be a problem. This was night time and we were being hunted.

It was pitch black now and what we were doing was almost suicidal. One false move could bring us crashing down to the sea and rocks below. The Germans came to our aid. They fired another flare. We were below the clifftop and could not be seen but it lit up, albeit briefly, the cliff and the rocks. I saw the spit of rocks leading out to sea. We were at the right place. Just thirty yards ahead I saw a rock overhang and somewhere for us to shelter. If we could reach it without one of us plunging to our deaths. Stepping carefully along the almost vertical path I made my way to the overhang. I climbed over the top and moved under its protective ledge. The others tumbled in behind me. We all fitted in lying below the rocks but only just. I opened my Bergen and took out my rope. I closed the bag and returned it to my back.

Scouse hissed, "That was bloody dangerous, sir!" I nodded and held my finger to my lips. He nodded and began to bandage his hand, bitten by the dog.

Sergeant Poulson took out his rope. He returned his Bergen to his back. There were still four hours to go. Two snaking ropes would be a giveaway and we had to keep them inside our shelter. After a short time, I saw lights playing down the cliff. The German voices appeared and seemed to be just above us. The sound of the surf on the rocks below made it difficult to hear but I did catch the word, "Kommando!"

Another twenty minutes passed and then I heard a shout. They had found my track down the path. Peering over the large rock which gave protection to one side of our den, I saw lights heading down the path. There were still Germans above us. I could hear them talking.

Another hour passed and then the lights approached up the cliff again. They stopped and played their torches on the overhang. My face was blackened and beneath the rock. This time I heard the words as an officer barked out an order. "Weber, fire a burst at the overhang!" He sounded close enough to touch but I knew he was at least forty yards away on the cliff path.

The gun sounded loud but the bullets striking the rock were both louder and more dangerous. Shards of rock ricocheted around us. I felt one hit my back. No one behind me cried out. When the bullets stopped the air was filled with the smell of gun smoke. Torches played down the cliff as they looked for evidence. The silence was broken by the officer again, "You two, make your way along to the rocks. See if there are bodies."

Another voice pleaded, "We would have heard them, Lieutenant. They would have cried out when we fired. It is empty."

"I gave an order. Investigate! They must be somewhere!"

A third voice said, "Perhaps they fell off the cliff, sir!"

"Then where are the bodies? Just do it!"

I risked looking over the rocks. The two Germans were some yards away. The other soldiers played their torches before the feet of the two men so that they could see their way to reach us. I readied my Luger. We would sell our lives dearly. The Germans' first five steps took far longer than we had taken. It was a second soldier who initiated the disaster. He slipped and instinctively grabbed his comrade's arm. They both cartwheeled to the rocks below. Their screams startled some seabirds which took flight and then there was a splash as one hit the water and a splat as one hit the rocks.

A German voice snapped, "Two good men lost, sir! There is no one there!"

"I want men guarding this cliff until daylight!"

He must have left because I heard one German say, "Prussian idiot! Hans and Karl dead and for nothing!"

The voices receded and it was silent once more. I checked my watch. It was almost ten o'clock. When I turned I saw that we had not escaped unscathed, Poulson and Beaumont had both suffered cuts from the flying stones. Scouse was tending to them. It could have been worse, much worse.

At ten-thirty, I tied the end of my rope around the sturdy-looking rock. I would delay throwing the rope over until I knew the launch was there. They would not signal us, Scouse would signal them. I tapped Poulson's arm and pointed to his rope. Sergeant Poulson, now looking like Frankenstein's creature, found another rock for his rope. He tied it on and held the coils. Fletcher took out his Aldis lamp ready to signal.

Although it was pitch black we peered into the darkness trying to see the white bow spray which would show us the launch. It was sharp-eyed Fletcher who saw it; he waved at me. They were early! I nodded as he began to signal. I threw the end of my rope over the side of the cliff and watched it snake down. I had tied the rope so I would test it. I wrapped it across my back. The hardest part was stepping out because the Germans might still be looking over the edge. I saw no white faces as I did so and then I began to lower myself until my legs were horizontal. Sergeant Poulson threw his rope out. As my body bent to ninety degrees I looked up. I saw no German faces. I lowered my body until my legs were straight. Then I began to walk down; I could have bounced and done it in three drops but there might be Germans watching. Sudden movements would attract attention. I looked up and saw Sergeant Poulson as he descended. I then watched my feet rather than the clifftop.

Suddenly a flare lit up the sky. The game was up. They had seen either us or the launch. I flexed my knees and bounced outwards. I let the rope run through my right hand. As I came in again towards the cliff I bounced once more and then began to cross my right hand to arrest my descent. As my feet touched the wall again I saw I was just ten feet from the slippery rocks. I jerked my hand across my chest and I stopped instantly. My climbing instructor in Oswestry would have been proud. I walked the last ten feet. As I stepped away from the rope I saw the muzzle flashes as the Germans fired blindly into the dark. They were firing at the launch and not at us. I drew my Luger and aimed it at the cliff. I targeted a muzzle flash. Poulson landed next to me followed by Beaumont. My sergeant drew his silenced Colt and fired at the muzzle flashes.

"Beaumont, where is the launch?"

"Thirty yards offshore, sir. She is holding off."

"As soon as Fletcher arrives get into the water."

A flash of light was followed by an explosion thirty yards to my right as a grenade was thrown. Shrapnel whistled past my head.

"Just get into the water both of you! I will wait for Fletcher."

They both jumped in when Fletcher fell the last eight feet, landing awkwardly. I ran to him. His left arm was bloody. He had been hit by flying shrapnel.

"Twisted me ankle too, sir!"

I holstered my gun and put my arm under him. "Come on! The water is lovely!" I half-carried him to the water and jumped in with him. There was a series of explosions as more grenades were thrown from the clifftop. Where we had stood before was now a killing zone. I put my left arm under his chin and using my right arm sculled backwards. I had to hope that the crew of the launch had their wits about them. It was so black and the water so rough and choppy that they might not see us. The air was thick now with bullets as more Germans joined those who were firing at us. The launch's' Lewis guns replied.

I heard a voice above me. "Here, sir! To your left!"

I changed direction and a few kicks later my head banged into the wooden hull of the launch. Fletcher raised his right hand as I kept him afloat. Poulson and Beaumont pulled him up. My bag was now sodden and threatened to pull me under. Then arms reached down and began to haul me aboard. I was only halfway up when the launch spun and headed out of the deadly bullet-filled water. I was rolled unceremoniously onto my back.

"Cutting it fine again, sir!" Beaumont was grinning.

I nodded. "Fletcher is wounded!"

"I know, sir. He is with the Sick Bay Attendant. Sergeant Poulson is there too. His face is a mess."

I rolled onto my knees noticing the two dead Lewis gun crew. The launch's crew had also paid a price.

Once in the mess, I felt a little safer. The wooden walls would not keep out bullets but this way I would not feel as though they were aiming at me personally. I shrugged off my Bergen to check my men. Poulson had had his cheekbone laid open by flying rock. He grinned "Hope the ladies like a scar sir. The Sick Bay Attendant reckons it'll be a pearler!"

The Sick Bay Attendant said, "I will keep the stitches small but it will have to wait until I have looked at your oppo."

I helped him take off Scouse's battledress. Like Poulson the wound was deep. His arm had saved his life. Had the shrapnel hit his chest who knows the damage which could have been caused.

"Not as bad as I thought. You can leave them with me now sir." He cocked an ear. "I reckon the shooting has stopped now."

I took off my own sodden battledress and headed back on deck. The young lieutenant and his coxswain were at the bridge. "Glad you made it sir. Whoever came up with that as an extraction point wants his head looking at!"

"I think they chose somewhere without mines either on the beach or in the sea."

"They have them in the sea sir. We will pass the minefield in about a mile. It wasn't there last month. The Germans are getting sneaky."

"I think the landings in Italy have put the wind up Jerry. Thanks for coming for us."

He looked surprised. "Orders, sir."

"Orders didn't tell you to come as close to the rocks as you did." I pointed to the dead gun crew. "And your men have paid a price too. Just so you know me and my lads don't take it for granted."

I stayed on the bridge to one side as we negotiated the minefield. They were intended to deter larger ships and with four lookouts watching we made good speed as we passed through. The rain began not long after we left the field. I went below deck.

A Leading Seaman popped his head in the mess. "Cocoa, sir?"

"That will be perfect."

Fletcher and Beaumont were both asleep. Poulson had an enormous dressing on the side of his face. He tried to smile but winced when he did so. "Not a pretty picture, eh sir? We nearly got away with it."

I nodded, "Perfect right until the end. One positive is that the locals won't suffer. They will know now who did it. They will know it was the Commandos"

"Did we make a difference? I mean they can repair the bridge before we invade. They will probably make it stronger too."

I could not tell my sergeant that was the plan. His disappointment showed me that the strategy might actually work.

"You should know by now that we do little bits. We can't see all the other parts. We have to trust in the planners in Whitehall."

"I suppose so, sir. The Sick Bay Attendant said I ought to get my head down." He laughed, "I will have to choose which side very carefully eh sir?"

I had the mess to myself as I sipped the piping hot cocoa. The crew of the launch were all on duty for we would have the danger of dawn soon and the daylight crossing of a very dangerous English Channel. In the end, it was the weather which came to our raid. The low cloud made it hard for the German aircraft to see us and we docked in Falmouth after dark. We had made it; we had survived.

Chapter 3

Beaumont was fit and ready for work but the other two were sent, reluctantly, to hospital. Gordy had made sure that the rest of the section were at their peak. I had chosen him as my number two as he was reliable and knew explosives. Emerson's skills with motors might come in handy too. As for John Hewitt, I had chosen him because he was calm under pressure and could see to our first aid. The two men in the hospital told me that I needed that skill.

I reported to Major Rose and Sergeant Major Dean made a transcript of my words. I did not have time to go up to London and then return. Time was of the essence. Major Rose had only been on one raid and that was the huge one to the Lofoten Islands with Lord Lovat. I think the thought of being behind the lines with just two or three others worried him. "You were lucky with the Kubelwagen. That could have gone the wrong way."

"I know sir that is why Colonel Fleming is so wrong. He believes you can plan these missions and that they will work to a timetable. If the Lieutenant had not brought his launch dangerously close to the rocks then Fletcher and I might have drowned. In Colonel Fleming's world men only die or return. They don't get wounded. You have to think on your feet. Luckily my lads can do that."

Major Rose nodded, "This one should be a bit easier. You don't have huge cliffs to negotiate and the target is marginally closer to the coast."

"With respect sir that adds to the problems. I know we weren't the only raid. I don't need to know where the others were but I can guess. Jerry will increase his vigilance. The closer we are to the coast the fewer avenues of escape are open to us."

"Oh, I see. And there are another two after this."

Sergeant Major Dean coughed, "That depends on the weather, sir. A boat can land men in any weather, just about, but if Captain Harsker is dropping from a Dakota then the weather has to be right. It seems to me this is the wrong season for dropping from the skies. Just my opinion, sir."

"And welcome too. Anyway, when you get back you should have some company. Captain Marsden and Sergeant Curtis will be here with their new recruits."

"Oh good. Will his whole section be new then sir?"

"No, about half will be new the rest are the remnants of his old section."

Captain Marsden had commanded me when he had been a lieutenant. He had been unlucky. Wounded at St. Nazaire he had missed the opportunity to go to Africa with us. Ken Curtis had been my Corporal and I had moved him to Captain Marsden's section so that he could gain promotion. He was a good NCO.

The second raid was delayed as three days of atrocious weather over the channel made flying hazardous and parachuting suicidal. The four of us spent the three days in the hangar at the airfield playing pontoon and patience. We had camp beds placed beneath the Dakota's huge wings. Flight Sergeant Wilson ensured we ate well but the waiting played on nerves. Gordy Barker had not dropped from an aeroplane for some time. It showed. He chain-smoked. We finally got the all-clear and we boarded the aircraft enthusiastically. We wanted to be away as soon as possible.

Our pilot appeared more relaxed than in the first mission. Flight Sergeant Wilson told me they had made two other drops since our first one. He gained confidence with each flight. He actually smiled when he was chatting with us. The delay in take-off enabled us to go through all the details with a fine-tooth comb. I knew this target would be more heavily guarded. Our escape would also be harder. We were closer to the coast but aerial photographs showed that the defences had been improved since the raid was planned. The only good thing was that we would not have to lie up during the day. We were close enough to the coast so that we could destroy our target and still make the extraction point.

Our target was a busy rail junction with railway lines coming from the north, south and west. There were anti-aircraft guns nearby. They would have dogs patrolling. It would not be as easy as blowing up a railway bridge over a road. There were more mines out at sea. Our pick-up, north of Boulogne, towards Wimereux would be more difficult. The cliffs this time were gentle almost like huge sand dunes. We would not have to abseil however there were more likely to be mines buried there. We could not see that sort of detail from the aerial photographs. We would be using a long rock shelf which jutted out into the sea to make our escape. That could not be mined but I remembered the danger that the ML had been in the last time. There were just too many unknowns. Major Rose's words still rang in my ears, "Be careful, Tom. Don't take too many risks. We shall need chaps like you in the real invasion."

I knew we did not approve of these diversions. I just hoped that they were useful. I wanted a purpose for the wounds and the deaths. The wounds to Fletcher and Poulson were healing but the two dead Lewis gunners would never see the end of the war. Perhaps Colonel Fleming had the right attitude. Think of the greater good and the bigger picture. Maybe I was holding the telescope the wrong way around. Certainly, the increased German defences made it seem likely that these diversions were succeeding.

Although the storms had abated the wind was still stronger than we would have wished for a parachute jump at night. We left before dark and would be picked up the following morning. We would not have to lay up for the day. For that reason, I left my Tommy gun with Poulson. I would rely on my Luger. The other worry was the actual drop zone. We were going to be landing close to the railway line. We chose a stretch of line where there were two tracks but few houses. The ground around would be open and we would have just a mile or so to walk back to the points and the signal box. We had two targets. Not only did they want the point disabled, but they also needed the signal box wrecking. Already hit in the early years of the war it had been rebuilt in concrete. It had withstood the RAF's many attempts to destroy it.

Barker and Emerson were in charge of demolition this time while Hewitt and I would stand guard. I saw Gordy's nerves as he drummed his fingers on the bench in the Dakota. Once his parachute actually opened he would be fine but it was these moments, in the dark, waiting which were the worst. The flak warned us that we were close to the target. Flight Sergeant Wilson tapped me on my shoulder. We were making a drop from a higher altitude to avoid the guns. It made life easier for pilots but the margin of error for us was much narrower.

I smiled, reassuringly, as I checked Gordy's parachute. His weak smile back was just for show. When we opened the door the rush of air brought in blasts of icy rain. Winter was already here. I realised that the rain might help although it would make for an uncomfortable drop and landing. The rush of wet, rain-filled air was like a slap in the face. I forced myself to look down out of the door. I stepped out into nothing as Flight Sergeant Wilson tapped me on the shoulder. The rain limited visibility but the wet had made well-used railway lines stand out. I had to fight the wind. I tugged and pulled on the cords to control my flight. I hoped that the others were managing; I dared not risk looking up. I stared between my feet because I was approaching the ground rapidly. This was not open scrubland; there were railway lines; there were telegraph poles; there were more things to hurt us than the first raid. More by luck than anything else I managed to land along the railway line.

I quickly folded and stored my parachute in my Bergen and drew my pistol. I watched up and down the line; as I did so Corporal Hewitt came in to land. He was slightly off line and landed on the embankment to the right. Fred Emerson landed on the line itself. It was a good landing. Of Sergeant Barker, there was no sign. I looked into the sky but I saw no chute.

When the others had joined me I signalled for them to follow me. I headed down the railway line. As the last to leave the aircraft it was likely Sergeant Barker had drifted further west. We had walked three hundred yards and there was still no sign of him. I began to worry. I heard a whistle. I look to the right to see that he had managed to get caught on a telegraph pole and line. He could not reach his knife to cut himself free, the cords were wrapped around him. I pointed to Gordy and then to Hewitt. My

Corporal used Emerson's cupped hands to climb up the pole. Using his own knife he cut Gordy free. Disaster struck when the wind caught the parachute and sent it high into the night. It was a clear sign to the Germans that commandos or paratroopers were abroad. We could do nothing about that but I knew it would come back to haunt us.

Gordy landed heavily but he did not look to be injured. I waved the section down the line. The delay in finding him and rescuing him had cost us fifteen minutes. We ran down the line knowing that the rain, which came in blustery gusts, would keep German heads indoors. I had just touched the right-hand rail with my foot when I felt the vibration. A train was coming.

"Train!" I hissed and pressed myself into the low embankment. Five minutes later the train thundered past, belching smoke and soot. It seemed to be quite a long train but I did not risk looking around to check. There was little to be gained. When it had gone we resumed our march. The embankment disappeared as I saw the line joining from the northeast. We were now close to the junction we had come so far to destroy. Even in the dark, we could see how big it was. Two hundred yards to our left I saw the snouts of a pair of anti-aircraft guns. I knew there were more to the north for I had seen them in the aerial photographs and they would be on our escape route out of the junction.

Our first target was a signal box. We did not know if it was manned by the French or the Germans. Either way, it needed disabling. There were no lights to be seen within it. That was not a surprise. The Germans would not wish to show aircraft where it was. Gordy had the silenced Colt and he led the way up the stairs. John Hewitt remained on watch as Fred and I followed the Sergeant up the steps. He held the handle of the door with one hand and the gun with the other. He burst in. I heard a shout of surprise and the 'phut' of the silenced bullet.

I entered, my pistol at the ready. Gordy had shot the German sentry. I saw the German's gun in his hand. My sergeant would have had little choice. The old French railway worker stood with his hands up.

I signed for him to put his hands down and spoke to him in French. "We are British. We will not harm you."

"But the Germans will think I helped you!"

"Do not worry. We will tie you and gag you before we leave!" I turned to Emerson. "What can we do here?"

He pointed to a conduit which led outside. "I'm guessing this powers the signal box. We will have to blow it." That ruled out leaving the old man in the box.

"Right, you set the charges here with fifteen-minute fuses. Gordy you and Hewitt set the charges on the points. Twenty-minute fuses."

"Right, sir. Sorry about the landing."

"Couldn't be helped, Gordy." I turned to the railway worker. "You better come with us."

He pointed towards the line. "There is a shift cabin four hundred metres down the line. You could tie me up there." He grinned. "I do not wish to be blown up!"

He had seen the charges we were using. Emerson was already taking them from his Bergen. They were not large but they would disable the line for some time. "Good. Lead the way." As I reached the bottom I said, "Gordy take charge. I will meet you back here."

The old man led me to the cabin. It too was made of concrete. He would be safe inside. I used parachute cords to bind his hands and feet. I was about to leave when he said, "You had better hit me. Give me a lump, eh Englishman, who speaks French so well."

"Are you certain?"

"If this is the only wound I suffer in this war then I will wear it with pride." I nodded and struck him on the temple with the grip of my pistol. It broke the skin and bled a little. He smiled, "Good, now bring your army back soon, we have had enough of these Germans!"

"You are a brave man. We will return. That I promise you."

I shut the door and left the old Frenchman safe in the concrete cabin. By the time I reached the signal box, Fred was looking worried. "We just have eight minutes left sir!"

"Then let's run." We headed across the spaghetti of tracks towards the gun emplacement. When we were two hundred yards from them I waved Barker and Hewitt to the right while Emerson and I went to the left. We crept closer to the sandbagged gun emplacement. We crawled around to the side furthest from the points and waited. We took out a grenade each and pulled the pin. I could hear the Germans talking. They were complaining about the air raids and the food. It was typical sentry talk.

The explosion lit up the sky. Without looking I knew that the signal box would have been lit up by the explosion. The Germans inside the sandbags shouted. We threw our grenades over the top. For grenades can do serious damage in a confined space. We dropped to the ground as the shrapnel from the four Mills bombs scythed through the gun crew. Air raid sirens began to wail as I hissed, "Let's move!"

We headed away from the busy junction. Soon it would be alive with Germans. On the road adjacent to the wire I caught sight of German uniforms disgorging from trucks lit by the glow of the burning gun emplacement. Even as we ran ammunition from behind the sandbags exploded sending a pyrotechnic display into the sky. It would draw the enemy there and with every footstep, we were further from danger. The real problem would come when we reached the edge of the railway lines. Just then there was an enormous explosion as the demolitions planted amongst the points exploded. I resisted the urge to turn. I knew what the effect would be. There would be the ballast and timber showering down from the skies and the metal would be twisted into fantastic shapes.

I saw a fence ahead. We had reached the edge of the junction and the railway lines. It was not a well-maintained fence and the other side was a wasteland of scrub. There had been buildings here but that had been many years earlier. Emerson and Hewitt had their wire cutters out in a moment and soon cut a gap large enough for us to pass through. I looked back across the tracks. Shells still exploded in the gun emplacement. It kept the Germans occupied.

I checked my watch. It had just gone eleven. We had to make the rendezvous by three. Four hours to make less than five miles may not seem much, except when Germans are trying to kill you. Being north of Boulogne and now northwest of the railway line we just had the main road from the north to contend with. The first half mile was relatively easy. We crossed the wasteland and then ducked through some workshops and what seemed to be fish storage buildings. It certainly smelled like it. Once we were through we had a small road ahead of us. It was bordered by small houses every hundred yards so. We could cross the road and then run over the fields. The shells behind us had stopped exploding but I could now hear the sound of vehicles. It would not be long until they investigated all the small roads. We passed the first house and ran down an overgrown lane. It led in the right direction. We emerged at another open patch of land and we hurried across that. We were making better time than I could have hoped. Once across the main road, we were within sight of the rendezvous. Once more we would scramble over the low cliffs and down onto the rocks.

The road appeared clear although it was so dark and the rain still fell sporadically that visibility was poor. It also made it hard to hear well. Barker had just sprinted across the road and Emerson was in the middle when a small truck came around the bend. Emerson dived across the road but the damage was done. The truck squealed to a halt and the German next to the driver jumped out and fired blindly into the dark. I pulled my Luger and fired three bullets into his back. Hewitt fired at the driver but although he was struck he still managed to drive off. I emptied my magazine but he continued driving. Pausing only to pick up the dead German's grenades and ammunition, we joined Emerson and Barker.

"That's torn it, sir!" I looked at my watch. Two hours until the launch and we were just a mile from the pick-up point.

"No use crying over spilt milk, Corporal Hewitt. Let's keep to the plan. Gordy cover the rear!"

As we hurried through the rain I ran through the options left open to us. The rain would make it harder for the Germans to see us but, equally, we would find it harder to see the launch. We would have to wait until the last minute to signal them or the Germans would soon spot us. Whichever way I looked there were problems. However, we were commandos and we would adapt.

We found the path leading to the rocks and the rendezvous soon after the encounter with the Germans. I saw that the path continued south to Boulogne and paralleled the road. These were really not cliffs they were just a rocky outcrop and sand dunes. I found the rocky shelf for the extraction one and a half hours before the boat was due. For once we had too much time. Had the German not got away it might not have been a problem. However, the death of the German meant that they would be looking for us and they knew roughly where we would be. We took out the ropes and tied them to two spindly-looking trees. We refrained from letting them fall. We crouched and we waited. The lack of noise on the road was reassuring.

Hewitt pointed out to the sea, whilst pitch black we could still see the whitecaps from the bowels of the launch in the distance. Once again the young lieutenant had come early. I was grateful for that. Gordy said, "Taxi is here, sir."

I nodded, "Lower the ropes."

Just then I heard a truck in the distance as the driver ground the gears. It was coming from Boulogne. The Germans were on the way. The other three looked around as they heard it too. It was now a race between the launch and the German truck. We stood. Fred and I wrapped the ropes around our backs. "You might as well go now, Emerson. We will take a chance on the rocks."

Just then the night sky was lit by a huge flash and there was a sound of an explosion as the launch hit a mine. There was no time for hesitation, recriminations or regret. We had to get away from here as quickly as we could. I let go of the rope. "Follow me!" I ran back down the trail towards Boulogne. I was gambling. The Germans would have seen the explosion. They would investigate. If we could pass them then we might be able to hide in the town where I hoped I might come up with another plan for us to escape. One thing was certain we would not surrender, the Hitler order guaranteed that. We kept low as we ran and remained below the level of the road.

As we approached the road where we had shot the German I saw the dimmed, dipped headlights of the two German trucks as they climbed towards us. I ran faster. We passed the corpse. I didn't see it but I knew it lay forty yards away at the road. Our trail ran parallel to the road. There was no cover here and we had to keep an eye on the faded yellow dots of light which climbed towards us. We dared not be picked out or it would be over for us. Two hundred yards down the road I yelled, "Down!" I threw myself onto the sodden, spongy grass. The two trucks ground up the incline past us and turned the bend. I peered over my shoulder and saw that they had not stopped but continued to the dead German. I jumped up. We ran at a reckless speed for the path led downhill. I needed to put as much space as I could between us and the Germans. The ground descended slowly. I could see, in the distance, a beach with fishing boats and then the harbour with two moles one on either side. It was in darkness behind us I heard the sound of machine guns. A shudder ran down my spine. Were the survivors from the launch being shot in the water?

The path had now descended towards houses by the beach. It was still the middle of the night but this was a port. Ships and boats came and went at all hours of the night. We stopped behind the back wall of a rundown, nondescript house. It was in bad need of repair and I was not certain if it was inhabited. I would have to reconnoitre.

I took off my Bergen and handed it to Gordy. I made the sign that he was in command. I headed towards the port. I knew that, although the main entrance would be guarded, sometimes locals created their own entrances and exits. I was lucky, I spied no one. I saw, forty yards away, a barrier with two German guards. They could be taken easily but they would be missed. I saw the Germans had erected a fence with barbed wire at the top around the harbour. It was new and would take some cutting. I turned down the back alleys of the houses which bordered the harbour. In more peaceful times they would have bars and restaurants there. Perhaps they still did. At each intersection, I peered out. Then I saw that the fence ended. I crossed the road. It was still dark but I knew dawn could not be far away. We had to be away before dawn broke.

At the edge of the sand, I saw a sign for mines. Once again I gambled. They would not risk mines close to the fence. I walked along the edge looking for the deadly indentations in the sand which would show me there were mines. I reached the sea. I saw that by wading I could get around the fence and there were fishing boats drawn up on the beach. More importantly, I saw similar boats heading out to sea. There were fishermen going out to fish.

I retraced my steps. My men were just four hundred yards away as the crow flies and I reached them in less than five minutes. I grabbed my Bergen and made the sign for them to follow me. Gordy took the rear. When we reached the road we went across in single file. I heard traffic further north. The Germans would extend their search soon enough.

Once on the beach, I said, "Stick close to the fence. Mines."

We reached the water and it was icy but our luck held. No one passed us. As I waded around the fence I saw that two more boats had gone in the ten minutes I had been away. There were just three left. They were sixty yards away from us.

I heard the fishermen's voices. I waved to the sand and we all fell flat. I saw a group of fishermen approaching the boats. It looked like our last chance of escape was about to be snatched away from us. It took them just ten minutes to drag two boats towards the water and then begin to roll out. I risked raising my head. There was one boat left. The two fishing boats were heading into the dark.

"Quick, let's become fishermen." We stood. Freddie started to run. "Just walk!" In the dark I wanted us to appear to be French fishermen. They would not rush. I began speaking French.

Gordy caught on and when I stopped speaking he said, "Oui."

The boat we approached had been the one furthest from the main harbour. It was a good thirty feet from where the others had been. The northern mole was four hundred yards south of us and I saw the heavy gun machine emplacement at the end. When we reached the fishing boat I saw that it was in poor condition. I spoke quietly to the others. "Put your bags in the bottom of the boat and then drag it into the water. We have less than an hour. It will be dawn by then. I am certain those Germans will have binoculars. When we get in, take off your battledress. Fred and John row. Gordy, be ready to hoist the sail."

"How sir?"

"Untie it and then haul it up. I will give you a hand. Just look busy."

We got the boat in the water and I held it while they clambered aboard. The water was icy. I jumped in as they began to row. I fitted the tiller. The mechanism was rusty and it groaned. This was not a well-maintained boat and had not been at sea for some time. I saw pools of water at the bottom. They looked ominous. Glancing to my left, the Germans in the machine-gun emplacement did not appear to be taking undue interest in us. I followed the course of the other boats although the nearest was a good three hundred and fifty yards from us. The sails had been raised and they were making good speed. Gordy was struggling with our sail. The poorly maintained boat actually helped us. The tiller was so rusted and stiff that I was able to leave it while I went to help Gordy. I quickly untied the sheet and began to haul on the sail. It creaked like the tiller. As a sail was raised I saw it had small holes in it. It confirmed that the boat had not been at sea for some time. "Gordy sit at the side and hold onto the sheet."

"It's a rope,, sir!"

"We call it a sheet. If I say go about then sit on the opposite side of the boat but keep this rope tight."

Emerson said, "What about us sir?"

"Keep rowing. This is not the best boat in the world." I returned to the tiller and took out my compass. I did not trust the one in the boat. The other fishing boats were heading south parallel to the coast. And then I remembered, mines!

"Hewitt, Emerson, ship those oars and get to the bow and keep your eyes open for mines! Give me a shout if you see them!"

I glanced to the east. Dawn was imminent. We would stick out like a sore thumb when daylight came for we would be alone and sailing in the wrong direction. We would be heading west alone into a minefield while everyone else was heading south. It would take us four or five hours at least to cross the twenty miles of the English Channel. We would not make it.

"You two get your guns and grenades ready."

They obeyed but Gordy asked, "Why sir? If a patrol boat finds us we are dead meat."

"Not necessarily. All of you take off your battled dress and put them in your Bergens. We will look like scruffy fishermen!"

"It's peeing down, sir. We'll get soaked!"

"Fred, just do it!"

I took my battledress off and rolled up my sleeves. I wanted to look like a fisherman. I lounged against the stern. First impressions were vital. If we were spotted I wanted us to look the part. It was a shame we were all dressed in khaki but that could not be helped. By the time dawn broke, we were a mile or so offshore

Emerson shouted, a little too loudly, "Mines, sir! Hundreds of the buggers!"

"Keep it down Emerson, I am only here. Gordy come about!" He looked at me blankly. "Go to the other side of the boat and keep the rope tight."

"Sir, water is coming in!"

"Thought it might, Hewitt. Find something to bail the water out with. Use your Dixie if you have nothing else."

"Sir!"

I turned the tiller so that we were heading west by south "Fred, keep calling out where the mines are. Silence means you can't see any."

"Sir!"

I had no idea how far the minefields stretched save that I doubted it would reach all the way across the channel. Dawn would bring new dangers. We were alone and close to a minefield. Even though it was overcast the German binoculars from the coast would soon spot us and send a launch or even worse an E-Boat to investigate. The weather might keep the aeroplanes grounded but not the boats. The wind was from our quarter and we made better time than I could have hoped for. Poor Hewitt was sweating profusely as he bailed.

"Emerson spell Hewitt."

"Sir."

As he came aft he said," Sir, there is a fast patrol boat, a mile astern. He's coming really quickly."

"If he comes alongside let me do the talking. How far away is the minefield?"

"Hundred yards sir."

"Good. Tell me when you are almost close enough to touch them." I suddenly realised we had no nets out. There were some at the bottom of the boat. They were wet and they were oily. They did not look as though they had been used lately. But they were nets. "Barker tie off the sheet around that cleat and then drape the net over the side. Make it look as though we are preparing to fish and light a cigarette!"

"They are damp, sir!"

"It doesn't matter. A Frenchman would smoke whatever the cigarettes were like." I glanced over my shoulder. It was a harbour patrol vessel. It was armed with a couple of heavy machine guns. "How far from the mines are we?"

"Forty feet, Sir! They look bloody huge!"

"If you have to fend them off don't touch the prongs." I reached into my Bergen and took out two grenades. I placed them in my lap and jammed my Luger under my left leg. We had travelled four miles from the coast but the patrol boat could easily catch us now.

"This net is a bit smelly sir!"

I sighed. We were trying to look like fishermen. "Just keep a miserable expression on your face, Gordy. You can manage that can't you?"

"Oh yes sir," he said cheerfully. Then he added, seriously, "A hundred yards more, sir, and they will be on us."

"Stand by, Hewitt," I pushed the tiller slightly and we headed for the black deadly prongs of the German mines.

A loudhailer sounded and a German voice told us to stop. I turned and put my hand to my ear and shrugged. I pointed to the tiller and said in French, "Thank God, the tiller has jammed and we are heading into the mines!"

I saw a hurried conference between two German officers as my words were translated.

I said quietly, "Ready with a grenade!"

The German officer said in bad French, "Be ready to take a line but beware my friend. You are in serious trouble."

I stood and nodded, "I know I can see the mines. Thank you for coming to our aid!"

The patrol boat came to within twenty feet of us. There were no mines to be seen close by us but that made the manoeuvre no less risky. As a line was thrown I raised my hands as though I would catch it. Instead, I brought up my Luger and fired, first at the bridge then at the machine-gunners.

Gordy shouted, "Grenade!"

I fell flat. The grenade went off. The deck was cleared and our holed sail gained some more speed from the explosion. The blast sent us into the minefield. We had no choice now. We had to get deep within it before a rescue boat was sent for the launch. I glanced over my shoulder. The burning German boat was drifting before the wind. Suddenly there was an enormous explosion as it hit a mine. Pieces of wood and debris from the launch fell from the skies.

"Mine!" Freddie's hand pointed to the right and I edged the tiller to port.

"How is the bailing?"

"We are keeping pace that is all, sir."

I noticed that the wind had veered a little and now that the patrol boat was no longer around I could risk heading west again.

"Gordy, come about!"

"Aye, aye, skipper!"

He was back to his old cheerful self. Then they were all back to bailing out the boat. The shredded sail caught the wind but we were travelling slower than I would have liked. The French coast was now a smudge on the horizon and I saw a thin dark patch which had to be England ahead of us.

"Seen any mines lately, Emerson?"

"No sir. Not for some time."

"Then help the others to bail."

By my estimate, we were in the middle of the English Channel. Had there been less low cloud and rain then we would have had fighters to contend with as well. At least that was in our favour. Hewitt looked up and shaded his eyes against the drizzle. "Sir I think I can see an E- boat."

I looked over my shoulder. It was an E-boat and travelling at speed. That alone told me they would not be near the mines. Our oblique course had bought us time but he would soon be upon us in less than half an hour at the most. He would just have to navigate around the edge of the minefield. I knew that the E-Boat had all the speed it needed.

Emerson said, "Grenades sir?"

I shook my head, "Not this time. As soon as they are in range they will open fire. Those were their mates we killed." The three of them nodded. They were prepared to die but not yet resigned to their fate. So long as we breathed then there was hope.

After fifteen minutes Barker said, "He's turning sir. He must have passed the edge of the minefield."

"Give him another five minutes and he will try a ranging shot. As soon as he does, sergeant, I intend to turn. That means you will have to come about. We need to throw his aim off." The choppy sea gave us a low profile as we dropped below the tips of waves. His machine guns would have an even smaller target. It was his shells we would have to worry about. The first shell fell well astern. I risked staying on the same course. The second sent up a waterspout thirty feet from our bow. The next would hit us.

"Come about you lads but watch your heads!" I put it on the larboard tack and the next shell struck twenty feet from our starboard beam. "Come about!" As I put my weight against the creaking tiller I wondered how much punishment the ancient boat could handle. As he went on the opposing tack I caught sight of the cliffs of Kent. We were now less than ten miles from safety. Now was a time for a break in the cloud cover. A couple of Spitfires would make short work of the E-Boat. The next shell came so close it half-filled the boat with seawater as it struck just twenty feet from us.

Hewitt shouted, "Sir, the planks have sprung! She is sinking!"

"Right, lads over the side. Use your Bergens as buoyancy aids. We have eight miles or so to swim." The thought of surrender never entered our heads.

As we jumped in Gordy said, "I like a paddle as much as the next bloke, sir, but eight miles! I hope there's a chippy by the beach!"

We kicked out. Already soaked and cold I wondered how long we would last in this icy water. Our four dead bodies would probably wash up close to Margate pier. The fishing boat took some time to sink. The German shells still came close. They were looking for us. Each kick of our legs took us closer to home. I could feel the cold permeating my body. I had read about this. They called it hypothermia. We should have left our battle dresses on. It was too late for that now. Behind me, I heard machine-gun shells finally sink the fishing boat as the E-boat closed with it. Now they would look for us.

Hewitt said, "Sir, Fred's stopped swimming!"

Emerson was lying face down in the water. His Bergen had long gone to the bottom. "Hewitt get to the other side and turn him over." Between us, we managed to put him on his back.

He opened his eyes. He was alive. "Just thought another five minutes sleep, sir!"

"None of that Emerson! Come on, all of you, let's sing." We began singing *'roll out the barrel'*. It sounded thin and weak but it kept us awake. We were swimming on our backs. My Bergen and that of Hewitt lay under Emerson's back. I saw the E-boat as it appeared and disappeared with the choppy waves. It drew on inexorably closer. It was going slowly as they were looking for us. They saw us. When it was two hundred yards from us I could see that they were not going to shoot us, not yet. We would be taken back and questioned first. Two sailors at the bow stood with boat hooks ready to pull us aboard.

The twin waterspouts on either side of the E-Boat took us all, Germans and commandos alike, by surprise.

"Bloody hellfire!" Emerson had woken up.

The boat turned, like a greyhound and sped east. More waterspouts erupted close by. I heard the sound of engines and saw a destroyer as it slowed down. Within a short time, it was next to us. Two sailors clung to a scrambling net from the side.

One shouted, "Here y'are chum. Grab my hand."

Hewitt reached out so the three of us pulled closer to the net. The second shouted, "What are four Pongoes doing out here?"

Gordy shouted, indignantly, as he was pulled up, "We are commandos! Not bloody Pongoes!"

Grinning, the sailor said, "My mistake. Whoever you are, you have the luck of the Irish. You were about to swim into our minefield!"

We made sure that Emerson was taken directly to the sickbay but they looked after us all well. They wrapped blankets around us and mugs of cocoa laced with rum were pressed into our hands.

A Sub Lieutenant took my elbow, "Sir, the Captain would like a word."

Clutching my cocoa I followed him to the bridge. The Captain was leaning against the side of the bridge. He held out his hand. "Captain Rupert Wild."

"Captain Tom Harsker, commandos."

He laughed and held his hand out. Lieutenant Commander handed him a ten-shilling note. "I knew it. Commandos are always resourceful chaps!" He suddenly frowned. "How were you supposed to get back to Blighty?"

"Motor launch. We saw it when it hit a mine." I shook my head."There were no survivors. We stole a fishing boat and headed into the German minefield."

That made him roar with laughter, "Rum buggers! We will have you in Dover in no time. I'll have Sparks send a message to your base."

Chapter 4

We spent the night in Dover. Sergeant Poulson arrived at six o'clock in the morning with the brigade car. He beamed, "Sergeant Major Dean told me to watch out for the car but I saw nothing at all on the road sir. Where is Emerson, sir?"

"They are keeping him in hospital for a couple of days."

"It was rough out there Sarge." Our voyage had shaken Hewitt.

"Well, you lads settle in the back and ...."

Gordy said, "You've been driving all night Polly. I'll drive."

Sergeant Poulson shrugged, "Up to you."

We looked scruffy as we settled into the back of the staff car. We were still wearing the jumpers the crew of the *'Hotspur'* had given us. We had lost our battle dresses in the channel. I was the only one still with a Bergen. We had lost three irreplaceable Tommy guns!

Hewitt sat in the front. I sat with Poulson. "How are things back at camp."

He smiled, "No sooner had you left the airfield when the rest of the brigade arrived. A bunch of lads couldn't get digs and had to stay in camp. The old hands aren't happy about that."

"We are fortunate to have Mrs Dean. We dropped lucky there."

"Too right, sir. She'll be glad to know you're all safe and sound."

As much as Reg's wife appreciated us, we needed and appreciated her far more. The boarding house was an island of peace in a world of war. It was our home in every sense of the word. The rooms were kept spotless by the men just as if they were at home with their own mums and dads. Mealtimes were cosy. In a world filled with rank, there was none around Mrs Dean's table. I received the same amount of food as the rest and I was not served first either. The only deference I received was that Mrs Dean always addressed me as Captain. I think she was proud that I was a guest.

I watched the countryside, grey wet and cold flash by. Poulson had had an easy journey for it had been at night time. We had the day. It was not a pleasant journey. It was well after dark when we reached our digs. We had had to change drivers twice. It had been a nightmare finding petrol. The war was over four years old and the U-boats were beginning to bite. Everything was in short supply. However, Mrs Dean did not subscribe to that philosophy. Her boys would be well fed no matter what the Germans did.

Sergeant Major Dean opened the front door and shouted over his shoulder, "They are here!" He took my Bergen and ran an appraising eye over me. "I can see you have had it rough again sir. Come on in and get warm. Mrs Dean has kept food for you and the lads will be relieved." He looked beyond me to where the others followed. "No Emerson then?"

"No Sergeant Major. He'll be fine but the seawater got to him."

The minute we sat around the table and tucked into liver and onions with home-made bread it was as though the war had ended at the front door.

"Thanks, Mrs Dean, you are an angel."

"No more than you deserve although why it always has to be you I have no idea!"

The next morning I got back into my old routine straight away. I packed my Bergen; it would need drying out properly and ran to the camp. It soon became obvious that it would not dry out any time soon. It was pouring with rain. I arrived at the camp looking like a drowned rat. I kept an old uniform there and I changed into it. I threw my Bergen to Private Larkin. "Be a good fellow and dry that for me."

"Right sir although it has seen better days!"

"I know. It is like an old friend!"

My men would be hard on my heels. Even Barker and Hewitt would not take a day off. Commandos weren't made that way. As I left the office, I saw two Commandos, I didn't recognise them, and they were getting out of a car. They waved amiably to the driver and then strode into the camp as though they hadn't a care in the world. They both gave me a lacklustre salute and headed to the canteen. My men, in contrast, ran in together all singing. They were soaked but each one had a smile on his face.

I went to the officer's mess to pick up my letters. John Marsden was there. He clapped me on my back. "Congratulations on the promotion and the Victoria Cross."

"I haven't got the gong yet."

"It is a shoo-in! And I hear you have had a couple of hairy trips across the Channel?"

I nodded, "Yes, we were lucky both times."

"I will have to get my section up to the standard of yours sooner rather than later. The trouble is the new chaps need the edge rubbing off them."

"Oh, they'll soon settle in."

"I don't know Tom. I have a couple of barrack-room lawyers amongst them. Poor Curtis is pulling his hair out."

I laughed, Curtis had been in my section. "I know he likes things done his way. Well if you need any help..."

"From what I hear you are destined for great things. Major Foster was here yesterday talking with the Colonel. Your name came up. The Colonel said you and your section were to be kept off regular duties until March. I don't think you will have time to give me a hand. Thanks for the offer though." He smiled, "I have got a lieutenant though. Toby Rankin. Seems a nice chap. Very enthusiastic!"

As I left the mess Corporal Anderson, who worked in the office said, "Beg pardon Captain Harsker but Lieutenant Colonel Dawson would like a word."

I went into the office feeling scruffy in my old uniform. I need not have worried. The Colonel smiled and held out his hand, "Congratulations on the medal Tom and the last two raids. Top-notch shows."

"Thank you, sir. Just doing what we always do."

"Sit down. Not true you know. They sent four teams in as well as yours up and down the Pas de Calais. Two didn't return. One didn't manage to achieve its objectives and the one that did only brought back two men and one is crocked. No, Tom, you did well. And it looks set to continue."

My shoulders must have sagged a little and my head drooped.

"What's wrong? Too much for you?"

"No sir, it is just...I hesitated.

"Go on Tom, speak openly."

"It's Colonel Fleming, His plans get people killed. We were lucky but the other three weren't. I will be honest, sir, what we did could have been achieved by a couple of Mosquitoes. And I am betting the other ones could have too. I don't mind putting my men's lives in jeopardy but I want it to be for a good reason not just to allow Colonel Fleming to become a Field Marshal!"

The Colonel laughed, "I agree with you, Tom. It looks like someone has realised that these raids were not as successful as they might have hoped. The other two you had been expecting have been cancelled. What you are going to be doing is different." I gave him a searching look. "Don't worry I have spoken with Major Foster. The work you will be doing will be vital." He picked up some papers. "To that end, you need to go to Carrick Roads and practice with canoes and rubber dinghies. It seems you need skills in that department." He smiled, "Although from what Sergeant Major Dean said you have skills in that department already."

"Well, I am happy mucking about in boats, sir. I'm just not certain that my lads are." He handed me my orders. I stood and saluted. "Thank you, Colonel."

"No, thank you, Tom."

I went to find my men. Poulson and Fletcher had been returned to duty although they both bore the scars from that raid. They were eager to find out what we were about. "Well, lads as it is such a lovely day I thought we would go boating!"

Jimmy Smith said, "Boating sir! It is peeing down!"

Roger Beaumont was his mate. An unlikely pairing for one was from what one would call a posh background while the other had a father who worked at Bristol docks. Roger said, "I think he means we will be getting wet anyway. Isn't that right sir?"

"It is."

Roger pointed outside. There were flecks of snow with the rain, "Besides we might need iceberg training!"

Gordy Barker said, "Haven't you had enough of boats, sir? That Froggy boat was nearly the death of us!"

"Having seen your skills, Sergeant, I thought they needed improvement!"

We spent longer with the canoes than with the rubber dinghies. For one thing, they were more fun and for another, I had a feeling that we would be using them rather than the more cumbersome inflatables. They were made of canvas and wood. Each held two men. They fitted tightly around the waist. Army Commandos rarely used them and we were instructed by two Royal Marine Commandos. Sergeant Geoff Betts and Sergeant Ray Garvey.

I had used them before and I think that Beaumont must have too for we were the only pair who found it easy. That first morning saw the rest of the section spend more time in the water than on it. Even my two sergeants struggled. The Royal Marines were very patient and by the afternoon my team had managed to follow orders and keep afloat.

By the end of the third day, we had made so much improvement that we were able to canoe across the width of Carrick Roads. Then came the skills of getting in and out under difficult circumstances. Sergeant Garvey said, "You will not always have the luxury of someone holding the boat for you."

That skill took another day and then we learned to maintain it. "Maintain it, Sarge?"

"Yes, Smith. These are robust craft but if they get a hole in them then they will sink. Now sometimes you might want them to sink. To hide them in a river like our lads did on the Gironde. That is no problem. Fill them with rocks and they will happily lie on the bottom or in reeds. Just make sure you use smooth rocks. Now if you are sixpence short of a full shilling then you might put a hole in it. Repair is relatively simple." He held up a tube. "This is a rubber solution. Cut a patch from your waterproof cape and stick it over the hole. Then Bob's your uncle, you float once more."

The two were the best instructors I had ever met. By the end of that week, we were cold but we were all confident canoeists.

Once we were back at the camp I set my sergeants to setting tasks for my men. I knew we would be behind enemy lines and I wanted them even more skilled than they already were. I did this because the Colonel told me that Major Foster was coming to the camp. He implied that I might be away for a few days. It looked like the operation was about to begin.

I sat in the lounge of Mrs Dean's boarding house and helped devise problems for the men to solve. "We will be behind enemy lines. They need to practise breaking into houses. Hiding in plain sight. Finding food. You know the sorts of things. Stealing vehicles."

The three of them nodded. Bill Hay said, "Pas de Calais again sir?"

"Possibly but don't count on it. France, the Low Countries; they are all likely targets."

The next day when we reached the camp, I saw Major Foster's car. I had seen it before. It looked like the next phase of the invasion of France was about to begin."

**Part 2
Normandy**

Chapter 5

Major Foster drove up to London with me. The roads were treacherous. Where the snow had been cleared there was deadly black ice.

"Don't you miss the action, sir? I mean you are the one who got me into all of this."

"I do Tom but if I'm honest I can achieve more where I am at the centre of the planning. Colonel Fleming has a somewhat cavalier attitude to men's lives. You have been lucky. Most of the other teams he sent in did not make it back. This new operation, well let's say that a few others have tried to rein in the reckless Colonel. You and your team will be involved before the actual invasion and when the show starts I will be watching from one of the supporting destroyers."

"You must miss leading the men, sir. They followed you anywhere."

"That's right, Tom, and most of them are either lying in Belgian graves or behind barbed wire. You are a success story."

"I know we lost. We were chased unceremoniously across the Channel but I'm proud of what we did back in 1940."

"As you should be. What you have done behind enemy lines is vital. That is why we are heading to London now. We want to pick your brains. We need to know how to help our chaps survive as you do. Now tell me about the Pas de Calais. You only get a flavour from the report. I need more."

I went through the two raids. The Major was a commando and I left nothing out. How he listened and drove at the same time I will never know. He was a skilled driver. Perhaps he had travelled the roads so often that they were like second nature to him. We were approaching London by the time I finished.

He nodded, "You have luck on your side, I can see that but you seem to have the ability to make your own luck. We can't teach others that. But I can see how we need people who can speak French and German. Can any of your team speak other languages?"

"Beaumont can. Poulson and Fletcher are getting better. The rest can understand more than they could but it is still a work in progress, sir. I run classes in the boarding house. It does help."

"Tell me, Tom, you have been on the last three invasions. You know more about the problems than anyone else. What can we do to minimise casualties? The brass needs to know."

"The Germans have laid mines across beaches which a couple of years ago were safe. We need to have some means of getting over mined beaches. The small landing craft we use are good but they need better protection for their crews. In a perfect world, you would have tanks paving the way. It was how Jerry chased us out of Belgium. Remember, sir?"

"Our tanks have come a long way since then."

"And so have the Germans."

He nodded forward, "I have arranged for us to stay at a chum's flat tonight. He is in Italy. Better than a club. We can have a night out. I daresay it has been some time since you let your hair down."

"To be honest, sir, I have never let my hair down. I was always quiet. I went from school to the 1st Loyals."

He laughed, "Then I can repay you for all your work thus far. I will show you how to have a good time!"

England might have been at war but the English are sticklers for rules. Large theatres and places of entertainment were all closed for the duration. However, the pubs stayed open. By the time we had put our bags in the flat, it was nine o'clock. The pubs would be shut in an hour and a half. The Major took me to one just half a mile from the flat. "The '*Crown*' is a nice pub. More importantly, girls frequent it. It is close to Whitehall and these days they use WRNS, ATS and WAAFs to staff it. All the blokes have gone to war!"

As we approached the doors I said, "We are here for one night. We will probably just have time for a couple of pints and then back home." I was pessimistic.

As we pushed open the blacked-out doors and before we had entered the pub through the blackout curtains we were assaulted by attacks on our senses. There was the smell of too many cigarettes and stale spilt beer. Then there was the noise. Women squealing and the forced laughter of men who were not certain if this was to be their last pint. London suffered almost nightly bombing raids. It was not as bad as it had been but having a drink in a pub was filled with risks.

After the darkness outside the pub, the bright light made me blink. Although it was crowded I could see that we would be able to sit. Most men liked to stand at the bar. I never had. "You go and get us a couple of pints and I'll find us some seats."

"What are you drinking, Major?"

He shook his head, "Forget the rank for tonight, Tom, call me Toppy. It is the nickname I have had since a kid and as for the pint, I'll have whatever they have. Beggars can't be choosers!"

I squeezed into the bar between a private and a sailor. The soldier turned around aggressively and then saw my rank and my ribbons, "Sorry sir. I thought you were one of them skiving wide boys. This area is filled with them."

"Don't worry, Private, their day will come."

There was a great deal of bad feeling amongst the men about the black marketeers and draft dodgers. They managed to get petrol, have good cars and clothes and throw money around as though there was no tomorrow. Every town had some but London appeared to attract more than its fair share. I was surprised that they would frequent a pub used by men in uniform. They would extract a fearful retribution.

The barman had to be seventy and I suspected he was the landlord. He took in my rank, "Good evening, sir. Sorry, I have no spirits."

I shook my head, "Two pints of bitter will do."

He leaned forward, "I would have the dark mild, sir. It's a better pint."

The Private had heard him and he nodded and added conspiratorially. "He's right sir. The bitter is donkey piss not fit for drinking."

I smiled, this was typical. Good landlords looked after their own and the Private was obviously a regular. "Two pints of dark mild it is then." I handed over the money. I took a swallow before leaving the bar. There was less chance of spillage that way. It had a dark nutty taste. There was a hint of milk stout about it. I nodded, "Nice pint. Thanks for the recommendation, Private."

"You are a Commando sir. As much as I hate wide boys I respect Commandos even more."

I turned to look for the Major. I saw his back at a table and an empty chair next to him. I headed for him. When I neared he turned and I saw that there were two ATS privates seated opposite. "Ah, here he is. This is Captain Tom Harsker. Tom, this is Doris and Susan. They are stationed in operations. Fellow operatives so to speak."

The one called Doris had bleached blond hair, and bright red lips from which hung a cigarette. She amply filled out the uniform she wore. She smiled, "Pleased to meet you I'm sure!"

The one called Susan looked like a frightened mouse in comparison. It was like Jack Sprat and his wife. Susan was thin and looked as though a strong breeze would blow her away. Her hair was neatly tied behind her head and she wore just a smudge of lipstick. She too smiled but held out a hand, "I am Susan Tancraville. Pleased to meet you. Toppy here was just telling us that you are in for the Victoria Cross. You must be brave."

I wished he had not mentioned the award. I had heard nothing more. I might not even get it. I didn't think I had done enough to deserve one. "Not brave. There are braver men than me but they lie in graves in foreign fields."

Doris rolled her eyes. "That isn't very cheerful is it?"

Susan smiled, "It sounds like a line from a Rupert Brooke poem." I nodded. It seemed that these two girls were different in every way possible.

Doris said, "I'll have to go and powder my nose. You coming, Susie?"

Susan wrinkled her nose at the use of the diminutive. "No that's fine, Doris."

Doris put her hand on the Major's knee, "Susie doesn't need a drink but I do. Could you be a dear and get me a port and lemon?"

"Of course."

When they had gone Susan said, "I have heard your name before tonight, you know?"

"Really?" I wondered if she had heard my father's name.

"Yes. I was in Operations for the Dieppe raid. I heard it then. You are wrong you know, you are brave. It isn't the medals that tell me that. It was the way the officers in operations spoke of your actions." She smiled. "I feel privileged to be talking to you." She briefly covered my hand with hers. It was soft.

I laughed, "Don't be silly." I quickly drank some beer and she took her hand away. She looked embarrassed. I realised I had been churlish. "Sorry, I don't get to talk to pretty girls like you very often."

"I am not pretty. I am plain. That's why Doris lets me come out with her. It makes her look even more attractive."

"Then why come out with her?"

"I wouldn't get out otherwise. We are the two youngest ATS in Operations. At least I see a bit of life here."

"Surely there must be lots of young men who ask you out? If I was here I would ask you out in an instant."

She smiled and suddenly her whole face lit up. She was more than pretty, "Then I will take you up on that."

"But I am only here for two nights."

Her face fell a little and then she smiled, "If you don't want to take me out tomorrow then just say so."

I felt awful. I shook my head, "I didn't mean that. I am just surprised that you would go out with me and I would be delighted to take you out tomorrow. In fact, I wish it was tomorrow night right now."

She laughed, "You are right. You don't go out with girls very often."

Just then Doris toddled towards us on a pair of very high heels from the ladies' room and we both pulled back. We had been face-to-face. Major Foster negotiated the bar which had suddenly become crowded as people came in for the last half hour of the night.

Doris took the port and lemon, "Bottoms up!" She swallowed a good half of it and then took out another cigarette. As she lit it she said, "So what brings two such handsome officers into this godforsaken pub?"

Major Foster smiled affably, "It isn't that bad. I have drunk in worse believe me."

"But you two are officers. You shouldn't be mixing with the hoi polloi!" She seemed outraged that we would be seen in such a working-class pub.

Mum and Dad would not have approved of Doris for one moment. They loathed snobbery of any kind and Doris was a snob. I took heart from the fact that Susan didn't seem to approve either. I now had the difficult task of arranging to meet Susan without Doris knowing. I don't know why but I suspected that she would make Susan's life a misery.

Before anyone else could speak the air raid sirens went off. Doris threw down the contents of her glass and, grabbing Susan's hands said, "Come on!"

I said, "Surely there is a shelter close by we can all use."

Susan shook her head, "Ours is just two streets away and we are under orders to return there. Sorry, I'll...."

I never heard the end of the sentence as Doris dragged her unceremoniously out of the door. The rest of the drinkers, mainly men it must be said, finished their drinks and began to leave in an orderly manner. They were used to this. The landlord shouted, "You two gentlemen are more than welcome to use my cellar."

Major Foster shrugged, "Why not? It should be safe enough!"

We took our beer with us and descended into the bottle and barrel-filled cellar. It had been some time since I had been in an air raid. Having faced danger and German fire so many times it should have been easy and yet somehow this was much worse. Major Foster emptied his glass and said, "This must be hard for you. When the bullets and bombs start flying then you fire and fight back. You have to just take it here."

I nodded, "You are right. The civilians have it much harder than we do. No wonder my sister became a ferry pilot. It is better to fight back than accept this."

The all-clear went two hours later. As we made our way back to the flat Major Foster said, "That Doris was a little frightening wasn't she? But Susan seemed a nice girl. Were you getting on?"

"We were. I had asked her out."

He clapped me around the shoulders, "Splendid! Where are you taking her?"

"That's the trouble. We didn't get around to the details. Doris came back in and... I don't even know her second name!"

"It is Tancraville and she told you!" He shrugged, "It is like ships that pass in the night. It reminds me of a play by Noel Coward I saw before the war, *'Still Life'*. That ends happily though."

"Real life isn't the same as films and books, Toppy." I gave him a smile, "At least I got to talk to a girl. That is a step in the right direction at least."

"It certainly is!"

On the walk back I took in everything I could remember about the girl. Perhaps when I came to London again I might meet someone half as nice as her.

We were early for our meeting. Major Foster had already told me that there would be some important people there. They could be late but a lowly Major and Captain had to be early. I was admitted a little quicker this time. It seemed the Major was well known. Hugo was already in the conference room and the lack of smoke suggested that Colonel Fleming was absent. Hugo smiled, "Yes the Colonel sends his apologies. He has a meeting with Eisenhower. He deemed that more important than Operation Bodyguard."

I had not heard the name before, "Operation Bodyguard?"

"Oh sorry, Tom, I forgot you didn't know. That is what you have been doing. It is the name we came up with for the operation to deceive and mislead the Germans. You have done splendidly!"

I shook my head, "I had no idea. No one bothered to tell me the results of what we did."

Major Foster shook his head, "That's my fault, Tom. Your two operations had the same effect as smashing a wasp's nest with a stick. The Germans have been racing all over the place. They have had to repair the damage you did as well as beef up their security on that section of the Atlantic Wall. Rommel himself has spent more time close to Calais. We have heard that he is beginning to change his mind about the intended invasion. He believed we would come through Normandy. Along with the other deceptions your two raids have made him doubt himself. They have moved two Panzer Divisions north! Believe me, that is a victory!"

Hugo grinned, "And they think we sent two companies in rather than four men!"

I had no idea how Hugo knew that. I suspected he was aware of information which was at a far higher level than was disseminated to me. I felt a little better knowing that the deaths of the motor launch crew and the wounds to my men had been worth it.

The door opened and a gaggle of officers entered. Most had red around their collar which meant they were staff officers and all, bar one, were of a higher rank than me. Had Hugo not been there I would have been the most junior. I saw no one I recognised but there were at least three American Lieutenant Colonels.

A youngish-looking staff officer came over to me, "I am General Marlowe. I am pleased to finally meet you. We shan't need you after this morning. I am certain a young buck like yourself has better things to do than listen to us old men. We need to pick your brains and then outline some ideas we have."

"Anything I can do to help, sir, of course."

I was then interrogated again. Without Colonel Fleming there I found it much easier. They seemed to value my opinion and I found myself answering questions from every part of the room. When they were satisfied we broke for a coffee break and everyone left apart from General Marlowe and his aide, Captain Webster. Hugo was still there. He had been taking copious notes, presumably for Colonel Fleming.

"We would normally have Major Rose here but I think we can rely on you and Major Foster to make sure that the orders are delivered to your brigade safely." We nodded. "We think you have done enough in the Pas de Calais area. We want you and your section to be familiar with Normandy. You will be spending a great deal of time over there between now and April.

When the actual invasion comes you will go ashore with Lovat and the rest of your chaps but then we want you to go behind enemy lines again. The difference is this time you won't have to get your feet wet to get to safety."

"That's a relief, sir."

The General laughed, "Anyone who can sail a sinking fishing boat into a minefield and manage to sink his pursuer has nothing to fear in France. I am confident that you and your men will do a splendid job." He looked at his aide. "Captain Webster."

The Captain unrolled a map. It was a small part of Normandy. "On the day of the invasion, code-named Operation Neptune, the 1st Special Service Brigade along with French Commandos will land here at Queen Beach on Sword. The task for the 1st Special Service Brigade is to join up with the Airborne Division who will have taken the bridge over the Orne. You, however, and your section will be tasked with getting through the German lines. You will be the first ashore." He smiled, "Lord Lovat is not happy about that. He wanted to be the first ashore but we need you and your chaps to get to the bridge over the Orne. You have to find a way through the defences to facilitate the rest of Number Four Commando. Speed is of the essence. Once you have reached the bridge then your work will largely be over."

"Sir, the beach will be heavily mined!"

"We know that. We have over forty swimming tanks. They are called Duplex Drive Shermans. DD for short. Some will be fitted with flails and they will clear the beach. We do anticipate that there will be heavy losses which is why you and your section have to lay the trail of breadcrumbs for Lord Lovat to follow."

Major Foster said, quietly, "It is why you and some of your section will be going over in February. As you showed at St. Nazaire prior knowledge can be vital. We want you to be as familiar with the area as possible."

The Captain pointed to a second map. This one was much better detailed. "This is what we know of the area around Bella-Riva. It has too many blanks. We want you to bring back detail, Captain Harsker."

"Without being discovered."

General Marlowe had the good grace to smile, "Yes, something of a magic trick I feel, but everyone seems to think you can manage it."

"How will we be extracted, sir? If I know that then I will be able to say if it will work or not."

He nodded approvingly, "Honest and forthright. I like that. Submarine. You will be dropped in the estuary, paddle ashore and then paddle back out again. That way you go in just after dark. We have chosen February. The nights are long and inclement weather may well aid you as it did on your last venture."

"That sounds feasible sir. I am guessing that we lie up during the day."

"That's right."

"The danger I can foresee is the submarine having to charge its batteries at night so close to the Atlantic Wall sir. There will be patrol boats, mines, listening devices."

The General smiled, "Exactly what the Lieutenant Commander of the '*Osiris*' said. He seemed to think that they could manage it but that it would be tight. You will only have a very narrow window of opportunity."

"And I am guessing it will be another four-man section I take in."

"Quite right. The submarine and the mission dictate that."

"From what you said earlier, sir, this will not be a one off."

"No, Captain. You will need to reconnoitre both sides of the bridge. That means two missions."

I began to write down ideas on a piece of paper.

The Captain coughed, "There are still some details I need to give you, Captain."

I looked up and smiled, "Like what?"

"Well, you will need to know what units are there and their weaponry for a start."

"I thought that we were going to find that out, Captain. If you have that sort of detail then it seems pointless sending four men in. It is almost two months until we go in. Anything and everything could change by then. I have more than enough information to begin to make a plan. Any more detail can wait until nearer the time. It will not affect my plan overmuch."

I saw the Captain open and close his mouth. He looked like a carp! The General smiled and said, gently, "Sit down Captain Webster. So, Captain Harsker, you have a plan?"

"I have the bones of one, sir. There will be a curfew and anyone wandering the streets at night will be stopped and questioned. We need to be invisible. My men and I acquired some German greatcoats and caps when we were in Italy. We will take them and German weapons."

The Captain jumped up and said, "But that means you could be shot as spies! It is madness!"

I saw the General shake his head as Major Foster said, "Adolf Hitler has ordered that any Commando who is caught will be shot on sight. What can they do? Shoot them twice?"

Hugo coughed to cover his laugh and the embarrassed Captain sat down. "You see sir, the rules that bind ordinary soldiers do not affect us. I have six weeks to teach my men enough German to pass muster although from what I understand the Germans have brigades made up of all sorts of nations fighting for them. My plan is not to hide but to move around in the open. In fact, sir, It might be easier if we are dropped closer to dawn and spend the day there."

"That is a little extreme, Captain."

"It will make life easier for the Navy sir. However, we will go in as planned for the first recce."

The General nodded, "And where will you acquire the German weapons?"

I grinned, "We already have them, sir."

He laughed and slapped the table. "I wish they would let me go in with you Captain. If you survive this you can eat for free for the rest of your life!"

I closed the notebook, "And that is the trick isn't it General, to survive?"

His face became serious, "Quite right, Captain. Now I need to go through some more detail with the Major. What say you and Lieutenant Ferguson have a wander around the building? We have just begun to put in place the team that will be supporting you and to whom you will be reporting. It might be good for you to get to know them."

"Thank you, sir, that would be useful."

"Of course, they were only moved from the other side of the building today. As they are all ATS girls I am guessing they may have their knickers in a twist already."

Hugo said, "I don't think so sir. Senior Commander Dunne, the ATS commanding officer, is a calm woman. She terrifies me. The girls call her Dragon Dunne. I think they will be like a swan sir, calm on the surface and paddling for all they are worth below the surface."

"You may be right. She terrifies me. Anyway, give us a couple of hours. We'll go to my club for lunch."

"Sir."

Chapter 6

Hugo led me down some dingy, ill-lit stairs. "They are down in the basement. We had some squaddies clearing it out. Now that it is painted it looks a little better. What the General meant was that there is a whole section dedicated to Operation Neptune. You are part of that. Your element will be called Operation Dormouse. They will be collating the information you bring back and adding to the information from aerial photography and the French resistance. We did have some SOE agents but we lost too many of them last year to make that source of information reliable."

"It is a pity we couldn't have **'Lady Luck'**. I prefer that to a submarine."

"I am afraid it was badly damaged last month. This time it is a right off."

"And the crew?"

"Alan and most of the lads survived. I have no idea what happened to them. They were a good team. I hope their talents were not wasted."

The problem was always that Alan could never keep his mouth shut. He argued with the brass too much. They don't like it.

We stood outside a pair of newly made double doors. There was glass in the top half. I could see that the ATS were still organising the room. A formidable-looking woman with severely cropped, greying hair stood in the centre barking out orders while the rest hurried around carrying files, maps, even tables and chairs. Others laboured under huge typewriters.

"They look a little busy, Hugo. Perhaps this is not a good time."

"It is the only chance you will have, Tom. From now on everything comes through Major Foster or me. Your little jaunts to London end today."

I sighed, "Very well." I knew it was important that we put faces to the people who would be responsible for us while we were away but I did not relish bearding the dragon in her den!

As soon as the door swung open Senior Commander Dunne turned around. She was stockily built and reminded me, bizarrely, of Gordy Barker. She raised a quizzical eyebrow and said, "Yes, Lieutenant Ferguson?" Her voice showed she was used to command but I detected a twinkle in her eye.

"General Marlowe sent us down, Senior Commander. This is Captain Harsker and he is part of the team."

"The team?"

"Yes, Senior Commander, Operation Dormouse."

I saw her swing her gaze to me. I was not certain if I was about to be devoured. She certainly looked capable of that. She held out her hand. "I am pleased to meet you, Captain Harsker." Her eyes took in my medal ribbons. "I can see that you are not a desk jockey like Lieutenant Ferguson." Poor Hugo blushed and looked for somewhere to hide. "I suspect this will be our only meeting." She turned and said, "Attention!" Reg Dean could not have done it better. She turned to me and shook her head, "Not as crisp as I would have liked but they are learning. Ladies this is Captain Harsker. He is a real soldier, not the lazy type you all seem to date. This is the only time you will see him but you will be processing the information he provides. He is here to see us and, perhaps, understand our work. Now get on with what you are doing. I want this room operational by the end of the day!"

It was as though a light had been switched on in a dark room as they scurried away. "Sergeant West?"

"A Sergeant of the ATS appeared next to me. She had her hair in such a tight bun that her face looked pinched, "Yes Ma'am!"

"This is Sergeant West. She is the nearest thing to a soldier we have." The Sergeant looked pleased with the backhanded compliment. "Sergeant West makes sure that every part of the operations room functions. We only arrived this morning and so far it is a shambles but we will make it better." She nodded to the Sergeant to continue.

"Yes sir, we will have a radio fitted in the far corner. I have a couple of girls who have been training on that. They will communicate with the aircraft and ships used in the operation." I nodded. "Everything else will be organised so that each piece of information which enters this room is recorded, logged, filed and cross-referenced."

She looked at me expectantly as though waiting for a comment. "Very efficient. I will have to make sure my writing is up to muster then!"

The Senior Commander said, "Not to worry, Captain. I was an English teacher and Deputy Headmistress for thirty years. I will be able to decipher your handwriting. Make no mistake."

I nodded, "And I take it you know the details of the operation?"

For the first time, she did not look as confident as she had. "Not the detail Captain." She waved a hand at the uniformed women who scurried around. "These are good girls and can type, file and cross-reference but they don't need to know where you are operating."

I smiled, "But you have an idea where we are going, don't you Senior Commander?"

A genuine smile appeared on her face for the first time. "I have a mind, Captain and I use it. I can guess but your secret is safe with me. Well then if you would like to wander around and talk to the girls I have so much to do!"

I nodded and was about to say that I had seen enough when I suddenly caught sight of Doris' bleached blond hair. If she was here then the chances were that Susan would be too. "Thank you Senior Commander. Right, Hugo let's go over there eh?"

He looked confused. I said, under my breath, "There is a girl I want to speak to. Watch my back. Make sure I don't attract the dragon!"

"A girl?"

"A girl! I am human you know."

I pretended to be taking an interest in the room but I was scanning for Susan. I saw her bending over a desk and putting files in order. I tapped Hugo on the shoulder and then nodded to her. He smiled. I walked up behind her and said, quietly, "So where would you like to go tonight?"

She turned around with a look of surprise on her face. "I didn't think you would remember me!"

I heard a squeal from Doris. Hugo was masterful. I heard him say, "Could you show me where the little boy's room is, Private."

"But I know him."

"Of course, you do, my dear, the Senior Commander just introduced you. Now come along. I haven't got time to waste." He used his hand to direct her away from us.

"I haven't got much time. I don't know the area. I am in your hands. Where should we go?"

"There is one restaurant, but it is really expensive. We could always have fish and chips!"

"I am not having our first date at a fish and chip shop! Never mind the price. What is this place called?"

"The Whitehall Grill."

"Good. I shall meet you there at seven-thirty. Is that fine with you?" I smiled and was gratified when she beamed back at me. She nodded.

"Captain Harsker is that Private bothering you?"

I turned and saw a glowering Sergeant West, "Quite the reverse, Sergeant, she has answered all of my questions perfectly. She is a credit to the ATS!"

"Excellent." She added, conspiratorially, "She is one of the better ones."

"Quite. Well, I have seen enough and I feel more confident having spoken to you all."

As I reached the door Doris and Hugo came in. She opened her mouth but Sergeant West barked, "Private Day please close your mouth. There is a bus coming and it might fall in! Now get back to work!"

Once outside Hugo said, "What was all that about?"

"I met her last night and I wanted a date with her. Thanks, Hugo. I owe you."

"I am not certain that the General would approve. Security and all that."

"Bugger security!"

I did not mind the wait for the General. I had thought I would never see Susan again and she was going out with me. I still might make a mess of it but at least I now had a chance.

When they came out he said, "See everything?"

"Oh yes, sir. It looks well organised. I am happy."

"Good. We'll head for my club. Roger, fetch the car around."

As we headed down the stairs he said, "Any plans for dinner, Captain? The Major said you were driving back tomorrow."

"I thought I'd try a restaurant called the Whitehall Grill."

The General turned, "Damned fine restaurant but very expensive. You can come to my club if you like."

I shook my head, "I think I need to live a little more, General. I should hate to go toes up with money in my pocket!"

He burst out laughing, "That's the spirit."

As we descended the stairs Major Foster asked, "What was that about?"

"Susan! I just met her again and asked her out."

"Good fellow." He suddenly looked worried, "You didn't tell that harpy that I was in the building did you?"

"No Major. She got nothing out of me."

"Thank God." He looked at my uniform. "When we have had lunch we must see about getting that sponged."

I nodded, "If we have time I could do with ordering another uniform. If I am to be at the camp and in France so much I shall need one."

Make do and mend was a national watchword. I did look after my battledress as much as possible. Mrs Dean often repaired it but I needed another set of Number Ones. As we pulled up at the club, close to Green Park, I saw that we were close to the tailors I used. My father had used it for years and it felt like an old family friend.

"General, I will be just five minutes. Do you mind?"

"Of course not."

By the time I had been admitted and brought to the General, they were all seated around a table where a doddering old retainer was apologising for the lack of fare. The General nodded me to my seat and said, "Not to worry, Jenkins. Just bring us whatever you think we would like. I trust your judgement."

The General had brought us to his club as it was a discreet place to speak. Without going through the details of the operation we were able to iron out the last of the wrinkles. "I am afraid that you will be doing the Falmouth run at least once a fortnight, Foster. With Lord Lovat back there we will be requiring constant updates."

"Don't forget the liaison with the Americans too, General. They need to be, what is the phrase they use? Ah, that is it, they need to be kept in the loop!"

Shaking his head the General said, "We share English but they speak a totally different language."

I smiled, "You can blame your namesake, Captain Webster."

"Mine?"

"Samuel Webster. He wrote a dictionary and changed many of the spellings for efficiency."

"You are an interesting chap Harsker. How can you possibly know that? Your background is in Engineering."

"Mum and Dad tried to bring us up as rounded as possible."

Hugo chuckled, "That's right, General. Did you know that the Captain is an excellent cook?"

"I have never met your father but I have heard great things about him. Remarkable that he did so much in the Great War and is now so vital in this."

I remembered my conversation with Alf, the landlord of the pub in which we had sheltered. "That's the trouble, sir. There are lots of chaps out there who have managed to avoid doing anything and actually profit from the war. I thought it was just my lads who objected but when the Major and I were talking with some civilians last night we discovered they are just as irate about the issue."

"I know. I just hope that they are brought to book once this damned war is over." We then talked about the changes the war had wrought in the country we all loved so much.

It was almost four o'clock by the time we had finished. It was a leisurely meal but I was anxious to get around to my tailors. They were expecting me but I doubted they would be able to do anything. When we emerged into a damp grey dusk the general said, "Do you want me to send my car back for you, Captain?"

"No sir. The flat is only around the corner."

Shaking my hand the General said, "Good luck Harsker. I have no doubt that we shall see each other again but I want you to know that what you are doing is important. More than that, it is vital!"

I had nipped in to the tailors and told them what I wanted. I hoped that we had enough time now to complete the uniform. As I walked into the tailor shop I saw a uniform already on the table. "Ah, Captain Harsker. We wondered when you would get here."

"But how did you..."

"We have your measurements. I doubt that you have put on weight, sir. Here let's try it on for size." Maurice had been a young assistant before the war now he was one of the senior fitters. As he fussed around me he said, "As I thought sir. You have lost a little weight. A couple of darts will do the trick. We have the Commando flashes and pips in stock but we will need some time to swap over the medal ribbons, sir."

"That's not a problem, Maurice. I am just pleased that you could work so fast. I have a function tonight in a restaurant."

He beamed, "Then you will be the smartest one there." As he took off the jacket to hand to one of his assistants he said, "A young lady sir?"

I nodded, "A young lady."

"Excellent! Your father will be pleased!"

Everyone, it seemed, was concerned about my lack of love life.

I was there early. It was cold and it was damp but I had my greatcoat and I sheltered under the portico of the empty shop next door. It looked to have been a shop selling high-quality foods. There was little of that around these days. I wondered if they would return after the war. Now that we had begun to take back pieces of Europe we could begin to hope that the war might actually end one day. The difference between this war and the Great War was the fact that the civilians had been affected far more. As the air raid, the previous night had demonstrated death was as close to those who used pubs as those who dropped behind enemy lines.

As soon as I had arrived I had nipped in to make sure they had a table for us. The owner, another who wished for the more profitable days before the war had assured me that there would be a table but he was less confident about the range of fare we could be offered.

As I waited I found myself panicking about tiny details. Had I shaved closely enough? Should I have had a haircut? What would we talk about? What if she didn't turn up? I shook myself. I could lead men behind German lines; I was about to do something so normal that just about every one of my section had either a girlfriend or a wife. If they could see me now they would laugh and quite rightly too. I said, out loud, "Pull yourself together Tom!"

Susan's voice, almost by my elbow made me start, "You know they say that talking to yourself is the first sign of madness?"

She looked up at me and her smile seemed to drive away the rain, "I wasn't certain if you would come."

She slipped her arm through mine and said, "I told you I would be here." Looking up at the rain-filled, black night she said, "Can we go inside? I am sure it will be warmer."

"Of course. How rude of me."

The blackout curtains had prevented us from seeing inside. It was lit by candles. Before the war this had been romantic; now it was practical. There were just two other tables occupied. One had an elderly couple while the other had another version of Doris and what was undoubtedly a spiv. The head waiter glanced over at the couple and said, "I have a nice quiet table over here, sir." He took us to a table which had a potted plant between me and the spiv. He took our coats and said, "I will bring the menu and wine list over shortly, sir."

I could not help grinning as I said, "You look gorgeous!"

She cocked her head to one side and smiled back, "In this light, it is difficult to say but you do look handsome." She reached over and touched the lapel on my uniform. "Is this new?" I nodded. "I am flattered. I hope I am worth it and that you aren't disappointed."

"How could I be? As you must have realised this is all new to me."

She laughed, "I can see that but you are a war hero. After you had left the Operations Room even the Dragon was impressed.

She kept going on about how you had been put in for the Victoria Cross."

I nodded, "But I may not get it. I am not even certain I deserve it."

"That was the other thing I heard about how modest you are. I am just a plain little ATS girl from Cheshire." She waved a hand around the room. "This is far grander than anything we have in Church Lawton."

"I don't get to this sort of place very often either."

The waiter returned with the menu. I leaned over to Susan, "Do you like wine?"

"I have had a glass of port once. Does that count?"

I laughed, "It is a start." I chose a red wine from the south-west of France. I had had it before. Mum liked it because it was soft.

The waiter nodded approvingly, "A good choice sir and if I might suggest?" He gestured at the menu.

"Of course."

"That wine would go well with the pâté." I nodded. "And then vegetable soup?" Again I nodded. "For the main course I would have suggested the liver but I can see that might spoil the evening. How about two omelettes with wild mushrooms and garlic?"

I looked over to Susan, she smiled engagingly, "That sounds splendid to me although I have never eaten garlic before. Doesn't it have a strong smell?"

The waiter said, "If it is cooked badly, miss, then yes. We have a good chef. I will bring the dessert menu later. Bon appétit."

Susan looked down at the array of knives and forks. "I am regretting suggesting this place now. It seems even posher than I thought. Where do you start with all of this?"

I smiled back at her. "Start from the outside and work in but don't worry. I am more interested in you than your ability to choose the right knife and fork."

She laughed, "Doris said you were both posh and she was right. She was jealous when I told her I had a date with you. She wanted one with the Major."

"I think she frightened him off."

"Doris is all right. The trouble is she has seen too many American films. She is desperate for an Errol Flynn or Clark Gable to sweep her off her feet and take her to his home in America. She can't cope with the rationing."

"I confess you do seem like an odd couple."

The waiter brought the wine and poured some for me to taste. It was fine and I nodded. When we both had full glasses I raised mine. "Here is to my first date. Let us hope I don't make a mess of it!"

She touched my glass with hers and said, "As it is only my second I will drink to that." She sipped the wine cautiously and then smiled. "Like port but not thick and cloying."

"It is one of Mum's favourite wines."

"Your mum drinks wine?" I nodded. "Does she work? My Mum helps out in the village shop now."

"No, Mum was a nurse in the Great War and we live in a small village too. We don't have a village shop."

We small talked about our homes and our families through the pâté and the soup. She had never had pâté before but said it was like her mum's homemade meat paste. I discovered that she had a brother who was serving in the Navy aboard a corvette in the North Atlantic. Her dad had been wounded in the war and was a handyman. By the time the main course arrived, I felt easy in her company. We finished the main course. A group of Americans had come in and were loudly ordering. I leaned forward to speak to Susan, "That was better than I could have hoped for in wartime England. How about a dessert?"

"Normally I wouldn't but why not?"

I was about to wave the waiter over when the spiv wandered over. I could smell him before I saw him. He reeked of cheap cologne, hair cream and cigarettes. He was a Cockney, "Nah then sir I can see that you and your little lady are a lovely couple. Can I interest you in a ring?"

I looked around and saw him close up. He was in his twenties and I wondered why he had not been called up. He had all the affectations of a minor criminal: the pencil moustache, wide-lapelled suit and gold watch. He had in his hand a tray of rings which he had produced from under his jacket.

I spoke even before I saw the look of distaste on Susan's face, "No, thank you. We are quite all right."

"Nah, come on sir! A smartly dressed officer like yourself. If you can afford a tailored uniform then a ring should be no bother. I'll do you a special deal!"

I turned so that I faced him, "We are not going to buy a ring from you so go away and peddle your wares elsewhere."

I had not spoken loudly but we had attracted the attention of the other diners. The room had gone silent and the American officers all stared.

I could see that the spiv was not happy with the attention. He hissed, "You think you are so high and mighty with your medals and your Commando flash. You wanna watch it mate! That's all. You just watch it!"

He turned and stormed back to his table. The Americans nodded approvingly. "Do you want to go now?"

Susan smiled, "No, that would look as though he had driven us out. I will have dessert. Apple pie and custard sounds wonderful."

The waiter came over and I ordered two and two coffees.

She stared over my shoulder as the spiv and his lady friend left. "I can't stand those types. I had never seen one until I came to London and they are on every street corner. It makes me so angry when I hear of brave lads being killed for this country and here, in London, these criminals get away with... well all sorts. I bet those rings were stolen."

I nodded, "Or worse, taken from dead bodies." She put her hand to her mouth and I regretted my words instantly. "Sorry. That was crass of me!"

She shook her head. "No, you are probably right. I just hadn't thought of that. It just makes me even more proud of the way you stood up to him."

I laughed, "I don't think our greasy friend would have been a problem."

When we had eaten and the waiter had delivered the bill the head waiter came over and said, quietly, "I would watch out for that man, sir. Joe Cameron is a dangerous man. He has thugs who work for him."

I suddenly realised that this Joe Cameron had not paid when he left. I had heard of this sort of thing. "And the owner has to pay protection is that it?"

The head waiter shrugged, "It makes life easier and the police have enough to do. When the war is over..."

I gave him some notes, "You shouldn't have to."

"I will get your change."

I shook my head, "Keep it. We both enjoyed the meal. Although I am not certain when we will be back."

He waved over the waiter who brought our coats and hats. "You take care, sir. We want a restaurant filled with officers like you after the war and not..."

I nodded, "Quite!"

One of the Americans came over. I saw that he, too, was a Captain. I saw his shoulder flash and identified him as the 1st Infantry Division. "Can I just shake you by the hand? I have heard what you guys do and from the medals on your chest, you don't hang back. I'll be glad when we get into this little fray."

I shook his proffered hand. "I met some of your chaps in Sicily; Darby's Rangers. They did very well. I am sure you will do fine. It is good to have some allies at last. It has just been us, the Russians and the Commonwealth for some time."

He nodded, "Believe you me there were plenty of guys back home who felt the same." He looked beyond me. "Say, do you and your young lady need any help? That guy did not look pleasant. There might be some trouble."

"He wasn't very pleasant was he but I think we will be fine. Just so long as I keep upwind of him!" I laughed, "We are not quite the Wild West!"

He shook his head. "I love your British sense of humour."

The rain had not relented and for that, I was pleased. Susan pulled in even tighter to me. She had chosen the restaurant because it was close to her barracks and we just had four streets to negotiate. Susan seemed very happy. "And to think you were in Italy not long ago! I bet you would like to swap right now!"

I leaned in more, "Right now I wouldn't wish to be anywhere else."

"Sweet!"

We had just turned into the narrow street which led to the barracks when three figures stepped out. One of them was Joe Cameron and the other two looked like his thugs. Although I had had a couple of glasses of wine and I was relaxed the Commando in me made me alert to danger in an instant. I moved Susan behind me and, stepping forward, began to gauge the opposition. This was not a friendly meeting.

I had correctly judged Joe Cameron; he was the boss. He allowed his two thugs to come forward. Both were in their twenties. Although they had the gnarled faces of two men who had been in fights I was not intimidated.

The spiv said, "You should have shown me more respect soldier boy! You showed me up in front of my woman and I can't have that. People were laughing; they were only Yanks but that makes no difference. The lads are going to teach you a lesson and then we will just lift your wallet as payment of dues for coming on my manor." I said nothing. I was weighing up which one would strike first. I saw the one to my left preparing his fist. He was wearing a knuckle duster. I took the glove off my right hand. The spiv saw it as a sign of weakness. "Frightened of damaging your glove eh? Get him boys and do him over good!"

The one on the left swung, as I had expected at my head. I stepped back and pushed his arm away with my left hand. I then punched him hard, twice in the ribs. I heard one crack. I punched him under the chin with my forearm and his skull cracked into the face of the other.

I stepped back and said, "Now go away boys before you get hurt!"

Joe Cameron snarled, "No more mister nice guy. Charlie, use your knife!"

Charlie pulled out a knife and moved his dazed friend to the side. As he lunged at my throat Susan took a whistle from her handbag and began to blow it. It did distract Charlie somewhat although I knew what I was doing anyway. As he lunged I grabbed his arm, turned into him and threw him over my shoulder. He sailed through the air and landed on his back.

"Harry! Use your knife!" I heard the panic in Cameron's voice. I was also dimly aware of voices approaching from behind.

As Harry pulled out his knife I turned and stamped on Charlie's right hand. I broke every bone in his hand. Harry was wise to my jujitsu throw and he was more cautious. What he did not expect, as he stepped forward, was for me to raise my heel and stamp at the knee of his leading, right leg. It folded back unnaturally and he fell to the ground, screaming in pain. I had no idea who was coming behind me but before I could turn Joe Cameron tried to run. As I pulled back my fist he pulled out a flick knife and slashed at my eyes. I ducked and hit him with every ounce of strength I had. He smoked and was unfit. I hit him squarely in the solar plexus and he fell to the ground, gasping for air like a stranded fish.

I turned to take on the next attackers and saw a policeman and an ARP warden.

"What the...?" The policeman stopped as Joe Cameron raised his head. "Joe Cameron! You finally bit off more than you could chew eh?"

Susan said, "They attacked us! They had knives!"

I knelt down and took out the box of rings. "I think these may be stolen property, Constable."

"You may well be right, sir." He began to laugh as the two thugs tried to rise. "And I have waited many a year to see you two cut down to size."

I said, "Will I have to come to the station, Constable?"

He looked at me and smiled, "I don't think so, sir. This looks pretty clear-cut to me. We have found three criminals with stolen property. It looks like they fell from that wall. It was just fortunate that we happened to be here eh Reg?"

The ARP warden said, happily, "Propitious I should say, Fred. We can get them to the hospital and then lock them up!"

The Constable saluted, "Have a pleasant evening, sir and I am sorry that you had to run into scum like this."

I nodded, "I have run into their type before. The difference was they were wearing grey uniforms with SS on their shoulders! And Constable, in case you didn't know, this piece of... well this chap has been taking protection money from the local businesses."

The Constable's face hardened, "That explains a lot. Thanks again, sir."

Susan took my arm and we hurried down the street, "Where did you get the whistle?"

"Dad was worried about London. He got it off a bobby friend of his. It came in handy."

"It certainly did."

"Not that you needed it. Three men with knives and you don't have a mark on you."

I held up my grazed right knuckle. "Not quite unscathed but I have had worse."

She laughed and threw her arms around my neck. She pulled down my head and kissed me full on the lips. I felt as though I had touched an electric cable. I stepped back. She looked afraid, "What's wrong?"

I shook my head, "I have never been kissed before!"

"And?"

In answer, I grabbed her and kissed her back. I think we would have spent hours there had not the ambulance for the injured criminals to come hurtling past. "I had better get back, Tom. The Wild West will be waiting!"

I did not want to go but I knew we had to. There was a sentry at the gate and our farewell had to be perfunctory. Her eyes were wide and I saw the hint of tears. "When will I see you again?"

"I am back to Falmouth in the morning."

She nodded and bit her lip, "Will you write to me? I mean you don't have to but..."

"Of course I will but you should know that sometimes I can't write because..."

"Because you are behind enemy lines and risking your life. I know. I finally find a man I can love and find that he has the most dangerous job in England." She shook her head, "It's not fair!"

"*'A man I can love'*, is that what you said?"

"Of course, silly! You don't think I kiss a man like that all the time!"

The sentry coughed, "Sorry miss, but Sergeant West will be out soon and she will chew me out as well as you."

I nodded, "I will write and Lieutenant Ferguson has my address."

She kissed me and stepped back, "Have you nothing to say?"

"You know exactly how I feel, don't you?"

She nodded, "I know but a girl likes to hear it."

I looked at the grinning sentry and said, "Well I do." It was then we heard Sergeant West shouting at someone in the building and, with a teary wave, Susan ran into the building.

As I headed back to the flat I wondered at the wisdom of this. My life had been dangerous enough before. Now I would be going into battle worrying that I might die. Auntie Alice and Charlie had been where I was and then Charlie had been killed. Would I be sentencing Susan to such a life? Any joy I had had in the evening evaporated by the time I reached the flat.

Major Foster was relieved when I told him what had happened. He had assumed the worst. "You can't avoid liking people just because there is a war on, Tom. Your Dad and your Mum fell in love during a war. You and Mary are the proof, aren't you? I think I know you well enough to know that it won't make any difference to you. You have this ability to be cold and detached when you need to be. I saw it in Belgium. You still have it. I personally think this is the best thing to have happened to you."

Chapter 7

There would be no Christmas leave that year. Everyone knew there would be an invasion sometime in 1944. I had a better idea than most but even Mrs Dean had an opinion. There were huge American camps all over Southern England and it was rumoured that a whole village in Devon, Slapton, had been evacuated to accommodate the Americans who used it to practise landings. I had to put Susan to the back of my mind for I had too much planning and training to occupy me. The German lessons were a priority. We discovered that the best time for such lessons were first thing in the morning. We would then have our run which seemed to be more enjoyable after the classroom. We then used the time after our evening meal to practise some more. Mrs Dean and Reg joined us.

"You never know, after the war is over we might get German visitors. I shall need paying customers once you lads go."

Scouse had said, "I can't see Jerry coming over here Mrs Dean."

"You never know."

It seemed slow at first but they were all willing. That was one advantage of having such a settled team. It became fun and that was always the best way to learn. Now that the whole brigade was together I was joined by other officers. Captain Marsden was an old friend and he took to running back, each night to our digs. His was just four houses away. We had found that running was more efficient if you talked as you ran. It kept your breathing steady.

You don't appear your normal cheerful self these days, John."

He shook his head, "It is some of these new chaps. They have widened the net for volunteers and, I think, lowered the standard."

I had heard this myself. "I think you might be right. The Marines look to be getting the better volunteers."

"Perhaps that is no bad thing given the new role we have. We will be landing with all the other units."

"True but we will be the first in and that is always the most dangerous." As we ran I learned more about the problems he was having with his section. I began to feel guilty; mine were perfect.

We had been training with our men separately but, as December drew to a close and the weather became worse we were sent to Devon to join the Americans and practise landings. We were each given a lorry to travel down. I sat in the front with Gordy and Bill Hay, the recently promoted Lance Sergeant. Sergeant Poulson rode in the rear.

"This could be messy, sir."

"Perhaps Gordy but it needs to be done. We need to learn how to go in with other landing craft. It won't just be us this time."

"But the weather sir! It's freezing cold and the rain is slashing down! We wouldn't land in weather like this!"

Bill Hay was a thoughtful sort. He liked to listen a lot but when he spoke he was worth listening to. "I think you are right Sarge but it might be that we have to go in when the weather is marginal. If we go in just using good weather that could be a disaster." Barker nodded. "Besides the bad weather stops Jerry from coming over and making a nuisance of himself."

"Would they do that, sir?"

"Everyone knows there is an army gathering ready to invade. If you were Jerry wouldn't you like to spoil the party? I think Hay is right. This weather is a boon!"

We were given tents when we arrived. For my lads that was no hardship. We had slept out in the desert, snow and rain. Captain Marsden had a problem with his men. Ken Curtis was his Troop Sergeant. He had been with me until he had been promoted. Their section had arrived first and he was allocating their tents as we pulled up. Captain Marsden was nowhere to be seen. I suspect he had gone to arrange food. He knew the value of a hot meal. Whatever the reason for his absence Ken was having to deal with some truculent Commandos.

"I am just saying, Sarge that this isn't right! We should have some Nissen huts! We'll freeze our bits off tonight and the ground is sodden! How will we keep it clean? King's Regulations say that we should be given decent accommodation. This is not fit for animals, Sarge."

"Osborne, you are a whinging barrack-room lawyer. Why in God's name did you join the Commandos?"

"For the extra money of course Sarge!"

I stepped out of the lorry. In the dark, my pips could not be seen. They all snapped to attention. "Is there a problem here, Sergeant Curtis?"

"No sir. Some of the men wondered why we were using tents instead of huts. I was about to explain."

I looked at the ring leader of the objectors. I recognised him as one of the two recruits I had seen getting out of that car at the camp. He was a big man and a cigarette hung from his lip. He had a sneer on his face. I had heard of his type before. They knew every regulation and used them to their own advantage. They were neither fair nor reasonable. There were increasingly more of them for they were latecomers to this war. My section had all been in from the start.

I turned to Sergeant Curtis. "The day we have to explain why a man should obey orders is the day we start to lose this war." I turned to Private Osborne. I pointed to the tent. "Those are your quarters. Far from being fit for a pig, they will be fit for His Majesty should he wish to visit and you, Private Osborne, will keep that tent immaculate." He stared at me and I saw his eyes narrow. "And take that cigarette from your mouth. I don't recall Sergeant Curtis giving you permission to smoke!" My days as a Sergeant were not forgotten. I saw him slightly ball his fists. This man was a bully. I stepped in close. "Get rid of that cigarette and unclench your hands or I will have you on a charge so fast that your feet won't touch the ground."

He threw away the cigarette and placed the palms of his hands down his legs. He flicked his head around, "Sir, with respect, you aren't our officer."

"I can see you have only been in five minutes so I will be a little more lenient with you. Perhaps you are a little slow, I am not certain. You look like you sat at the back of the classroom but I will say this once. You do not have one officer; you have every officer! Understand?" I tapped my pips. "You salute and obey these. This is the British Army and not some ragtag bunch of malcontents!"

"A problem Captain Harsker?"

"No, Captain Marsden. I was just reminding this Private that he obeys the orders of every officer who wears the King's uniform."

He saw who it was, "Private Osborne! I might have known. Insubordinate again!"

"No, sir, I was not. I was..."

"Sergeant Curtis put this man on a charge."

"What charge?"

Ken Curtis growled at Osborne. "Sir."

"What charge, sir?"

Captain Marsden pointed to the still-glowing cigarette at Osborne's feet. "Smoking whilst on duty for a start." He put his hands on his hips and roared, "Now get your gear stowed and stop embarrassing the Sergeant and me!"

They turned and hurried to their tents. Sergeant Curtis said, "Sorry about that, sir."

"These aren't the men we led in Africa, Curtis. You will have to be a bit harder."

"Captain Harsker is correct, Curtis but it is my fault. I have tried to mollycoddle some of them. Better we break them now or they might break us on the big day!"

I turned and saw my men watching. Gordy Barker said, "What he needs is a good old-fashioned hiding."

Bill Hay shook his head, "He is a barrack-room lawyer. That is just what he wants. He knows King's Regs inside out and he will use them! I served with a bunch like that. I am just glad we have none in our section!"

The incident created a foul mood. The weather suddenly seemed worse. When we went to the mess tent I could see that Captain Marsden's section was divided. There was a small group who obviously supported Osborne while the rest were behind Captain Marsden. It was not a good situation.

The next day we were taken to Dartmouth to embark on the landing craft. We saw them in the harbour. They were big ships and designated LC(I). With a couple of Oerlikon guns and a crew of twenty-four, they were substantial vessels. At a hundred and sixty feet in length and almost twenty-four feet, wide they were nothing like the E-boat we had been used to. We disembarked from the lorry carrying our equipment. We still carried our Bergens. Their replacements had not been issued yet. We were in no hurry to change them. Two detached themselves from those bobbing about in the icy water and headed for the quay. They were numbers 523 and 527.

I turned to make sure that my men were ready to board in an orderly fashion. In truth, I was not worried but the behaviour of some of Captain Marsden's men had planted seeds of doubt in my mind. When I turned back the coxswain of 523 waved cheerily. It was Bill Leslie.

Lance Sergeant Hay said, "There is a cheery and familiar face!" The two Bills had been friends when we had served in the Mediterranean.

Lieutenant Redmire was the skipper. He looked young and wore the RNVR flash. I suppose for such a small boat that was the norm. He shook my hand, "Welcome aboard, sir. We are your taxi for today and, so I have heard, for the big show. Exciting, what?"

I smiled at his enthusiasm. "It certainly is. We will rattle around a little in here I am afraid. How many do you normally carry?"

"Rammed to the gills we can manage two hundred but it is normally one-eighty. You are our first passengers so to speak. Today will be our first little jaunt."

I turned to my sergeants, "Have the men sort themselves out. Any chance of a tour Lieutenant?"

"Delighted!" He took me to the bridge. "This is the business end. We are lucky to have Petty Officer Leslie. He is very experienced."

"I know, Bill and I have served together before."

"That's right sir. How is the *'Lucky Lady'*?"

"I am afraid her sailing days might be over but Wacker and the Lieutenant are still around."

"Good. I miss my old shipmates. This is a fine ship, sir. Solid as a rock. We'll get you ashore safely."

The Lieutenant was keen to show off his command. I suspect it was his first. "Quite. Now we have two Oerlikon guns. They are not manned at the moment. There is a mess and we can accommodate some men below decks but I am afraid most will have to suffer the elements." He took me to the bows.

To my surprise, there was no ramp. "No ramp Lieutenant?"

"No sir, you go down these two gangplanks at the side. They get lowered at the last minute I believe."

He did not sound confident. "You haven't tried them yet?"

He shook his head and said, quietly, "I think that is what the next couple of days will be about sir. Trying things out and seeing what problems arise."

"Good. Better than finding out when Jerry is firing at us. Well, I am looking forward to this. I have taken up enough of your time. I shall go and talk to my chaps." When he had returned to the bridge I waved my sergeants forward. "It seems they lower these two ramps and we disembark either side of the bow."

"Interesting sir. I am glad we are having a play with these oversized bathroom toys." Sergeant Poulson always enjoyed new challenges. He had not changed much since he had first joined my section as a keen young private.

I nodded, "Today I will lead one half down the left-hand ramp and Barker you take the right. Poulson and Hay, you chivvy them up."

"A bit like jumping from an aeroplane sir."

"With the added delight of Germans firing at us."

"All ready Captain?"

I turned and waved, "Whenever you are, Lieutenant!"

As we left the harbour for the short journey around to the sands we would be using my sergeants and began to arrange my men into some kind of order. I could see that we could not possibly simulate the real thing. There were just thirteen of us for one thing. Getting off would be easier than when jostling with a hundred and eighty others. I could see why this exercise had been arranged. If Lieutenant Redmire was new to this too it was better to iron out the smaller problems. I looked over at the other boat. Captain Marsden had twenty-one men in his section. He would have slightly more problems than I would.

The men were carrying their new Lee Enfield rifles. Crowe and Davis had the two Bren guns. Smith and Herbert would be their loaders. No matter what the orders when we went in the day of the invasion we would take any Colts and Thompsons we still had. If we could get our hands on the ammunition then we would also take the American rocket launcher we had been given by Colonel Darby. We respected the enemy too much not to take as much advantage as we could. For this exercise, however, watched I had no doubt, from the shore by senior officers, we would play the game.

We were used to travelling by E-boat or motor launch. Sixteen knots was not slow but it was compared with our other mode of travel. We did, however, have steel bows. We knew the effect of German heavy machine guns. We would have some protection. I saw now that these had an advantage over the smaller landing ships which had a ramp. They would be far slower.

Lieutenant's voice sounded, "Ready Captain; we land in ten minutes!"

I raised my hand to show that I had heard. Fletcher, Crowe and Smith stood behind me. "Let's make this as realistic as possible eh lads. If there were Germans waiting for us then they would have guns firing at us. Zig-zag up the beach and when I hit the deck you follow on either side. Crowe, I want that Bren ready to fire as quickly as possible."

"Yes sir."

Fletcher's Scouse drawl always sounded vaguely disrespectful somehow. "Aye sir, we'll need to put on a good show for the brass." He pointed to the high ground above the beach. I saw a huddle of khaki. It was as I had thought. The new ships and men were being evaluated. My inside knowledge from my meetings with the General had given me a better insight into the whole operation. The general and the planners were keen to avoid any kind of disaster. By beginning training early and using small-scale operations then minor problems could be identified. When we had the whole brigade involved it would be a logistical nightmare.

I put those thoughts from my head as I saw the beach grow closer. Four sailors ran alongside us to prepare to lower the ramps. I saw a problem right away, "Fletcher, watch those sailors and see what they do. In the real assault, they might get shot. They are brave men!"

"Yes sir." He nodded for he had seen the problem too. They would be exposed to enemy fire while they lowered the ramps into position.

I frowned when I saw them joking as they went forward. As we had learned at Dieppe and St. Nazaire, if you did not take training seriously then it cost lives when you went into action.

The Lieutenant was using a loud hailer. "Lower ramps!"

The two ratings began to lower the ramp. It was too slow. I moved behind them. One looked behind me with surprise on his face. The ramp was beginning to lower. They let the ropes slip through their hands quicker. The front of the ship bobbed up and down in the surf. Even before it was down I ran down the ramp. One of the sailors was knocked into the water. I jumped clear of the surf and jinked to my right and then my left. Lyme Bay swept around us. The headland and low cliffs were over a hundred yards away. I ran for forty yards and then dropped; the shingle and sand were soft. I cocked my Lee Enfield and aimed it up the beach. I pushed sand and shingle up before my face. My men did me proud. They dropped next to me seconds after I did. My line of men spread out along either side. Technically the exercise was over. We had only been sent to practise the landing but this was too good an opportunity to miss. I spied the twelve officers on the low cliffs a hundred and fifty yards away.

"Sergeant Poulson take half the men right. The rest follow me left. We will take those officers prisoner!"

Fletcher chuckled, "That's great sir!"

"On three! One, two, three!"

I leapt to my feet and ran left for ten yards and then right. The shingle and sand gave way to some rocks, more sand and shingle before the low cliffs rose gently up to the vantage point the officers were using. As an obstacle, it would merely slow us down. I turned right and ran. When I turned left and ran up the slope my feet slipped slightly on the slick stones and grass. If we had been wearing boots then we might not have found our footing. We ran obliquely beyond the officers and when I turned and shouted, "Charge!" the noise of our collected shout made some of the officers start.

We levelled our guns at them. I saw one older officer with a white moustache open and close his mouth. Beyond them, I saw Sergeant Poulson and the rest of my section.

General Marlowe began to clap. Major Foster, grinning, joined him. I lowered my gun and my men did the same.

The General stepped forward. "I am not certain that was in the orders for the day, Captain."

I nodded, "It seemed a waste just to land on the beach and build sandcastles. We are Commandos. This is what we do."

"The officer with the white moustache pointed to the beach. "Not all Commandos, it seems." He pointed down the beach. Half of Captain Marsden's section appeared to be sitting on the beach and smoking. The other half were advancing towards us.

I shrugged, "My section, sir, has been in action longer than most."

"And they follow you no matter what." General Marlowe nodded. "Well done gentlemen. I think we can safely say that you do not need to practise the landings any more. I believe you will have other tasks to complete but well done. Major Foster here has told me already of your exploits and your reputation. It is well deserved."

I turned, "Take the men back to the beach, Sergeant Poulson."

After they had gone General Marlowe said, "How are the landing craft then Harsker?"

"Fine sir but when the ratings stand to lower the ramps they are exposed. I think we could lower them if the ratings fell in action."

Major Foster laughed, "Or if they are pushed out of the way by over-eager Commandos."

"If there are Germans firing at you, and I guarantee there will be, then you stay still as little as possible."

"I can see that. Thank you, Captain."

I walked down the beach. I saw Captain Marsden and Troop Sergeant Curtis berating the men who had sat down. I was not surprised to see that Osborne and his cronies were amongst them.

When we reached the landing craft I saw the rating I had pushed into the water, "Are you all right?"

I saw, behind him, Bill Leslie. When the rating spoke I guessed that Bill had had a word with him. "Yes sir. Sorry about the delay. I thought it was just training. You were right to shove me." He glanced behind at the Petty Officer. "I'll be quicker next time."

I nodded and shouted to the Lieutenant who was standing at the top of the ramp. "Could my men have a go at lowering the ramp, Lieutenant?" I pointed to the headland, "If there were guns there then your men might be hit. Another practice eh?"

"Fine by me! To the helm, Coxswain."

Bill winked at me with a grin on his face, "Right sir! All aboard the Skylark! Trips around the bay a penny a passenger!"

As we climbed up the ramp I said, "Fletcher, Smith let's see how fast you could do it."

Fletcher pointed as we passed the top of the ramp. "If we ran down when we reached here sir then the ramp would fall faster. Mr Bird our Science teacher taught us that. It is called gravity!" He seemed proud that he remembered something from school. From what the others had told me those occasions when he had been in school had been rare!

By the time we had headed back to Dartmouth, we had made four more landings and each time the lowering of the ramp had been better. The ratings quickly adopted the methods used by Fletcher and took to sheltering beneath the ramp. Bill Hay had pointed out that they had more protection from bullets there than on the top of the ramp.

Back at camp Captain Marsden came over to me. He had a troubled look on his face. I had felt bad all the way back to Dartmouth. I had not wanted to embarrass John. I had been concentrating on my part of the operation. As he came towards me I said, "Sorry about that John. I was not trying to show off or anything."

He nodded and lit a cigarette. "I know. It did take me by surprise but Curtis said he expected something like that from you. No, it was the right thing to do and, in many ways, it has helped me."

"Helped you?"

"Well, you saw Osborne and his cronies. I saw the problem right away. If it was just one man I might be able to do something about it but there are seven of them."

"You could have them transferred to other sections. Give Osborne to me. My lads will sort him out."

"Thanks, Tom but it is my section and I will sort them out."

"Remember Waller, John."

He nodded. Waller had been a really bad apple. I had been forced to shoot him after he had gone on the rampage during a training exercise, taking Captain Grenville hostage in the process. "I know. I think I will enlist the help of Reg Dean."

"I think that is a good idea."

He laughed, "I remember when you were my Lieutenant. I saw then that you were a real leader and look at your section now. I would take those twelve against any other fifty Commandos. They are a good team."

I nodded, "I know."

The practice attack spurred my men on and we were out in all weathers and times. We ran before dawn and after dusk. The incident with Osborne seemed to have galvanised them even more. As the month of January began to pass I summoned my sergeants.

"Next month we have two or three operations planned."

Sergeant Poulson said, "Three sir? I thought you said there would be just two."

"Now that we are closer to the time and the operation I can give you more detail and you will see why it might be three. We are to land at the Orne River in Normandy. We will scout out the town on one visit and, on the second a week later, the west side of the river. We will be going in by submarine and we will be dressed as Germans. If we do not manage to get what we need in those two then we will have to return for a third."

Bill Hay said, "German uniforms sir?"

Gordy shrugged, "They will shoot us if they catch us anyway."

"Precisely so, with that in mind, I have an operation for us here in England. We are going to scout out Plymouth dockyard with weapons but without papers."

"The sort of thing we had to do as part of our training?"

"Right Bill. When we go over to Normandy we will be in teams of four. I will be one of the four. I intend to take those who evade capture." I looked at them. "That includes the sergeants."

They nodded.

"I want proof that you got into the dockyard." I smiled, "Other than your capture of course. There are thirteen of us. You each pick three men to be in your team. I will choose one of the teams to accompany. Regard me as an umpire." They laughed. "When we go to Normandy I want us to be able to walk around in German uniforms observing and recording but we also have to evade capture."

Gordy asked, "Are we dropping this time sir?"

"No Gordy. Submarine."

"Sergeant Poulson shuddered, "A steel coffin then, sir."

"I am afraid so Sergeant. At least our extraction should be easier."

"Are we going to go in to Plymouth by boat?"

"That is up to you. We will be making the attempt tomorrow night. The first raid is scheduled for two weeks from today." I could see they were eager to be away. "Off you go then. Submit the names of your teams to me by tonight please."

I went to the adjutant's office and told him what I had planned. "A risky strategy. Suppose they get caught? Won't that ruin the morale?"

"If they do get caught then we can modify the plan. Better to fail here rather than in France. Here we would be embarrassed. In France, we would be dead!"

Sergeant Major Dean was summoned. We told him what we had planned. "I will take the lorry down to the docks then, sir, in case anybody does get picked up. If you ask my opinion, sir, I think it is a damned good idea. And it will ginger up the dock guards when they find out we have been inside their fence."

Chapter 8

The names of the teams were given to me as we finished dessert. I had already decided to go in with Bill Hay and his team. I knew the other two would pick the most experienced men and Bill, as the lance sergeant, would be left with the rest. I stood and addressed the room. Mrs Dean and Reg were doing the dishes.

"Remember chaps, that Plymouth tomorrow is enemy territory. This is neither a lark nor a bit of fun, Next week three of you will be coming with me to go behind enemy lines. Don't fail tomorrow."

They nodded. Fletcher and Crowe grinned. To them anything like this was fun.

"I will go in with Lance Sergeant Hay's team." Peter Davis, John Herbert and Roger Beaumont were all new lads. They were good but new. We went to the sitting room. "Well then Lance Sergeant, what is your plan?"

He looked at me with a querulous look, "My plan?"

"I told you I am the umpire. I am going on all of the missions anyway. I want to see how you and these lads do under duress."

He took a deep breath. "Actually sir I was going to pinch your plan. Get a fishing boat and instead of sailing out, sail in."

"Get a boat?"

"Er borrow one so to speak."

"Do you have a boat in mind?"

"There is an old chap I sometimes drink with at the *'Dog and Gun'*. This time of year he doesn't use his boat much; he's in his seventies. If we get some fuel for it I am sure he will loan it to us. We could go in and sail up the Tamar. It is about forty miles or so to the coast. I reckon that is about six or seven hours. If we leave early we could do it with time to spare. We could do a bit of fishing on the way and get there towards dusk. We can pretend to have a bit of engine trouble and one of the lads could go and get some spare parts."

"Who?"

Beaumont piped up, "Me sir. We worked out that they might not expect fishermen to have papers with them or we could say we lost them overboard." I cocked my head to one side. Roger was a bright lad. "We would make sure we had no jackets on, sir."

I glanced at my watch. "It sounds like a plan but the clock is ticking and you have no boat."

Bill jumped up like a startled rabbit. "Beaumont, you sort the lads out and get fishermen's gear. I'll go and see old Eric."

To Beaumont's credit, he did not ask how or where he would obtain the clothes he just rose. He had the nerve to say, "I take it you can get your own gear sir? Umpire's?"

I smiled, "I will work something out."

The others had gone to their sergeant's rooms to continue planning. I was looking forward to this. I could observe the men I led from close quarters. Hay's plan was sound but not without risks. I went into the kitchen. Reg had just finished drying. "Everything sorted sir?"

"Just about. Hay's team will leave before dawn and I will be with them. I'll just go and get some old gear to throw on. We are fishermen. I need to look the part. I think I will just use my oldest and smelliest clothes!"

Mrs Dean wiped her hands. "I have something old and smelly. I was going to throw it out but I didn't have the heart."

Reg was curious, "What is it, love?"

"My brother John, he died in the Great War; at Jutland. He was on the '*Invincible*'. Well, he was a fisherman before the war. He had all the equipment, sou'wester, oilskin, sea boots, and sweater. You are more than welcome to use them but they might be..."

"Disgusting?"

She laughed. "That is about the size of it, Captain. They are in the cellar. They have been there since 1916."

When she had gone Reg said, "Captain Marsden is still having bother with that Osborne. He is being sly. Just this side of insubordinate. Curtis is becoming frustrated.."

"Has he asked for your help?"

"I think they are both a bit proud. Don't want to be seen as failures."

"Waller."

"Exactly! I think I shall intervene. If they don't like it they can lump it."

"If this is still a problem after I come back I will have a heart-to-heart with both of them. To be honest we can do without this sort of distraction; forty-four is going to be a busy year."

Mrs Dean appeared with a large hamper. She dived into it. She was right it did have the damp, decayed and musty aroma of clothes left for too long out of the air. The jumper had holes in it and she was about to return it when I said, "Whoa there, Mrs Dean. That is perfect. If everything else is like that it will do for me." The sea boots were slightly big but I just used a couple of pairs of socks. "I'll return them when we get back."

She smiled and it was a sad smile, "I think John would just be happy he was still doing something for this country. He was a real patriot. If he had been alive he would have loved to listen to you and your lads." She began to fill up and Reg put his huge arm around her. I slid from the room. I was surplus to requirements.

Knowing that we were out before dawn meant Mrs Dean had breakfast on the go even earlier. We had porridge in winter. Seasoned with salt it kept us going far longer than bacon and eggs. I did not see the other teams at breakfast but there were four empty bowls, neatly stacked which told me that one team was on the road.

I had not seen Hay before I went to bed and had no idea if he had succeeded in his mission. Not only did he have to get the boat, but he also had to get fuel for it. I was finishing my breakfast when he came in. "There you are, sir." He pointed to the empty bowls. "We ate a while ago. We are on a tight schedule. Our boat awaits."

We did not have far to go. Bill had moored the twenty feet long fishing boat close to the lodgings. We clambered down the rusty ladder which was attached to the sea wall. At the bottom of the harbour wall, an ancient mariner stood smoking his pipe. I guessed it must be Eric. He knuckled his forehead, "Thank'ee for the baccy sir. Young Billy told me what you are about. Good luck I say!"

As we headed out to sea I asked, "Baccy?"

"Old Eric wasn't bothered about fuel sir but he likes Navy issue tobacco. We gave him four ounces and promised him another four when we get the next rations."

"Well done. And fuel?"

He chuckled. "We went back to the yard where *'Lady Luck'* was moored. We knew where there were eight cans stashed. We have more than enough and we can still leave Eric with a full tank."

A harbour patrol boat loomed up out of the dark. "Where are you going? That is Eric Roger's boat."

Bill pointed to the harbour wall where Eric waved. "I am his nephew. He asked us to go fishing for him. Poor old sod needs the money the catch will bring."

The young Lieutenant nodded, "You should have asked first."

"Me and my mates are on leave and we only arrived late last night. Sorry, sir."

The apologetic attitude worked and we were waved out of the harbour.

As we struck the bay I said, "Well done, Hay. That was smart thinking. Can you do it in German?"

"Some of it sir but I am not confident like." He pointed to Roger who was bent over the engine. "Now buggerlugs there, he has more bottle than a dairy! He rattles off Kraut like he was born German."

"Do you Beaumont?"

"I did it at school, sir. I like languages and when you do science and engineering it helps."

The boat was faster than we had thought although Hay explained that Beaumont had not been to bed. He had been cleaning and servicing the engine. Eric would be getting back a better boat. We stopped at about eleven and I worked the tiller while the others fished. It was not the greatest catch in the world but it was a catch. They packed it in boxes provided by Eric and then we continued to Plymouth.

The invasion plans could be seen clearly as we approached the port. There were barrage balloons everywhere and the fields, inland, were covered in tents and camouflaged guns. We knew what to look for otherwise they would have been hard to spot. It was coming on to late afternoon when we approached the entrance to the harbour. We were less than four hundred yards from it. I had no doubt that glasses would be trained upon us.

"Right, Beaumont; do your magic." I was impressed that the team had worked everything out to the last detail.

He knelt over the engine and fiddled on. Suddenly the engine began to cough and splutter. We still had way but we were now down to less than three knots. As we passed the entrance a harbour patrol vessel appeared from our starboard side, "Who are you?"

Bill had the glib answer ready, "***Padstow Rose*** out of Falmouth sir. We had a bit of engine trouble. The young lad thought he had fixed it but..."

"Have you the ship's papers?"

"This is my uncle's boat sir. You can check with Falmouth if you like, sir. We spoke to a young Lieutenant there before we left."

We had timed it well. It was almost the end of a shift and the crew of the harbour patrol were ready to go home. "There is a chandler's along there not far from the dockyard. Make sure you stay away from anything with a barrier or wire!"

"Right, sir. Will do!"

We headed towards the other small boats which had tied up close to the dockyard. Some of them obviously had official business there. We did not. I wondered how they would get into the actual restricted area. Bill pulled her over close to the end boat. There was a stair which led up to the gate leading to the dockyard. He and Herbert headed up the stairs. When they reached the top Herbert took out a pipe. There was a sign which clearly said, **'No Smoking'**. I saw Davis wandering up the steps as well. The Royal Marine Sergeant approached Herbert and began to shout at him. Without actually hearing I knew that Herbert would be saying the pipe was not even lit. He did not smoke! I guessed he had borrowed it from Eric. Bill Hay joined in the conversation and I saw David approach the gate and appear to be taking an interest in the conversation.

Suddenly there was a small explosion from the engine of our fishing boat and a plume of smoke rose, alarmingly from the engine. It made me jump! Herbert and Hay looked over the top. They would not have been human if they had not looked too and the sergeant and the Marine peered over. It would have looked odd if I had not gone to the engine and I rushed over as I spied Davis nip into the gate and the Guard Room.

"I take it this was planned, Beaumont?" I spoke quietly.

"Oh yes, sir. A tiny amount of explosive, a little oil-soaked cloth and Bob's your uncle. As Shakespeare said, *'Full of sound and fury, signifying nothing!'*"

The Royal Marine Sergeant came down a couple of steps. "What the bloody hell is going on? We have fuel up here! Are you trying to blow up the whole bloody dock? You are worse than saboteurs!"

Beaumont put on a slow voice. He sounded like a country yokel. "Zorry, zir. I 'as sorted it out now!"

"Well make sure you have." He turned and glowered at Herbert and Hay. "And you two can sling yer hook an all!"

I saw Davis standing behind them. Hay said, indignantly, "I thought this was a free country we were fighting for! You have a little accident and you get accused of all sorts. We don't need this. Come on lads! Let's go home!"

They boarded the boat and Beaumont miraculously made the engine sound as sweet as a nut. We all adopted a dignified pose as we sailed out of the harbour towards the setting sun. When we were clear Bill Hay asked, "Well?"

Davis produced some items from his pocket, "A copy of the guard roster for the Dockyard. A rubber stamp and the Sergeant's cheese and pickle sandwich!"

I laughed along with them. To be fair they did not need to have produced anything for I had seen Davis enter and then leave without being seen but I was proud of the fact that they followed the rules. They would do. We arrived back not long before midnight. The patrol boat was suspicious until Bill gave the young lieutenant a couple of the fish we had caught. Half of the catch would go to Eric as payment and Mrs Dean would make fish and chips for the rest of us. I have to confess that I was curious about the other two teams. I had not seen them in Plymouth; perhaps that was a good thing.

When we reached the lodgings the others had not arrived. Although Mrs Dean wrinkled her nose at the smell she was delighted with the fish. "Reg, take that box of fish. I shall fillet them now. We don't want them stinking out the house."

"But look at the time!"

"I thought you were a soldier. Come on, chop, chop!" He rolled his eyes as he picked up the box.

I smiled. I knew that Mum would have used the bones and other bits to make a fish soup which would have been wonderful. The Mrs Deans of this world did not even contemplate that! They would end up over the sea wall.

I said, "You chaps can have the day off tomorrow. You have earned it."

"Thanks, sir!"

I went upstairs to change. I had a good wash too but I knew that I would need a bath. My body reeked of clothes that had not seen the light of day in almost thirty years. Thirty per cent of my team had been successful. I wondered about the rest.

I fell asleep downstairs in the armchair waiting for the rest to arrive. I felt like a parent waiting for a child who had stayed out too late! I was awoken at five-thirty by a timid knock on the door. It was Sergeant Poulson and his team. He looked disappointed that I had answered. "Bill Hay succeeded then?"

I nodded. "And you?" In answer, he held up a menu from the dockyard canteen. "Any casualties?"

He smiled, "We didn't get caught if that is what you mean, sir. We are tired. We used bicycles to get back."

"How did you get there?"

"We took the bus." He grinned, "It helped as it dropped off close by the gates and there were workers from the bus going through. It was easy. Their security is not what it should be." He looked around. "No Gordy?"

"No Gordy! Tell your lads they have the day off. I have already told mine and it is fish and chips for tea tonight."

His face lit up. "Where did Mrs Dean get the fish?"

I gave him an enigmatic smile, "That would be telling."

I was getting worried about Gordy and his section. It was eleven o'clock and they had still to return. Reg had gone to the camp and promised he would send word if he heard anything from them. I think we both thought that they had been captured. It would be sad but as eight men had passed the test it was not a total disaster.

At twelve they wearily entered the boarding house. They arrived together and they were sweating profusely. "You had me worried, Gordy, where have you been?"

"We got there on the train but we left too late to come back on it sir. We ran."

"Forty-six miles?"

"It felt more like sixty, sir but I'll take your word for it."

"And?"

In answer, he grinned and shouted, "Scouse!"

Fletcher, still grinning despite the exhaustion, reached into his pocket and pulled out a large bunch of keys. A label attached to them said, *'Property of R.N. Dockyard, Plymouth- do not remove'*!

"Well done! I'd say get your heads down but..."

Gordy rubbed his hands together, "Is that fish and chips frying?"

"It is indeed!"

"Then a quick sluice down will do, sir!"

Chapter 9

Although I gave my men the day off I went up to the camp after Gordy's team came back. I ran. When I reached the camp I went to Sergeant Major Dean's office. As soon as he saw me he grinned. "Sir, if you could just pop in and see Major Rose."

I nodded, "Right, Sarn't Major." I turned to go, "Oh, by the by, Gordy's team came back." I handed him the keys. "You might want to ring the dockyard and tell them that their security is a little bit lacking!"

Reg held up the keys. "I am guessing that this was Fletcher?"

"It was. He managed to get them out of a locked drawer too."

I knocked on the Major's door, "Come." As soon as I walked in the Major strode over to me and grasped my hand. "Congratulations, Tom!"

"Thank you sir but I had every confidence that my men would perform the mission. I suppose I..."

He shook his head, "Not that although that was well done too, no, the gong! It has come through. You are to be given the Victoria Cross. The ceremony is next week at Windsor Castle."

"But we go on the mission the week after sir!"

His face became a little serious, "I think, Tom, that is one of the reasons. We have had too many posthumous awards. I think they want a live recipient."

I nodded. That made sense. If I died on this mission then I would be a dead hero. I had no doubt that the newspapers would be involved. That had happened to Dad in the Great War; I had no doubt that the Government was as keen for the publicity and propaganda as anyone. "Which day next week, sir?"

"Tuesday. You will be telling your family I take it?"

"Yes sir."

"You don't sound excited about this. You realise that the only other Commando who was awarded the Victoria Cross was killed in action in 1941. You will be the first to receive the medal. That is an honour!"

"I know sir but there are other chaps who have performed far more gallant acts than I have."

"Tom, I haven't known you for long but even I have seen, in that short space of time, that you are special. I had a long chat with the Quarter Master. He told me all about you. Enjoy your day." He handed me the details of the ceremony.

"Sir."

I went through to the Sergeant Major's office. He had the telephone ready. "I take it you want to ring your parents, sir?"

"My mother. I think Dad is in the Far East still." Mum was, of course, delighted and told me she would be there. As I had thought Dad and Mary were on active service. I put the phone down and hesitated.

Reg said, "And your young lady, sir? Are you going to tell her?"

"My young lady?"

"Major Foster told us that you had met a young lady in London." He looked unabashed as he said, "I help to sort out all the letters sir. She has a very nice hand."

"But I only took her out once!"

"And she writes to you twice a week sir. Trust me she is keen. Mrs D is excited too."

"Mrs Dean knows?"

"Of course sir. No secrets between a man and wife."

I nodded, "Get me, Major Foster, in Whitehall then. He will have to be my go-between."

It took some minutes for him to reach the telephone and when he heard my voice he was worried, "Something wrong Tom?"

I suddenly felt foolish. I was ringing the War Office about something trivial. "Sorry to bother you but I have been given the Cross."

I heard the relief in his voice, "I know. I heard. Sorry, I couldn't tell you."

I was suddenly aware that Reg, while apparently reading reports was listening. "Look, do you think Susan would want to come to the ceremony? It is at Windsor Castle and I can bring two guests. There will only be Mum and..."

I heard the laugh on the other end as he interrupted me, "And you want me to ask her for you! Of course, she would love to come. Every time I pass through Operations she asks about you and I am certain that the Dragon will give her leave! Give me the details."

I read them out to him.

"Good. I am pleased for you, Tom." He hesitated, "The training is still going well?"

"Oh yes. The hardest part will be choosing the three I will take with me."

"General Marlowe never tires of telling all and sundry how he and his staff were captured by you and your team. Enjoy your day and leave the rest to me."

Reg put the papers down and smiled, "Everything sorted sir?"

I nodded, "Everything sorted."

"I'll get Larkin to book you into a hotel in Windsor, sir. Do you want me to arrange one for your Mum and your young lady too?"

"Mum said she will drive. It isn't far and the train service from London is a good one so I think they should be fine. Thanks, Reg."

He nodded, "We look after our own here, sir."

Larkin had come up trumps. He had booked me a room in the Garter Inn which was directly opposite the castle. I arrived the night before so that I was able to reconnoitre my route. It was ingrained in me now. I was able to see the town, castle and river. They were all impressive. Although the staff were well used to the hotel being used for such ceremonies they still made a fuss of me. With most of the young men at war, it was old staff, brought back out of retirement who worked there. The old soldiers from the Great War recognised my medals. Dad had told me that those who had fought in the Great War never forgot.

The ceremony was set for eleven o'clock. Toppy had rung to tell me that Susan would be coming and would be arriving on the nine o'clock train. Mum would park the car at the hotel. I had a dilemma. Did I wait for Mum or go to meet Susan? I was finishing my breakfast at seven-thirty when Mum appeared in the doorway. She rushed over and threw her arms around me, "I am so proud of you!"

The ancient waiter said, "Would madam like breakfast?"

"A cup of coffee would be wonderful, thank you." She sat down as he whisked her coat away.

"You must have left early."

"You don't think I was going to have you receive the medal alone! Your Dad and Mary will both be sorry to have missed it. You will have one person there, at least."

I could not keep the smile from my mouth nor the blush from my cheeks as I said, "Actually, Mum. There will be two."

"Two?"

I told her how I had met Susan. I left out the incident with the thugs. I watched her face as I finished. The waiter had brought her coffee. She looked down at the cup and when she looked at me I saw that her eyes were filling with tears. She said, huskily, "I was already happy this morning, Tom but this news is even better!"

"Mum! I took a young lady out on one date and we have exchanged a few letters."

"And yet you invite her here and she is coming, on her own, from London! A mother knows. What time is her train due in?"

"I think it is nine forty-five."

"Well, we shall be waiting for her at nine-thirty!"

I was not the only one to be receiving a medal and there were others who were being given awards. The train from London was more crowded than it might have been. Mum had linked my arm as I stared down the platform looking for her. What had seemed like a good idea was now turning sour. Suppose they didn't get on? Would I be scaring Susan away? After all, a trip to the castle was one thing but the presence of my mother implied so much more.

I saw her and she waved. Mum said, "She is pretty!"

I smiled as she drew close, "Susan, this is my Mum. Mum..."

Mum disengaged herself, "Give her a hug, you goose!"

Feeling as though the whole station was watching I put my arms around her and squeezed. As soon as I did I realised that I didn't care who was watching. We both turned our heads and kissed, "Thank you for coming."

She stepped back and stared at me, "Are you serious? This is wonderful and I am honoured that you asked me." She held her hand out, "Pleased to meet you Mrs Harsker. Has he always been like this?"

Mum laughed, "Always, and call me Beattie."

The two of them took an arm each and I was marched down the platform. They spoke across me as we headed out of the station towards the castle. Mum began telling Susan of me growing up and I found myself colouring despite the chill January air. As we approached Windsor Castle with the Guards, now in khaki, waiting for us they subsided. Mum asked, "Will it be the King who makes the award?"

I said, "I am not certain."

Susan looked at the other small groups who were queuing to be admitted. "Are these all getting medals?"

"If they are in uniform then yes."

"Any other Victoria Crosses?"

"I don't know."

We were taken to a waiting room before an equerry sent us in to the hall where the ceremony would take place. The order was precise. The awards would lead up to mine. I was the only Victoria Cross. It was to be the King who would make the presentation. The Queen was in attendance too. I thought that the King looked drawn but then I had only ever seen photographs of him. Some of those who went up to receive the D.S.O, D.F.C, M.M. and M.C. had been wounded. There were representatives from every service. I saw nurses there too. I felt like a fraud. Some of these had wounds and I had barely received a scratch. The only other Commando to have received the Cross was Lieutenant Colonel Geoffrey Keyes. He had been awarded it posthumously. He had been my age when he had died. I felt a prickle across my neck as though someone was walking on my grave.

When my name was called and I stepped forward I felt every eye on me. I was the last award. I followed the instructions given to me by the equerry to the letter. The King smiled and spoke quietly with just the hint of a stammer. "It is good to see someone even more nervous than I am."

"Sorry, Your Majesty."

"Don't be. They tell me that your father has one of these too." I nodded. "This country is lucky to have such brave warriors fighting for her." He looked behind me, "Is that your mother?"

"Yes, Your Majesty. She was a nurse in the Great War."

"She did her part too. Any other family?"

"A sister, Mary, Your Majesty, she is an air ferry pilot."

He shook his head, "We will never forget what all of you have done for this country and this Empire. The sacrifices which our people make never cease to amaze us." He leaned forward, "Make sure you survive this war, young man. Our country will have need of the likes of you in the days when this is over."

I remembered his words long after the memory of the ceremony had faded. I felt he had meant them and that touched me.

Mum was like a schoolgirl as we left. "We must have lunch! My treat!"

Susan looked at her watch. "I have to get back to London. I was given the time off to come but I have to be on duty this evening."

"Nonsense, I shall drive you back. It is only five minutes to London from here! Besides, that will give us the chance to chat away from my embarrassed son!"

When Mum had the wind in her sails she was a force of nature but I took heart that Susan and she seemed to get on. We had a lovely lunch in the hotel. The staff made a real fuss of the three of us and we could not have had better service. When Susan began to look nervously at her watch Mum said, "I will pay the bill and then fetch the car around." She pecked me on the cheek, "You two can talk!" She shooed us away.

"I like your Mum."

"Really? I didn't know if you thought it was a bit much, I mean we have only just met."

"Your mum is right! You might be a good soldier and a hero but you have not got the first clue about women! I knew from the moment you spoke that you were the only man for me. And if you don't know that I am the only woman for you ... well, I shall just have to change your mind."

I felt relief, "Well of course but... I mean... I thought these things took much longer."

She nodded as she rose and the waiter brought her coat, "That was peacetime when we had time for such luxuries. This is war and you snatch happiness where you can. I have got you now and believe me I am not letting you go."

She cuddled into my arm as we left. Amazingly I was not embarrassed. Mum was at the front of the hotel in the shooting brake. Susan turned and kissed me hard on the lips. She said, quietly, "I know where you are going. When you are over there remember that I am watching everything that you do. I will be praying for you the whole time. Come back safely, my love! I love you, always."

I could not speak. If I had tried then I would have made a fool of myself. Mum must have realised too for, as I went round to her door she squeezed my hand, "Take care, son. We are all proud of you."

And then they were gone and it was back to the war for me.

Chapter 10

I chose my first team carefully. I knew that I had disappointed the ones I did not choose. I chose Sergeant Poulson. He was calm, dependable and had mastered German better than the other two sergeants. I chose Roger Beaumont. His German was almost perfect and he had shown himself to be resourceful. The last one I chose was Scouse Fletcher. He had already impressed me but stealing the keys from the dockyard had been the act of a magician. I felt I would need those skills. His German was not the equal of the others but it was better than the rest of the team. When I told the others of my decision and the reasons I saw the resolution on their faces as they determined to become as proficient in German as the ones I took.

We travelled to Southampton in our regulation uniforms but we had the German ones and guns in kit bags. While Gordy remained with the rest Bill Hay came with us to act as liaison. We had not operated like this before and I needed someone in Southampton who knew the way we worked.

The submarine was moored at the end of a line of three submarines. We boarded by crossing to their tender and then descending the ladder to walk across the other subs first. Bill came with us, helping to carry our bags. He would wait while we changed and then take our bags back.

Lieutenant Commander Reid was a regular officer. He was older than I expected with flecks of grey in his hair. He had been watching our approach from the steel hull of the vessel. "I thought there were just four of you, Captain?"

"The sergeant here will be taking back our gear once we have changed."

"Good. It will be a tight squeeze as it is. Come on in then."

We entered a hatch by the aft torpedo room. "This will be your nest until we land."

"Right lads, let's get changed."

The Lieutenant Commander looked amused as we stripped and then dressed in German uniforms. "Risky, wearing German uniforms."

"They shoot Commandos anyway." I turned to the other three. "Make sure you have no papers on you." I knew they had none but it paid to be careful. "Right, Hay. You look after the bags and, hopefully, we will see you when we return."

He took the two kit bags. "You watch out for yourselves eh, sir?"

He threw the bags through the hatch and then clambered up after them. The Lieutenant Commander looked at the uniforms. "Where did you get those and the guns?"

"This is not our first time behind enemy lines. We are magpies."

"Right. Well Captain, if you would like to come with me I will go through the operation with you. You chaps make yourself comfortable."

Scouse said, "You got a shroud then sir?"

"A shroud?"

"Aye sir, to go with this coffin we are in!"

As we walked forrard the Lieutenant Commander said, "I take it your men are not fans of the submarine."

"None of us are. We have done this before. We even had to lie off the bottom close to the Channel Islands and suffer depth charges."

"Then you have experience. That helps." We had reached the control room. He waved forward his navigation officer, "This is Lieutenant Dixon. He will be responsible for getting us to the right place."

The Lieutenant pointed at the map. "We were going to drop you here to the west of the mole close to the beach."

I shook my head, "The beach will be mined. The closer to the mole and the sea wall the better. How are we getting ashore? Dinghy or canoe?"

"We have two-man canoes for you."

The amount of training we had received had prepared me for that. "Then the sea wall will be fine. We will put stones in the canoes to keep them below the water. And the pick up?"

"We will lie a mile north of the low-water mark. We surface at dusk and we will watch for your signal." Fletcher did not have an Aldis but we had a heavy-duty German torch.

"How long can you wait for us?"

"We will have to be away an hour before dawn. Sorry."

"Don't be. If we aren't back by then we aren't coming."

The Lieutenant flashed a look at his superior who smiled, "These are commandos, John. They know the score. Right, Captain. You will want to get your head down. We have a long voyage ahead of us."

We had practised with both dinghies and canoes. I preferred canoes; they were faster and easier to hide. When I told my team they were pleased too. "Check your weapons. I hope we don't have to use them but you never know."

"And we still lay up during the day?"

"We do Sergeant although I think we will lie up in plain sight."

"How do you mean sir?"

Beaumont was still new to this. "We are dressed in German uniforms. There will be cafes and bars. We find a quiet one and nurse a couple of drinks."

"Like we did in North Africa, sir."

"Exactly Sergeant. We will use the money we lifted from the dead Germans. As we won't get much sleep over there you might as well get as much shut-eye here as you can."

Scouse shook his head, "I can't sleep in a sub, sir. I feel like the walls are closing in on me."

"Well get as much rest as you can. Tired men make mistakes."

After I had checked my Luger I lay down on the mattress they had provided. It was not the walls which got to me it was the smell. The stale air smelled heavy and was filled with oil, battery acid and sweat. As this was the start of the voyage the smell would only get worse. As I closed my eyes I reflected that it would only last until France and then we would have fresh air and the danger of death. I must have slept although Beaumont did point out that the carbon dioxide in the air would have made it more likely I was semi-conscious rather than asleep.

We were brought food an hour before we surfaced. It too tasted of battery acid and stale air. We ate because we needed to rather than because we wanted to. My three men had German rifles. Poulson had a Mauser pistol secreted in his German battle dress. I just had my Luger. As I had the proper holster for it I looked the part. Our German greatcoats would hide most things. We did not don them yet. We would wait until we left the submarine. The hatches were narrow.

The Midshipman came along, "Sir, the Captain says it is almost time."

"Thanks, Middy."

I led my men through the length of the submarine. We paused at the conning tower. "Everything set?"

I nodded, "Fletcher here has the signals. With a bit of luck, we will see you in twenty-four hours."

"Good luck!"

"Thanks."

I saw nods from the crew as we went along. It was as though they were saying farewell to condemned men. For my part, I was just glad to be getting off the submarine. I would never get used to them. When the hatch closed above you it felt as though they had screwed down a coffin lid! We moved into the forward torpedo room. The two canoes were taking up most of the space and I suspected that the torpedo room crew would be glad to see the back of them.

Lieutenant Dixon stood, waiting. "Are you sure these will do? We can inflate a dinghy if you like."

"These are fine. We want to be in as quickly as we can. What is the weather like up top?"

"Raining with flecks of snow and sleet. Sorry."

"Don't be those are perfect for us." We made our way to the hatch and stood with the two seamen who would open it.

We waited and then heard. "Prepare to surface." The lights went to red and we heard the hiss as the tanks were emptied. We must have been at periscope depth as we heard, almost immediately, "Open forward hatch!"

The two sailors reached up to open the hatch and an icy flood of water showered them and spattered us. It was a reminder that this was still winter. I climbed out and crouched on the pitching deck. I could see nothing ahead and that was a good thing. It meant we could not be seen either. I put on my greatcoat and moved to the bow to allow the others out. I watched while my men and the two ratings manhandled the canoes onto the submarine's deck.

Beaumont said, in German, "Ready, sir." From now on it would be German only until we boarded the submarine again.

I went to join Fletcher who was in the bow of the first canoe. It tipped alarmingly when I got in but they were a very stable craft as had been shown in the raid up the Gironde in forty-two. Fletcher handed me my paddle and we set off into the darkness. The submarine was pointed towards the mouth of the river. If Lieutenant Dixon had done his job then we just had to paddle straight ahead. The wind and the rain were in our faces. It would take longer to complete the mile or so to the shore. I did not take my eyes off the bow. "Are they on station?"

A moment later Fletcher said, "Yes sir." His accent was terrible. The less he spoke German the better. At least he understood more these days.

We soon got into the rhythm. We had practised with both a canoe and a dinghy. The canoe was easier to use. As the blades dug in we began to make better progress. I heard an engine to our left. I did not stop paddling but peered into the dark. I caught a shadow of a boat-like shape. Suddenly a searchlight stabbed into the black of night. Fortunately, it was pointing out to sea. They were looking for the submarine. We had heard they had underwater listening devices. This was proof. It might cause a problem getting out but that was for the future. The searchlight had allowed me to see that it was a minesweeper-type ship called an R ship. They had depth charges and a cannon.

I saw a fleck of white ahead and used that as a guide. It identified the sea wall. We were less than half a mile away. The presence of the ship and the proximity of the sea wall made me dig even harder with the paddles. Soon the sea wall became clear. I could see the flatter water of the canal and river mouth to my left and I turned us more to the right. This was the most dangerous part of the whole mission. If they had an eagle-eyed sentry and we were spotted then this would all be over before it had started. The weather helped us. The actual wall was only narrow and I could see sand on the right of it. The wall came at us far quicker than I had expected and we had to backwater and turn beam onto it. It was hard getting hold of anything. Each time the sea surged we cracked against the rocks. Then I spied an old piece of rope. It must have had something attached to it for it was jammed between the rocks. I grabbed hold of it. It held us tightly against the stones at the base of the wall. Fletcher leapt out of the canoe and then held on to the side of it so that I could get out.

I saw that Poulson and Beaumont were having the same problem. I pointed further along the rocks and Fletcher and I carried our canoe so that the sergeant could land too. I held the canoe under the water while Fletcher gathered smooth rocks and began to put them in the bottom of the canoe. As the water filled it then it began to sink. We did not need many; just enough to keep it below the surface on the bottom part of the sea wall. One of us would have to strip off and empty the rocks when it came time to leave but we would deal with that problem when we came to it. As the water filled the canoe I watched anxiously. It disappeared. I lay down on the rocks and put my hand below the water. I could feel the top of the canoe. It was just two and a half feet below the surface. As the tide came in the canoes would be in deeper water. When it came time for us to leave it would be low water again.

We waited while Poulson and Beaumont sank their canoe and then we began the difficult job of climbing the sea wall. It was made harder by the awful conditions and, for the first few feet, the seaweed. I had the easiest task as I had no rifle to encumber me. As I neared the top I slowed down. I did not risk putting my hands over the top. Instead, I slowly raised my head. There was a sentry hut. It was next to the mouth of the river and canal. The mole was just fifteen feet wide and the sentries were just ten feet away. There was a brazier and I saw the backs of two sentries. The fire would have ruined their night vision and I gambled that we had time to move beyond them. I quickly clambered over and waved the others up. We moved towards the beach as quickly as we could. The sentries were watching the sea and not this stone mole.

Our mission began now. Our job was to find the beach we would be assaulting and then find a way through the town to the bridge over the canal. We discovered, to my surprise, that there was nothing to stop us from getting down to the beach. As we dropped to the sand I quickly looked for signs of any mines. I saw twenty yards away barbed wire and to the right of it a darkened sign. I guessed that the minefield was there. I led us up the beach, keeping the wire to our right. The sand was soft and I did not think the tide reached this high.

I stopped for I had spied a tobruk. These were concrete foxholes the Germans used to protect machine-guns and heavier pieces. Occasionally the Germans embedded the old turrets from tanks captured from the British and the French in the early days of the war. This one had a machine-gun in it. It was unmanned at the moment. I saw a second thirty yards to its left separated by a concrete bunker. All of them were aligned towards the beach and not the river. I was about to move off when I saw the snout of a 50mm gun. They were surrounded by wire. I waved my men forward.

I almost fell into the anti-tank ditch. It ran from the side of the mole into the distance. It was too dark to see how far. We clambered down and then climbed out. It was intended to stop tanks, not infantry. Once we had passed the ditch we were in the town. I saw a huge building to our right. That, I already knew, was the command centre for the beach. It would be manned. I did not want to risk passing it in the middle of the night and I took us along the canal. Every building we saw was sandbagged. I spied a hotel with a German flag hanging from it. That would be a barracks for their troops. I headed for it. I did not run but walked as though I was heading back to our quarters. As luck would have it we saw no one.

I was feeling confident and would have walked past the command centre until Beaumont tugged on my sleeve and pointed to the glow of the cigarette. There was a sentry in the doorway. That route was barred. We ducked between the hotel and the Command centre. It took us down a residential street but the doors and windows were boarded up. The civilians had been moved out. We kept moving into the small town of Ouistreham. It was quiet. After a couple of hundred yards, we passed a couple of cafes. They were closed but I stored their location for later. The roads had no concrete barriers. Tanks could move down them. Then I stopped for I saw a large empty square. I guessed it would be where the market was held. I waved left and we headed back towards the canal and river. I had found a route for the brigade. There were no obstacles once we had passed the ditch and command centre. We now had to get to the bridge over the canal.

When we turned left the wind abated for there were shops and houses to our right. It meant we could hear better and I heard the stamp of boots. It was a German patrol. I saw an alley leading behind some shops and we dived into it. There were dustbins and empty boxes. We sheltered behind them as the eight-man patrol, led by a sergeant, marched past the end of our hiding place. Their heads were down as they tried to avoid the snow-flecked rain. I gave them five minutes and then we emerged, cautiously. We had seen one patrol and I doubted that we would see another any time soon. We made the canal and we halted. I could see derricks and bollards. There was the shape of a ship tied up too. I stopped. We would march down the road which ran along the canal as though we were a patrol.

I tugged Fletcher next to me and we began to march. As we turned down the road I saw a sailor on one of the boats. He was throwing something into the river. I did not wave. A German would not do that and when the man disappeared quickly I knew he had been doing something he shouldn't have. We marched down the road and passed more vessels. Most of them looked to be without a watch. The odd one which did have a watch just watched the German patrol heading along the canal road. The houses thinned out and we were marching down a tree-lined road which began to move away from the side of the canal. I stopped. To our left was a well-worn path. It stood out in the rain. I headed for it and found that it led to the canal and ran alongside it. This was a bonus. It had not shown up on the aerial photographs. Trees overhung it. We had our way to the bridge. We reached the canal. This was a deserted section. Half a mile later I saw the cafe which stood next to the canal and the bridge.

It was a swing bridge. We stopped two hundred yards from it. I could see that it was heavily defended. We could have turned around and gone back to the canoes. However, we had to wait now until the next night. I stopped. We needed some shelter from the rain and from observation.

It came to me that if they had boarded up the houses close to the beach they might be good places to hide. We had managed to do something similar in St. Nazaire. I whirled my hand above my head and began to retrace my steps. It was probably the safest route as the German patrol we had encountered probably had a circular route. They would be looking for French Resistance and, no doubt, Commandos. The rain and sleet showed no sign of letting up. Occasionally it became marginally lighter but then another squall would bring a heavier downpour. Our greatcoats were already soaked.

The open square was the most dangerous section but we walked up the side confidently as though we had every right to be there. It was, however, with some relief that we entered the street with the cafes and bars. When we entered the residential street I glanced at my watch. It was almost four. Although still some hours from dawn it was getting close to the time when the Germans would be up and about.

We stopped and, leaving Beaumont on watch, we entered the overgrown garden of one of the houses. The front door had a piece of wood hammered over the lock. Leaving the other two to search the front I went around the back. I saw that the rear garden was not overlooked. Garden trees had been allowed to grow unchecked. The French normally copsed them for firewood. Here there was an overgrown climbing rose on the side of the house. Whoever had nailed the wood across this door had not risked the rose thorns and there was the slightest of gaps behind the wood. I had a German knife. I took it out and slipped it between the wood and the lock. By levering back and forth the wood began to move away from the frame. As soon as I could get my hands in the gap I pulled it away.

Fletcher and Poulson appeared. I stepped away to allow Fletcher to gain entry. I pointed to the front and the Sergeant went for Beaumont. It did not take Fletcher long to force the lock but the door had been closed so long that it took almost as long for us to force it open without making too much noise. Poulson and Beaumont joined us as we entered the house. It smelled musty and dusty but it was dry. I waved Fletcher and Beaumont upstairs while the Sergeant and I checked down. The windows had their shutters closed and so the house was pitch black. We checked by touch. There was a cellar door. I did not investigate; who knew what obstacles lay in the dark. The kitchen had been cleared of all food. The Germans were efficient. We met the other two in the hall.

"All clear upstairs. There are beds but no bedding."

"And no food either."

"The tap still works. We have water."

"Good. We can refill our canteens before we leave. Sergeant, you have the first watch. Wake me in two hours."

"Right sir."

We were safe to talk in the house but we still used German. It was good practice and if anyone actually heard us they would not be alarmed. I went into the first bedroom I found. The bed was an old fashioned one with a metal frame which creaked when I sat on it. The mattress was old and lumpy. I took off my greatcoat and hung it on the frame at the bottom of the bed to allow it to dry. I also took off the German tunic. It too was damp. Putting my gun beside me I lay down and tried to sleep. We did not have enough information yet. We had seen much more of the town of Ouistreham, in the rain-filled night, than I could have expected but there was more we needed to know. We would be landing in daylight. If we were to be Lord Lovat's pathfinders we needed to inspect the beach and that would not be easy. I finally fell asleep running through the different idea in my head.

Chapter 11

When Poulson shook me awake I had no idea how we would achieve our ends. As the Sergeant took my place on the bed he said, "All quiet sir. Still as black as."

I took my tunic and greatcoat along with my Luger and headed downstairs. A fire would have been good but that was impossible. My coat would not dry out completely. I went into the kitchen and put it on the table. I emptied my canteen and refilled it from the tap in the kitchen. After putting on my tunic and holster I wandered around the house. It was more to keep me occupied rather than from any need to investigate it. As I neared the front windows I realised that getting out of the house would be harder than getting in. If there were any Germans in the street then we would have some explaining to do.

Although there were shutters on the windows they were old and as a grey dawn broke they allowed a few thin shafts of light to penetrate the darkness. I had decided that I had had enough sleep and I allowed the others to get their rest. I explored the downstairs. I risked going outside. The garden was not overlooked. After donning my field cap I opened the back door as quietly as I could. The rain had actually stopped but the air still felt damp. The house might have been unheated but it was warmer than the outside. I regretted not putting on my greatcoat.

I saw that there was an outbuilding. I went over to it and rubbed away the cobwebs and dirt from the window. Inside was an ancient Citroen. When we had had holidays in France I had often seen them. Suddenly I heard footsteps and German voices outside the house. I froze. The gate creaked open and I heard footsteps. Were they coming to investigate the house? Had we been seen?

The footsteps stopped and I heard the hiss of the men urinating. One must have finished before the other for he said, "Hurry Karl or the sergeant will have our bollocks for this."

"When you need to pee you need to pee. I will be glad when we are back on day patrols. At least we can use the toilets in the bars!"

"Do not worry. It will soon be eight and then we can go off duty."

The footsteps receded out of the garden. I had taken enough chances and I returned to the house. I had been given an idea. The Germans obviously used the cafes. I had been worried that they might be off-limits to German soldiers. We could use them now. I let the men sleep until eleven. I reasoned that the German shifts looked to be twelve until eight, eight until four and four until midnight. If we made our move at twelve noon there was a good chance that the Germans would be having a meal break. We could not stay in the house until night time. We still had much to do.

I shook them awake not long before noon. Fletcher looked at his watch, "Sir, you let us sleep."

"I needed to think. Come on we are going to move." When they were gathered in the kitchen I explained my plan. "Right now let's smarten ourselves up. Sadly it has stopped raining but our damp clothes might make it look as though we have been on duty and are ready for our meal break."

We fastened buttons and tightened belts. I made sure that their field caps were straight and then led them into the garden. Rather than sneaking, we marched purposefully towards the gate and then opened it. To my relief, there was no one around. We turned right and then we marched towards the beach and the defences. This time we would be able to walk past the command centre. As we emerged on to the road which ran along the beach I saw how impressive the defences were. They had looked good on the aerial photographs but, looking beyond them to the sea, I saw that it would be a bloodbath getting through them. Those in Sicily and Italy were like sandcastles compared with these.

We turned left to march down the road towards the end of the defences. There was a road which ran along the beach. Glancing to my right as I did so, I saw that the wire was like the maze at

Hampton Court. An attacker would see it as an impenetrable barrier but I saw the Germans using paths hidden from the sea. In an ideal world, we would investigate them. Poulson hissed and I looked ahead. A patrol of four Germans was coming the other way. It was led by a sergeant.

I began to talk to Poulson. "The letter from my wife has disturbed me."

The Sergeant caught on, "Really, sergeant, why?"

"I think there is something wrong with the house but she is not telling me." The German patrol was almost next to us. I nodded to the sergeant as we passed but kept on talking. "I know that the roof had a leak but I thought she had had it repaired."

Then we were passed them. I did not risk looking around. That would have been a mistake. When we reached the end of the section of wired off beach we stopped. There were two machine-gun tobruks close by. They were forty yards from us. I saw the two crews were closed up and watching out to sea. I saw, close to the beach itself were a pair of seventy sixes.

I looked back towards the canal and the river. The German patrol had reached the Command Centre and were turning down the street. I saw a ship, it could have been the one we saw the previous night, as it sailed across the mouth of the estuary. I wondered what they were doing and then I saw a spout of water. They were dropping charges off their stern. I guessed they were making sure there were no frogmen or miniature submarines hiding beneath the sea. I was glad that *'Osiris'* would be further out at sea and lying safely on the bottom in much deeper water.

I said, quietly. "We will walk down to the road and then along the front of the beach defences."

Poulson said, "Risky sir. What if we are stopped?"

"We march. If we are stopped I will think of something."

I had already seen that there was a road which led to the beach along the wire. The defences were concentrated around this end of the Riva Bella site. We would be marching the perimeter. Having seen the other patrol I guessed it would be normal for the Germans to be vigilant. As we passed the two machine-gun tobruks one of the gunners shouted, "Are you off for a paddle, Sergeant!"

His mate thought that was funny. I turned and snapped, "Unless you want to spend the next week on night duty I would get back to watching for the English and Americans!"

"Sorry Sergeant!"

I turned to my men, "And you can all take that smile off your faces! March!" I quite enjoyed playing Brian Donleavy in Beau Geste.

We reached the end of the wire. I saw footprints leading around the perimeter of the wire. They looked to be German boots. I risked following them. Perhaps, by luck, we had ended up following the right path. We passed in front of the Russian 76mm guns and a personnel casemate. Behind it, I could see mortar tobruks. I saw a larger one ahead and there were German soldiers there. They were without their tunics and hats. They looked to be cleaning it out. The Sergeant who commanded stood with his hands on his hips as we approached. Two of his men stopped cleaning and he snarled, "Get on with it! Just because the patrol is early is no reason for idling! Captain Schwarz will have my stripes if this is not spotless when he inspects." He turned to us. "Are you early or late?"

"Neither." I gestured with my thumb at my men. "These were getting a little lazy. I took it on myself to stretch their legs. It will do them no harm to wait for their lunch! They are getting fat here! It is all that cheese!"

The Sergeant laughed, "You are right there. Have you tried the *'White Horse'*? They have beer which is almost drinkable. Better than the French muck they serve elsewhere."

"No, we only arrived yesterday! We have not found our feet yet."

He nodded, "Tell them Sergeant Eisner sent you. You will get full measures that way!"

"Thanks and if I see you there I will buy you one!"

"You are on."

I turned. "Come on, march! Just because your betters are talking is no reason for you to slack off!"

The fact that we were seen talking made the rest of our inspection of the perimeter easy. I was able to observe the huge 155mm guns and the 75mm. There were six of the bigger ones and four of the smaller. They would make a mess of any of larger ships who approached. I could now clearly see the minefield. It lay just thirty yards from the wire. That made sense. They would not want exploding mines to rip holes in their wire. As we approached the canal and river again I saw that there was another armoured shelter and more armoured tobruks. We turned and walked along the edge of the canal. I glanced down to see if I could see the canoes; I could not. The tide was in. That was reassuring. Of course, when we took them out there might be damage. That was the chance we took.

We were almost back to where we had started our 'patrol'. I looked at my watch. It was gone one. I headed for the cafes we had seen. The streets were busy now. There were off duty German soldiers. I realised that would be a problem for us. We had to avoid any further, unwanted, conversation. Luckily the first two we encountered were too full. I stopped at one table. "We are new in town. Sergeant Eisner said the *'White Horse'* served decent ale. Where is it? These are all a bit crowded."

The private pointed down towards the square. "Go down to the end of the square and turn left, Sergeant. It is at the corner."

"Thanks."

The walk afforded us the opportunity to inspect the rest of the town. The narrow streets would not help our tanks when we attacked but once past the beach defences I could see no obstacle to stop infantry. The problems of the mines remained. There was no way to outflank them. The narrow path we had taken would be a death trap. I hoped that the planners had come up with something to disable the mines or we could lose many more brave and irreplaceable soldiers.

The *'White Horse'* was, fortunately, almost empty. There was just a handful of Frenchmen drinking and smoking. They scowled at us. I glared at them and they looked away. "Sergeant Eisner said you had a decent beer here. Four large ones."

I spoke in German and the barman ignored me. I leaned forward and repeated it in French adding, "I know you understand German! Next time serve me the first time or it will be the worse for you." He pulled four beers. "That's better." I glanced up at the tariff and put down the right money. "No tip!"

We took the beers to the furthest and darkest corner of the bar. We drank the beers quietly. Although we were all hungry none of us were willing to risk the food. At best they might spit in it and at worse...

"So what do you think of our new posting?"

As the most confident speaker Beaumont answered me. "I have had worse. The beer is drinkable but I prefer the Munich beers."

I nodded, "Why they cannot make wheat beers such as we have at home I do not know."

It was now almost two in the afternoon and the French, having finished their lunch, departed leaving us and the barman. I had given money to the others and Beaumont went to the bar to buy the next round. He spoke to the barman quietly and in French. I guessed he was playing the good guy to my baddie! He winked when he returned. He had learned something. We would have to wait until we were alone to discover what. It would be dark at about five-thirty but the port and the watch would be alert. We had to be ready to leave once it was closer to seven. **'*Osiris*'** could lie off the estuary at periscope depth but the minesweeper we had seen had me worried.

We nursed our beers until four and, as the bar filled up, this time with Germans, we left. I said loudly for all to hear, "We had better report to Captain Swartz." I had heard his name and guessed that he was something of a martinet. "We wouldn't want to get into his bad books the first day at a new posting."

We were halfway up the street when we met Sergeant Eisner and four other non-coms. He smiled, "Well, what did you think of it?"

"The beer was fine but I prefer Munich wheat beer."

He nodded, "Don't we all. Where are you off to? I thought you were going to buy me a drink."

"I would but our officer is due to arrive at six. We are to meet him at the Command Centre. He is a Prussian. He even has a monocle!"

Eisner spat, "I hate those Teutonic types. They are the ones who get good men killed. Another time then."

We headed up the street. Once we reached the quiet, empty residential area we darted back into the garden and re-entered the house. Having established that no one was near we gathered in the kitchen. "What did you learn, Beaumont?"

"Just confirmation that Eisner does drink there but he sounds like the character you were playing. Throws his weight around and pretends it is his private drinking club. I got the impression that they plan to do something about him."

"What makes you say that?"

"The barman said I seemed a nice young man and I ought to stay away from the likes of you and Eisner when not on duty. He said it would be safer."

"You may be right then. I spread my hand around the kitchen. "We have two hours to kill here. We have seen all that we need to and more. I don't want to risk an officer seeing us and asking us what we are going here."

We ate some dry rations we had. It was not much but it stopped our stomachs from grumbling. We had only gone twelve hours without food. We had taken on board plenty of liquid. We would come to no harm.

We knew when dusk had fallen for the house became pitch black again. We left at six-thirty. We did not have far to go. I hoped the tide was right. It would not be as low a tide as when we had hidden the canoes. We might have to swim for them. This time we marched confidently down along the wire to the stone at the end of the mole. The sentry on the top waved to us. We marched to the minefield and when we saw the two sentries had retired to their guard hut we went back to the wall. Once we had scrambled on to the rocks we were hidden from sight. They would only be able to see us if they peered over the side and there was no reason for them to do that. Even a ship entering the canal would not see anything unless they used a searchlight.

I took off my greatcoat and tunic. Our disguises would no longer be needed. I rolled up my sleeve and lowered my hand into the water. I managed to touch the top of the canoe but that was all. I mimed for Fletcher and Poulson to hold my legs and I immersed myself in the icy water. The surges of the waves made it hard but I eventually reached down and lifted the stones out of the bottom of the canoe. I had moved four when I needed to take a breath. I managed to empty it on the next immersion. When I went down for the third time I grabbed the canoe by the seat and pulled. It was hard at first but it began to move. Beaumont grabbed the bow and it became much easier. Once out we turned it upside down to drain the water. Sergeant Poulson emptied the second, aided by Fletcher and Beaumont. I packed the greatcoats in the bow and the stern of the canoe. It would not do to leave them for the Germans to find.

While Poulson and Beaumont emptied their canoe of water I nodded to Fletcher. This was the time for an act of faith. He sent the coded signal five times. Had we seen anything in the dark then he would have stopped but the black night remained empty. The Lieutenant Commander had said he would be there and we had to trust to him. Fletcher climbed in the canoe while I held it. Poulson held it while I got in and then Fletcher and I held their canoe so that they could board. Once we were ready we began to paddle. If the sentries saw us we would know it. For that reason, we kept our strokes slow and smooth so that we did not splash. We would have to go at least a mile beyond the end of the mole.

There was little point in hurrying. We would get there when we got there. The receding tide aided us and what little wind there was came from our backs too. After twenty minutes of steady paddling, I risked looking behind me. The mole could only be seen by the glow of light from the sentries brazier. We stopped paddling and waited. If the submarine was there they would see us and surface. If they were not then I would give it an hour and start to paddle home.

As we bobbed up and down I was convinced that I could see the periscope but each time I was wrong. Then I heard a dull sound from below. It was the submarine's electric motors. There was a maelstrom of bubbles as it surfaced just twenty yards from us. We paddled towards it and then I heard a louder noise from behind us. It was a ship and it was leaving the river. Eager hands grabbed us and others held the canoes. I took out my German dagger and slashed holes in the bottom of my boat. We did not have the time to recover it and if we left it floating it would warn the Germans that we had been there. Poulson saw what I did and he did the same. I slid the canoe down into the water. It began to sink but still too slowly for me. We hurried through the hatch. The deck crew had heard the ship too and we were unceremoniously pushed into the forward torpedo room.

The hatch was slammed shut quickly but even so, we were showered with water as the submarine crash-dived. We were turning at a sharp angle and diving for the bottom. I found it hard to keep my feet. The leading hand said, "Steady on sir! Don't want to lose you just yet."

I heard the engines of the R ship as it passed over us. I wondered if this was a coincidence or had we been spotted?

The Midshipman who waited for us said, "Could you come with me, sir. The Captain wants a word."

"Take charge, Sergeant."

"Sir."

The watertight door was slammed behind us. It sounded like the crack of doom. "Sorry we were late, Captain Harsker. Our little friend up there chased us last night and it took longer to get back on station."

"Does he know we are here?"

"I am not certain. Jerry has been developing underwater listening devices. I don't think it is as good as ASDIC but... Did you get the information you needed?"

I nodded, "And more!"

"Good. Number One, take us to the bottom. Pass the word, silent running." He looked at me. "I would rather travel on the surface if I am able. We will see if we can lose him."

I leaned against the side of the submarine as we touched the bottom. We canted over at a slight angle and then we waited. We heard the engines of the German ship as they passed over us and then they receded. I smiled. Lieutenant Commander Reid shook his head and pointed up. I looked at my watch. After twenty minutes I had begun to sweat. I watched condensation drip from the steel sides of the boat and then I heard it. Faint at first it was the German ship and she was returning. In the silence of the submarine, the noise of the engines sounded deafening and then they receded. Another twenty minutes passed and then the captain said, "Bring us up to periscope depth, Number One. We will have a look-see."

We rose slowly. The Lieutenant Commander wiped the condensation off the periscope with a towel and then turned it slowly through three hundred and sixty degrees. "Bring us up so that we can run on engines. Deck watch to the guns." He smiled as we rose a little. "Captain Harsker might appreciate the fresh air, Middy. I don't think he is a natural-born submariner."

I nodded, "Each to his own, Lieutenant Commander."

"If you nip to the wardroom I am sure we can give you a drop of something to warm you up. I'll just go topside."

A seaman said, "If you would follow me, sir." I almost laughed at the wardroom. It was a table with a bench and a curtain. "Take a seat, sir. I'll go and get some mugs. Are you hungry?"

I was but I knew I would not enjoy sandwiches with the acid taste of battery upon them. "No thank you, Killick. A drink will be fine."

The Lieutenant Commander joined me as the leading hand brought the mugs and a bottle of gin. "By way of celebration. I thought Jerry had us last night. I'll just have the one though! I'm driving."

I pointed upwards, "Who has the con then."

"Number One. I am lucky. He will have his own boat before too long and I will have to train up another." He poured the gin into the mug and added some Angostura bitters. "Bottoms up!"

I was not a gin man but I had been brought up well by Dad. "Bottoms up."

He swallowed half and smacked his lips, "So, what is it like?"

"The beach?" He nodded. "A death trap. There are mines, concrete emplacements, 155s, 75s and Russian 76s. Their big guns can pound ships which are thirteen miles offshore. And we only looked at part of the beach one mile by three hundred yards. It looked the same all the way down." I supped my gin. It was like drinking medicine. "I was on the Africa, Sicily and Italy invasions. They didn't have one-tenth of the defences I saw. They looked awesome enough from the aerial photographs. On the ground, they look positively impossible."

He downed his drink. "You are a cheery soul. Will you be taking part in this attack or are you the scouts?"

"Oh we will be in and we will be the first to land."

"But you chaps are good. Everyone says so."

"No matter how good you are, machine-gun bullets don't discriminate. They kill the good and the incompetent just as efficiently."

"You have survived behind enemy lines many times, I am told."

"A few times, yes."

"Isn't that more dangerous?"

"No, not by a long chalk. I have the greatest admiration and respect for any soldier who assaults a beach. I am not returning with good news but at least we are returning. One step at a time eh?"

Chapter 12

Major Foster came down to debrief me. We would be returning to reconnoitre the other side of the canal in ten days and he was anxious that I should not have to trek up to London and back. I wished he had let me. That way I could have seen Susan. After I had given him my report and drawn the map of the beach as I remembered it he said, "It sounds like a tough nut to crack." He smiled, "Still you got in and out in one piece."

"This second raid increases the risk you know? I am not certain what can be gained. If we are to find a path for Lord Lovat then we have done so."

He leaned back, "This is Colonel Fleming's baby. He is keen to know what dangers are presented by the land to the north of the canal and river. The Airborne Brigade have to hold that flank along with the 1st Special Service Brigade. The main break out will be further south. He asked for you specifically. He has great faith in you."

"I wish he wouldn't. He is reckless you know, Toppy. He thinks any price is a price worth paying."

"Well, it will be the last one. Have you chosen your team?"

"Bill Hay, Ken Shepherd and Alan Crowe."

"Why those?"

"I am acutely aware that on the last two raids before this one, my men were wounded. These three haven't used all their luck up yet. Besides, there is woodland country where we can hide and their language skills will not be as important."

"So you are the antithesis of Colonel Fleming?"

"I bloody hope so!"

"Surely you don't believe in luck, Tom. You plan and organize so well that I would think you had eliminated luck."

"Luck is as important as anything. We aren't superstitious or anything like that; not really but the fact remains that luck does play a part. When the invasion takes place and the machine-guns start to scythe down the men on the beaches it will be luck which determines which men fall. You can't dodge a German bullet. Remember the retreat through Belgium?" The Major nodded. "Think of the men who were killed by flying shrapnel and those who survived. We all marched down those lanes and we all scattered when the Stukas dived. There was no skill in survival. It was luck."

"Well, Captain Marsden appears to have his fair share of bad luck. He is still having trouble with that small bunch of malcontents."

I shook my head, "That's not bad luck sir and the problem is solvable."

"How so?"

"Move the bulk of the men to other sections and get rid of the ringleaders."

"Get rid?"

"Send Osborne and the other leaders to regular units. He said himself he was in it for the money. Move him and make him someone else's problem."

"Perhaps you are right. It is wearing down the captain and demoralising the rest of his section. I will have a chat with Major Rose before I go."

"And I will go and see Daddy Grant."

All the way back from Normandy I had run through what I needed to make life easier when we returned. He smiled when I walked through the door. I think he regarded me as a surrogate son. I know he was as proud of my promotion and medals as my mum. "Back safe and sound eh sir? What can I do for you today?"

"Have we still got those German waterproofs we brought back?"

"Somewhere. I'll have to search them out myself. Special equipment I tend to hide. There are some thieving buggers around here."

"In the Commandos?"

"They have the skills, sir. It has only been since the whole troop returned. I suppose it is inevitable; I mean there are more men. We have had pistols and ammunition stolen. Expensive binoculars too. I reckon someone is selling them on the black market. Major Rose is quite concerned."

"I can understand that. Was it Colts?"

"Yes sir. That is why we are so short. They are easy to get rid of on the black market. Your section has eight left and that is more than any other section. Poor Captain Marsden only has two in his. His own and Sergeant Curtis. We have thieves in the Brigade."

I shook my head. "The service is changing eh, Daddy?"

He nodded, sadly, "When do you need these waterproofs sir and how many?"

"Just four and we need them by the end of the week."

"I'll have them by tomorrow." He took in my words. "Going back, sir?"

I nodded. "Once more unto the breach!"

"Gordy going with you?"

"Bill Hay."

"He is a good lad. Are you well off for ammo sir? I still have some German stuff."

"We didn't need to fire a shot in anger this time."

"Well, I shall keep it safe and sound for you, sir."

As I went to gather my men and tell them who I had chosen I realised that this was the first time we had not had to use any violence. I hoped the next mission would end up as successful. Although disappointed that they had not all been chosen the men who would remain behind were not resentful. Crowe and Shepherd had not been on the last three raids and were beginning to feel left out.

"So you three it is down to the river and canoe practise."

Ken Shepherd was another of our explosives experts. "Will we need explosives, sir?"

"No Shepherd but I want the three of you to speak in German from now on. Beaumont, you keep testing them."

"Yes sir."

We would have the same journey by canoe as we had had before. It was important that each pair worked as one. I had studied the aerial photographs of the northern section of the river. I planned on hiding the canoes on land. I had been aware that without the bad weather of our last raid, we might have been spotted. I took Crowe with me. I intended to have three days of intensive training in the canoes before we spent the next three studying maps and photographs. Canoeing is all about rhythm. We paddled from the old E-boat dock up as far as Lamorran. It was a hard paddle upstream. We had no rain but it was as cold as I had ever known it. We used fingerless gloves but the icy river soon soaked them. Hay and Shepherd had to learn to stay in our wake and follow my every move. To do so in silence was equally hard.

Once we reached the small island on the Fal I stopped. We had some dry rations which we ate. Crowe rubbed his shoulders. Bill Hay laughed, "Are they burning?"

"German, Lance Sergeant, German."

He concentrated and said, in German, "Your shoulders, they are burning."

I smiled as Crowe concentrated, "They are hot, yes."

"You need to be more natural when you speak. You look as though you are thinking about every word you are saying."

"We are, sir."

"Don't then Lance Sergeant. Keep it simple. Short phrases are the key. Listen carefully. That will help your German. You need to think like German. They have a sense of humour but they don't smile much." Sergeant Poulson and the others had told them all of our experience. It had both excited and worried the rest of the section.

When I deemed they had enough time to recover from the hard paddle up the river I led them to the canoes again. "Right now when we go downstream I want to see if we can do it in half the time. I have my watch ready to time us. The day after tomorrow we do this same journey but at night. We will be landing in Normandy at night and that is much harder."

By the time we paddled down the Fal in the middle of the night, we were faster and quieter. I had learned lessons from our first landing. Their German improved as quickly as their paddling skills. That was down to Beaumont who haunted them when they were in the digs. He took to stalking them and listening outside their rooms. If they spoke English he leapt in and snapped at them in German.

Bill Hay came to me to complain, "Sir there is nowhere to get any peace. Shepherd was on the bog the other day and asked for toilet paper. When he asked in English Beaumont shouted in German. Poor bugger needed more toilet paper after that sir."

"Bill, one slip over there and we don't come back. Beaumont might be young but he handles himself like a veteran when we are in France. The lads are getting better but we can't just be good, we have to be perfect."

Daddy Grant had come up trumps for us. Not only did he have the waterproofs he also had more equipment. In the last push in Italy, many prisoners had been captured. Through his contacts, he had managed to get hold of some of it. He had German wallets for us and more German money. He had a proper sergeant's uniform and greatcoat for me and a corporal's for Bill. He even had four German identity cards. As they were for Italy they would not bear close inspection but they would buy us some time if we had to use them. Finally, he had some German field glasses. They were like gold!

Gordy Barker drove us to the submarine. I knew that he was a little disgruntled at not being chosen but he accepted it. "The rumour is, sir, that we will be going over this summer, to France I mean. Not just us but the whole troop."

I smiled, "And you know I won't confirm that, Sergeant."

"I know sir but what I wanted to know is when do we start training with the rest of the troop? Sure as shooting we won't be going in by aeroplane or submarine. The rest of the troop has been using that beach in Devon. When do we start?"

"When I get back I will see Major Rose. And not all of the troop has been practising. Captain Marsden's haven't."

"That is because they have too many bad apples in it. I am surprised at Ken Curtis. Why doesn't he give that Osborne a good hiding?"

"Because Osborne is a barrack-room lawyer. He is waiting for Curtis to do just that. He knows his rights and he will use them. No, we get rid of Osborne but we do it by the book."

Gordy shook his head, "Time was we would have sorted out our own problems. When we joined the Commandos we were proud to be part of something. Now the likes of Osborne just want shoulder flashes and extra pay."

Gordy was right and I could not help but agree. However, I was an officer now and I kept my counsel.

Lieutenant Commander Reid greeted me like an old friend. "We have the canoes in the forward torpedo room. I thought you might as well go there directly rather than using the rear torpedo room."

"Won't that make it more crowded for your lads?"

"They are going to use the aft torpedo room. It was their idea."

"Thanks."

I was the only one who had been in a submarine before and I knew that the others would be feeling nauseous as well as a little fearful. When the hatch was slammed shut and the dim lights came on it was like being buried alive. To keep their minds from it I took them through the German phrases we might need and had one last look at the maps. We didn't need it but it kept their mind from the claustrophobia. We had to check out the battery at Merville and then the route to the bridge over the canal. When their nerves were settled I told them to get some sleep. We would be landing, as we had the first time, in the middle of the night. That would allow us to get to the bridge over the canal by dawn and then work our way back for a dusk pick up.

Lieutenant Dixon came forrard to tell us we were close. "The weather is helping again, sir. There is a fog."

Crowe was our signaller, "Sir what about the signal when we return? If there is fog it might not be seen."

I nodded, "We cross that bridge when we come to it. So the sea is calm?"

"Like a millpond. The Captain is a little happier with this beach. We should be away from the patrol route of the minesweeper. We will surface in thirty minutes and make the most of the voyage on the surface." He smiled, "The air will be marginally fresher!"

We got ready. Already dressed we put our weapons in the canoes and kept our greatcoats to one side. We would use them to sleep on and then put them in the canoes. We had corned beef sandwiches and hot cocoa. They would be the last food and hot drinks we could guarantee until we returned to the submarine. I rested and told the men to sleep. It would be a long and slow journey across the Channel. We dived a couple of hours short of our destination. The Captain had heard aeroplanes and we did not want to be spotted.

We began to surface early. I looked at my watch. The lieutenant returned with the torpedo room crew, "Sorry about this, Captain, there is a minefield. You will have further to paddle. The Captain is surfacing but he wanted to know if you wanted to abort the mission?"

"No, Lieutenant. We will just have a longer paddle. I take it this is a new field?"

"It wasn't here when we last came. We sailed quite close to the coast to avoid the minesweeper."

"Then I think we made them suspicious the last time. How much further out are we?"

"You will have a mile and a half to paddle sir. Are you certain about this?"

"The mines are there to catch big boys, not canvas canoes. We will just take it steady. We allowed time in case there were problems. However, the extraction may be more problematic. We might paddle out to the edge of the minefield and then signal you. That way the signal will be easier to see."

The leading hand opened the hatch and a blast of icy air filled the boat. I scrambled up and moved to the bows. The other three followed me and then the canoes were manhandled out of the hatch. The Lieutenant was right. The sea was calm but you could barely see ten feet in front of your face. The leading hand pointed beyond the bows. The captain had brought us as close as he had dared. I saw one of the deadly, black mines bobbing in the water. The Killick shook his head. We donned our waterproof capes. They would give us some protection from the cold.

I tapped Crowe on the shoulder and we dug our paddles into the water between us and the submarine. We headed towards the mine. By keeping the mine in sight we would avoid another. Methodical Germans laid them in straight lines. It was the detonators which looked like hedgehog's quills which were the danger. I kept them at least four feet from the end of my paddle.

The fog shielded us from sight but made navigation more difficult. I had to use my compass more. I was suddenly aware of something to my right. A mine had broken free from its mooring. It was less than three feet from my paddle. I dug in and turned us closer to the mines on our left. They were tethered and safer. I hoped that Hay had his wits about him.

Once we had cleared the rogue mine I corrected our course and headed towards the beach. The mines stopped and I knew we were close. I heard the hiss of water on sand and shingle. We ground on to the beach. I jumped out with Luger at the ready. Hay and Shepherd slid up next to us. We grabbed the toggles at the bow and stern of our canoes and began to run up the beach. I stopped for I saw, above the high water mark, a depression in the sand. I lowered the canoe and took out my knife. I cleared away the sand and saw the mine. I didn't know if this was the edge or the middle of the field. Had we had better visibility then I would have headed for the river but the mines at sea had forced our hand.

I crawled forward on my hands and knees looking for another. When I spied, just ten feet ahead, the dunes I realised that we had found the edge of the minefield. Retracing my steps I returned to the others. I picked up the bow toggle and we followed my footsteps to the dunes. Instead of heading inland, I took us east, along the sand dunes. Here there was no wire and we made good progress. The dunes descended and I knew that the river was close. I lowered the canoe to the sand and began to unpack our equipment. Once emptied we buried the canoes in the dunes. Bill Hay went to find some stones and he placed them in an apparent random pattern. It would help us find them when we returned. Using the river we headed inland. We had four or five miles to go to get to the bridge. I knew that during the day it would be busy. We had to examine the site the planners had chosen for the gliders to land.

After crossing some scrubby, sandy land we found a road. I stopped the men and made sure we looked like a German patrol. I said, "March!" Our first mission had made me more confident about this part of the operation. There seemed to be few defences on this side of the river. I saw little evidence of wire. Of course, the land to the north of us was higher, not much but enough to enfilade this side of the river with machine-gun fire. The fog both helped and hindered us. We almost stumbled into the German checkpoint. Had they not spoken then we would have. I held up my hand as I heard, "Erik, this is the worst coffee I have ever tasted. Did you put any coffee essence in it?"

"You make it next time."

I waved us to the left and we headed across the farmland which lay there. I looked at my watch. It was almost five o'clock. I guessed that the bridge over the Orne River was close to the checkpoint but we needed confirmation. I closed my eyes to visualize the maps I had studied. There was another road which ran parallel to the river and then beyond it the main road from Cabourg. There was also a village there, Bréville-les-Monts. If we had the time I would investigate that too but the priority was the land between the canal and the river and the battery of guns. I led my men to the other side of the field and, sure enough, found the road. We headed down it. It met the main road from the north. This was more dangerous now. I risked marching down it towards the river.

As we walked I saw that the fields had not been flooded as the planners had feared and, more importantly, the anti-glider posts had not been erected. The fog was thicker closer to the river. As we approached the bridge I heard muffled voices ahead. I saw a small side road and we took it. We passed a farm. It was boarded up and then we found the track which ran along the river. We used it. There were plenty of trees and bushes for cover. I made my decision. We would wait there until dawn and then examine the landing zone in daylight. We had shelter and the abandoned farm meant it unlikely that we would be stumbled upon. I circled my arm. My men found cover. I found a bush and lay beneath it. Then we waited.

The weak winter sun was still enough to burn off the fog and we could see all the way across to the canal. We were less than two hundred yards from the bridge over the river and the landing zone between the river and the canal was clearly visible. It was flat. There were no obstacles. We had a perfect view and I used my pilot's eyes to assess the landing. It would be challenging but possible. There were no telegraph or telephone poles and although not totally flat it was possible to land a Horsa glider there.

Part one of our mission was completed. Now we had to get to the Merville Battery and identify the guns that resided there. Our first problem was to get beyond the road. I chose to use the same method as we had in Ouistreham. We would march. We headed back up the track to the farm and then turned back along the road. Once we reached the road I turned right to head up the Cabourg road. We managed a mile before we met another patrol. It was coming in the opposite direction.

I began to talk to Hay as soon as I saw them. "So I said to Captain Schwarz, 'when do my men get leave'."

Hay caught on, "And what did he say?"

"Oh, you know him. He is all spit and polish. He said we had to finish the defences first."

I saw that we had almost drawn abreast of the eight-man patrol. Hay shook his head, "We have almost finished them."

I waved to the sergeant of the other patrol and said, "I know but we will have to wait a while longer."

We continued the conversation until we could no longer hear their boots. I saw that the land between us and the coast was filled with little copses and wild bushes. It was pastureland and had dips and hollows. As soon as I could I led us across a field boundary and headed towards the nearest cover. I knew that the battery, which was still under construction, was just a mile and a half from where we had hidden the canoes. I estimated that it lay a mile from where we were.

Using the compass we headed across country. The maps and aerial photographs indicated that the battery lay on some high ground. I saw the wire ahead. There was some cover less than half a mile from the wire. We hid ourselves and I took out the field glasses. I could see that they were still building the concrete emplacements. It was obvious to me that there were no guns yet installed. There were, however, anti-aircraft guns ringing the battery as well as many machine-gun pits. The emaciated workers I saw building the battery were forced labour. The news that it was still being built was good news but the fact that we did not know the calibre of guns posed a problem. The planners had hoped that we could discover what aerial photography could not.

I turned to the others. "We have seen enough. I intend to get closer to our beach. I don't want to push our luck any more than we have to." I had wanted to scout out Bréville-les-Monts but time was pressing and the German patrol we had passed was a warning. It was not worth pushing our luck. Our main objectives had been achieved.

We headed to the north-west. The land fell away. It was scrubby bush and tree-filled but there looked to be no mines. We were within sight of the sand dunes when there was a sudden and enormous explosion out at sea. It looked to be where the minefield was.

Hay said, "Have they got the sub?"

Shaking my head I said, "I think it was that loose mine we saw last night. It must have drifted and struck another mine." I took out the glasses and looked back at the battery. It was as though an ant's nest had been disturbed. I turned the glasses to look at the estuary. The R boat emerged from the harbour and headed for the minefield. She stopped well short and I saw a boat lowered and sailors rowed slowly towards the minefield. Two divers slipped over the side and disappeared beneath the waves. It took some time but after a few dives, they returned to the ship. Alarmingly the ship dropped its anchor. I wondered what was happening.

Three hours later another ship emerged from the harbour. This was a smaller version of the R-boat. I saw immediately what they were doing. They were replacing the mines which had exploded and, what soon became clear, they were enlarging it. It took until the middle of the afternoon to complete the job and then the two ships left. I didn't think that it would hurt us for we had negotiated the minefield in the fog. As they had tethered the new mines we should be safer.

It was the Todt workers who created problems for us and stopped our escape being as it was planned. As dusk approached we heard firing from our right and drew our weapons. We saw a handful of the emaciated figures fleeing the battery and heading for the sea. Rifles and machine-guns fired at them but they seemed to bear a charmed life. The six of them managed to reach the sand dunes. I do not know what they thought to do but they ran on to the beach. We could not see them for they were below our eye line. But, once again, it seemed they were going to make it for some managed to get halfway to the water before they were unlucky enough to step on a mine. There were a series of small explosions as mines were triggered. The silence was followed by the cries of the wounded. We saw, from our cover, German soldiers standing on the sand dunes. An officer pointed and shouted something. machine-gun fire ended the cries.

If I thought that had ended the danger I was wrong. German patrols began to search the dunes. Obviously, there were Todt workers who had not been blown up. I looked at my watch. It was less than an hour to dark. There was no way we could approach the beach while they were watching. I prayed for dark. Just before dark, we heard the crack of a German rifle. Soldiers ran to a spot to the north of us. I took the opportunity to move closer to the sand dunes. We had just reached the edge of the dunes when the German soldiers began to march south again. They were in a skirmish line and searching the dunes. When darkness fell they were eighty yards from us.

The lights from their torches meant danger again. We crept towards the dunes. I gambled that they would not risk the mines. We had to get to our canoes and then risk the minefield. As we moved there was the crack of a Luger. I heard a German voice, no more than thirty yards from us, shout, "Weiss, do not shoot at shadows! You might hit one of us. They are not armed!"

"Sorry, Sergeant. I saw a movement."

"It would be a rabbit! We hunt men, not rabbits!"

We waited a few moments and then moved towards our canoes again. I took out the Luger and kept watch while the others dug out the canoes and emptied them of sand. It took a long time as they had to do it carefully. I heard another shot. This time it was further up the beach. Then there was a fusillade and a shout. It was too far away to make out.

Hay said, "Ready sir."

A pair of Germans rose from the dunes just ten yards from us and one said, "Who is there?"

I had no time to think. I fired four shots from my Luger and both men fell dead.

"What is that?" The voice came from further up the beach.

I shouted, "It is Weiss, Sergeant, he shot at rabbits again!"

"The both of you are on a charge. Get over here where I can watch you!"

"Right Sergeant."

I waved the others to the beach. Grabbing the rear toggle of my canoe I followed Hay. There had been no wind and our footprints were still visible. Hay followed them, risking the mines. When we stepped on to the damp sand I breathed a sigh of relief. We were through the mines. Behind me, I heard a whistle as the two bodies were discovered. I heard voices. We quickly clambered into the canoes and began to paddle. If we would see our footsteps in the sand then the Germans could too. They would follow. This time we had not slipped in and out unseen. I just hoped they would think we were two of the Todt workers. The hidden Germans opened fire at the beach. They were firing blind. There was an explosion as they set off a mine. We were almost in the sea minefield and I hoped we were hidden. A German officer shouted, "Cease Fire!"

I had been so preoccupied by the enemy behind me that I had almost forgotten the mines ahead. I saw the detonators of one just a paddle's length from me, to the right. I hissed, "Paddle right!"

Once we had cleared it I steered a course between them. Now that the rogue one had detonated German efficiency and straight lines came to our aid. We kept paddling until we were clear of the field. "Crowe, send the signal."

I looked back to the beach. I could see torches as the Germans continued to look for the escaped workers. I hoped that our diversion had helped them. If they were caught then they would be shot. Perhaps they were so desperate to escape that was the preferred option. As Crowe was facing to sea and the night was black he continued to send the signal. After half an hour he said, "Are they not coming, sir?"

Before I could answer I heard the sound of engines coming from the river. It was the E-Boat. They must have been summoned by the German hunters. A searchlight began to play on the water methodically sweeping from side to side as the ship gingerly approached the minefield. Eventually, it would spot us.

Now that we had cleared it we could paddle quickly. I gambled that the ship would move slowly so as not to miss us.

"Let's paddle."

As we paddled I wondered where the submarine was. Had they been scared off? A second searchlight was switched on. The two of them began to play upon the water. A fluke of the waves and the operator picked up the stern of Hay's boat. I heard a shout from the ship. We were seen. We could do nothing save paddle as the ship began to increase speed. The machine-gun on the ship began to fire. Suddenly there was a flash of light followed by a huge explosion. Had the ship struck a mine? As it settled in the water and we continued to paddle away the answer became clear as the submarine rose from the water and began to head towards us. They had torpedoed the German. We had to move quickly for I knew that there were other boats in the port but we would not have to crash-dive and await depth charges.

Lieutenant Dixon said as he helped us aboard. "The Captain says to sink the canoes. We have no time to recover them."

"Right." Taking out our knives we hacked into the canvas and then threw them overboard. They would soon sink. We slid down the ladder into the forward torpedo room and breathed a sigh of relief when the hatch was closed.

We waited in the forward torpedo room as the captain took us away from the minefield. I think he gambled on the fact that we had only seen one vessel on our previous mission.

The Midshipman came for me. "The Captain can speak with you now, sir. If you would come with me."

Lieutenant Commander Reid looked pleased with himself as well he might. "We are going to go out on the surface and charge up the batteries. That was damned close. We had been watching for some time. We couldn't come in any sooner; we heard the engines of that minesweeper. We had to wait until you were clear before we fired."

"Well, it was a good shot."

He grinned, "And we have a kill!"

Chapter 13

Although we managed to make good time sailing on the surface, it was still late at night when we docked in Southampton. I doubted that we would sail with **'*Osiris*'** again and we said a fond farewell to the crew. There was no doubt that they had saved our lives. Had the German ship picked us out with his searchlights then we would have been an easy target for his machine-guns.

Sergeant Poulson drove us back. "How was the French Beer, Bill?"

"We didn't get any!"

Poulson laughed, "You have to pick your missions, old cock!"

"We survived. I will live with that."

By the time we reached our digs, it was the middle of the night. We were so exhausted that we crashed into our beds. My body, however, could not sleep beyond six and I was up not long after Mrs Dean who was cooking breakfast. "Could you not lie in then sir?"

I laughed, "Believe me I wanted to but here I am up."

"Reg has the staff car if you want a lift up to the camp?"

"No, I will run up after my porridge."

After two cups of Mrs Dean's tea and a generous bowl of porridge, I slipped my Bergen on my back and ran to the camp. It was a cold dry day and the icy air brought colour back to my cheeks. I needed the run to get the smell of the submarine from my nostrils. The sentries grinned as I ran through the gate, "Thought you were off camp, sir!"

"Couldn't keep away." As I ran through the gate there was a honk from behind me as the Sergeant Major brought the staff car back. He was waiting for me as I arrived at the office. "The Major said to take the car, sir, and give you a lift this morning."

There was a hint of criticism in the Sergeant Major's voice, "I needed the run but I wouldn't mind a cup of tea while I write the report."

"Coming right up."

By the time the Major arrived, I had had three cups of tea and finished the report. Major Rose looked bleary-eyed. He was no action man that was for certain. "It went well, Tom?"

"We were lucky again." I gave him the highlights of the mission and handed him the report. "And now I guess we prepare for the invasion. At least my team have an idea of what to expect over there. This will be no picnic."

"Lord Lovat wants you to give a briefing to the officers in a few day's time. He thinks it is important that they have the benefit of your knowledge."

"I take it he didn't approve?"

"He thought it was a risk that was unwarranted. I get the impression he doesn't get on with Colonel Fleming."

"Few serving officers do." I stood, "I'll take my men up to the mine and have practice assaults. We will use the new weapons and machine guns. It is time we became familiar with them."

We had not been issued with the standard Bren gun but the Vickers K light machine gun. Smith and Herbert were designated as its operators and they had practised with it. It differed from the Bren in two respects: it was not as accurate but it had a higher rate of fire, a thousand rounds a minute. With a tripod, it would more than make up for the Thompson. We still had eight Thompsons and we still had enough ammunition for them. The eight Colts were similarly prized. One weapon we did like was the Lee Enfield Number 4 sniper rifle with the telescopic sight. It could hit a target at three thousand yards. Peter Davis had proved the most accurate of our men and he had spent a fortnight training to use the deadly weapon.

We marched with full Bergens to the mine where we liked to train. After dropping our Bergens I addressed them. "We will be part of the assault team when we return to Europe." I saw nods and winks from them. They all had a fairly precise idea of where we would be landing but I still played the game of being vague.

"When we land it will be in France. That means we can accurately replicate the land upon which we will be fighting." I pointed east where we could just make out a beach. "We will spend as little time on the beach as we can. The beach is a killing zone. Look around and see how you can blend into the background. Davis, if we are to use your skills and your new weapon well then you need to be camouflaged."

He nodded, "Yes sir. Sergeant Poulson suggested I make a cape from the camouflage netting."

"Good. Then I want you to hide yourself within half a mile of us. You have two hours and then we come looking for you."

He grinned, "Hide and seek! I love that game."

Gordy Barker growled, "The difference is here, old son, that Jerry will shoot you if he catches you!"

Unabashed he loped off to find a good hiding place. I did not doubt his skills with the weapon but that was only half of the story. "As for the rest of us, we will be attacking strong points. That means grenades. I intend to take as many grenades as we can carry. Crowe, you and your grenade launcher will come into their own. Remember those tobruks we saw? They are built to defend around and not from above."

"Yes sir. Beaumont has taken the charges from a couple of grenades and I am going to practise with those."

"Good. Now we have a mixture of weapons so let us use them wisely. The K gun can clear the enemy from before us so we use that and keep the Thompsons for those places where we have to be mobile. The Lee Enfield might not have the firepower of a Thompson but it is more accurate. You won't be firing at over a thousand yards like Davis will but you can kill at five hundred yards. That is your objective." I looked around. "Now make sure it is blank ammunition you load. Today is all about working in your teams. Sergeants!"

My three sergeants gathered around me. "You know your teams." They nodded. "I don't need to tell you that we will lose men when we go ashore. Gordy your lads have the K gun. You need to be able to fire that as well as they can."

"Aye, sir."

"Sergeant Poulson you have Scouse and the radio. Up until now, it has not been important but it will be in France. We can call in aeroplanes and armour. You may well have to make that call."

"Sir."

"And Hay, you have the grenade launcher. Make sure Emerson and yourself can use it as well as Crowe. As for me, well I will have to see how good I am with the sniper rifle. We have two weeks of training here. Major Rose tells me that the brigade will be moving to Southampton soon."

"Does that mean us as well sir?"

"No, Gordy. We are going to Devon. The French Commandos are there. We will be going in with them. We need to learn to work with them. We will be joining the Brigade in May."

They looked at each other. They were all bright lads and could work out that meant a late May or early June invasion. It was the middle of March. Time would fly.

"You have an hour. Gordy, I want you and your team to play King of the Castle. Hay and Poulson you will assault. My team will umpire. Then we go and find Davis!" I called over Hewitt and Beaumont. "We get to watch. If you think one of them is dead then tap them on the shoulder and tell them so."

"Sir."

Although Gordy had only two men under his command they had automatic weapons. With a rate of fire of almost seventeen bullets a second then they were a frightening prospect. The problem would come when they had to change magazines. Each magazine held ninety-six bullets. Dad had told me they had a similar problem in the Great War when they had used the Lewis gun. I would be interested to see how Gordy coped with that.

Gordy shouted, "Ready sir!"

Sergeant Poulson and Lance Sergeant Hay needed no instructions from me. They worked in tandem. They needed to get Crowe close enough to drop a grenade close to the K gun. Gordy and his men had used the debris around them to make a defensive emplacement. It would take a lucky bullet indeed to take them out. While Sergeant Poulson sprayed his Tommy gun Fletcher and Shepherd tried to get around the back of the emplacement. Emerson and Hay tried a frontal attack. Crowe took advantage of the cover to get as close as he could.

The K Gun, when it fired, sounded like a buzz saw. Hewitt tapped Emerson on the shoulder, "Sorry, you are dead, Fred!"

Shepherd and Fletcher had got around the back. There was a ripple of Thompson fire and Beaumont said, "Dead, Shepherd."

As the magazine on the K gun was changed Sergeant Poulson tried to attack. Gordy rose above the gunners and fired a burst. Hewitt said, "You are dead Sarge."

If this was real life and an actual attack, then half of the attacking force was already down. I saw that Crowe had crawled and hidden behind Emerson who lay back smoking, feigning death. He carefully aimed the grenade launcher and fired. He had been chosen for the task as he was able to judge ranges well. Beaumont shouted, gleefully, "Boom! Sorry, Sarge but you and your lads are dead!"

We all gathered at a flat part of the mine. Hay shook his head, "I wouldn't like to take on a German machine gun in a concrete tobruk. You have no chance."

Gordy said, "If I had had two more men then Crowe would not have been able to get that close."

Roger Beaumont was a clever lad, "Davis would have made the difference."

Gordy said, "Why?"

"When you stood up, Sarge then you were a target. You sprayed your gun around and that would have cleared the ground around you for a couple of hundred yards. Suppose Davis was a thousand yards away or even eight hundred. You would have been dead and then when the magazine needed changing Sergeant Poulson would have closed with you."

"He is right. Smith, you need to change the magazine yourself. Herbert your job is to use your rifle to fire while the magazine is being changed. You have ten rounds; Smith I want you to be able to change the magazine by the time he has fired four rounds. Just get the old one off and the new one on. Don't bother about being neat and tidy."

We spent some time practising changing the magazine and Crowe demonstrated his skill with the launcher.

"Right, we have given Davis long enough. Leave the bigger weapons here. Rifles, pistols and Thompsons. Look for signs. We have one advantage we would not have in real life; we know he is within half a mile of us. Spread out in a long line. Gordy, you anchor the line up here at the top, Sergeant Poulson down at the bottom. Watch for places he might choose to hide. He is one of us and we know the kinds of places we like to choose."

With fifty yards between us, it was not as efficient a sweep as it might have been but my men were good. Even so, it was a good four hundred yards until we found the first clue. Scouse spotted the footprint and held up his hand. He was like a dog on the scent. He pointed towards a small copse seventy yards from us.

Herbert, next to me said, "This will be easy."

Beaumont said, "Don't forget, John, that in real life, Davis would be firing at us. We have travelled four hundred yards. We would all be dead or hiding on the ground and then he could move off."

That set me to thinking. I would have to modify the exercise. It took us almost an hour to find him. The small copse proved a good hiding place. We searched the tops of the trees and every bush we could. It was Scouse who found him. He was on the ground. He had found a dell close to some tree roots and by using his camouflage net and dead wood, disguised himself well.

"If it was summer sir then it would have been easier. I had a bead on you from eight hundred yards away."

"But you were low down, Davis. You would have lost sight of us a few times."

"You are right sir but I thought I was supposed to stay hidden."

"You were but you need to pose a threat. We will try this again. I want you to use live ammo."

The whole section looked at me.

"And I want all of us to attach a piece of wood to our backs with a target on it. The wood will stand up two feet above your backs. If Davis hits it then you are dead."

Gordy said, "And if he misses then we could be really dead!"

I smiled, "Do you remember training and rock climbing, Gordy?" He nodded. "You trusted the Commando above you to belay you. Do the same with Davis. I trust him. Beaumont was right. This was too easy. We found him too quickly. German snipers are good. Davis, find your spot. The rest of you back to the mine and we will eat."

As we ate I said, "When you are hit. Let the rest know."

The men were resourceful and with the use of tape and wood, we managed to make the targets. While we ate Davis went to find another hiding place. As we began to move towards the hidden Davis I saw that having the target above our heads made us move differently. We all crouched more and moved less fluidly. This time we knew where he was when he opened fire. Gordy's target was hit, showering him with wood, "Bloody hellfire!" He shook his head. "I am dead sir."

I dropped to my knee as another bullet zipped through the air. I did not hear anything strike and I held my position. I dropped to the ground and crawled. Bill Hay was the next to be hit. As he sat down, feigning death he said, "He is in the wood four hundred yards away."

In real life that would not have happened but I could understand Bill. He was annoyed at having been shot. I found myself alone as I crawled. Sergeant Poulson and Scouse Fletcher were hit in quick succession. Then Hewitt and Beaumont fell. It was painfully slow crawling. I had to use whatever cover there was; rocks, bushes, longer pieces of dead grass. Davis was right. Late winter did not help us. In the summer we would have more cover and so would the German snipers. Emerson and Smith were the next ones struck. I moved obliquely to my left to take advantage of a bush. Herbert bought it. That left just three of us. Me, Crowe and Shepherd. I heard the sound of a bullet hitting wood as Shepherd was killed but I saw the flash from the muzzle of the bullet. He was no longer in a tree but behind it. As I raised my head to fire the target above me was hit and then Davis shouted. "That's me dead, sir! Good shot, Alan!"

As I stood I saw Crowe triumphantly raise his grenade launcher and whooping like an Indian. Gordy growled, "I thought the captain said just rifles and pistols?"

Crowe feigned innocence, "This is a rifle grenade, Sarge!"

"He is right Gordy. That was a good exercise. Well done Davis."

"To be honest sir I could have had you a couple of times but I had no clear sight of the target. I didn't want to risk hitting you for real."

Gordy sniffed, "It was a bit much going for the sergeants first."

"Actually, Barker, that is what snipers are trained to do. Davis' second shot was at me. It was why I hit the deck. The NCOs and officers will be the first targets."

As we sat, back at the mine, we went through the options we had. "What we could have done sir, was to go in pairs. A bit like the light infantry do. One fires and the other runs."

"That would work."

Sergeant Poulson injected some cold water, "Except that one man has to be hit to find out that there is a sniper. If we were attacking a machine-gun emplacement the Germans could have snipers close by. I have to tell you, sir, that I think the odds are with the snipers."

Beaumont was always Mr Positive. "We have our own sniper, sir. Why not use Davis to take out the enemy snipers?"

Davis liked that idea. "I would know where the best place was for the sniper to be. They will move sire. I did. But when you move you have to show yourself, however briefly. That gives us a chance."

As we marched back to camp I felt that the day had gone well. Crowe had impressed me. He had not obeyed the rules but then we were Commandos. We made our own rules. I decided that we would equip ourselves as we saw fit. As we passed the camp I called in and made a request of the armourer sergeant. "A bit unorthodox sir but I will see what I can do. The day after tomorrow all right?"

"That will do, Sergeant."

I had to let Sergeant Poulson take the men training the next day as Lord Lovat had the other officers assembled for my talk on the beaches. I was not allowed to mention Normandy but I think that most of them guessed our target. To be fair the defences we would be attacking, no matter where it was, would be the same as the ones we had seen at Riva Bella. I saw some of the younger officers writing copious notes as I told them of the mines, the wire, the tobruks and the command centres. My sketch of the beach had been duplicated and they all had a copy.

"The Germans will have a good view of us as we come in and they will direct their fire at us." I used my experience landing from an LC(I). "When the ramps are lowered you will be exposed. In my view, there will be only two types of Commando left on that beach; the quick and the dead."

I received a good round of applause. Major Foster and Lord Lovat took me to one side. "Well done, Harsker. That was just what I wanted. Too many of these chaps seem to think we will waltz in and take the beachhead easily."

"I think, sir, that it will be bloody." He nodded. "Sir, we have been training up at the mine and practising assaults. Do we have to go in with regulation weapons?"

Lord Lovat cast a curious look in my direction, "What do you mean, Captain?"

"My men are used to being behind enemy lines and adapting to changing circumstances. Some of my men have German pistols and other weapons acquired during our raids. We would like to take advantage of every opportunity to defend ourselves and attack the enemy."

Lord Lovat's face cracked into a smile, "I shall be going ashore with my trusty hunting rifle, my Winchester. I wouldn't dream of allowing every officer to do as you are, Harsker, but you have proved time and again that you get the job done. I will be relying on you and your men to get me to the bridge over the Orne. Do it any way you can."

The Brigade left the next day leaving just Captain Marsden and myself at the camp with our men. Major Rose, Daddy Grant, Reg Dean and the rest of the support staff were preparing to head to Southampton and our new quarters. The armourer saw me just as he was loading the last of his equipment. He handed me a wooden box. "Here you are, sir. If anyone asks you found it when it fell off the back of this lorry."

"Thank you, Sergeant."

He grinned, "I have no idea why you need a second sniper rifle but I am certain you will put it to good use, sir!"

Poor Reg Dean was like a bear with a sore head. Private Larkin bore the brunt of the Sergeant Major's ire. Reg shook his head, "Mrs Dean is not happy, sir. Not only are you lads leaving but I am too. And when Mrs Dean is not happy then I am a bad man to cross."

"We are still here for another couple of weeks, Reg."

"I know but then you go too and she will be rattling around in that big old house."

I remembered Mum when we all left home. "Why don't you suggest she has the house redecorated. Mum did that. It gives them a challenge and they can take their frustration out on the decorators."

He brightened, "Good idea sir. She has been going on about the wallpaper and with the lads all smoking every room needs doing."

When the Brigade had gone it was like being in a ghost town. Our two sections had a couple of weeks to train and then we would be off to Devon for assault training. It brought into focus the problems of Osborne and his cabal. There were now just six of them who were being obstructive but they were a hardcore who knew their rights and played everything by the book.

Captain Marsden had had enough. "I am going to break him or transfer him out."

"Just transfer him. You have more than enough grounds."

"I can't inflict him on someone else. He is our problem and the Sergeant and I will deal with it. It will help the fact that we are training with your men."

We were outside our digs and waiting for our men. Reg and Major Rose were doing a sweep of the camp before they left for Southampton. They hoped to find some of the stolen gear from the Quarter Masters. The bags of the brigade had all been searched before they left but nothing had been found. It was hoped that the major would find the stolen items hidden in the camp. I had my doubts. Whoever had done this was clever. They would probably keep any unsold gear close by them. It might even be in their bags.

John and I had full Bergens. We wanted to replicate the conditions we would find in Normandy. I had my sniper rifle and my Thompson. I wondered if I would regret it. However, when we landed in Normandy, we would need every piece of equipment we could carry. I pointed up the road. "If you lead with your section, we will follow on behind you."

"Are you certain, Tom? Your men are far fitter."

I grinned, "I think it will be better if we follow, don't you?"

He saw what I was getting at and nodded.

Our men arrived and fell in. "Sergeant Barker if you would care to run up alongside me this morning."

"Of course, sir." He looked at me curiously but said nothing. We knew each other well.

Captain Marsden led his men up the hill at a fast pace. We could run faster but it was a healthy pace. As I had expected Osborne and Harris, his close friend were at the back and within ten yards had dropped back two yards. Their Bergens appeared to be over packed. I wondered what they had brought.

Gordy soon cottoned on. "Move yourselves you lazy pair!"

Osborne turned with a sly grin on his face. "I am going as fast as I can. Overtake us, sergeant!"

In answer, Gordy and I speeded up and our knees crashed into the thighs of the two men. "Hey up! What are you doing?"

"Running! Now get a move on or you will be black and blue!" Our knees struck them again and they began to speed up.

I heard Osborne chunter, "I am going to put an official complaint in about this. It isn't right!"

I snapped, "If you can talk, Osborne, you are not running fast enough!"

Once again we closed with them but the two realised our intention and ran faster. Their other four confederates had dropped back a little too. I smiled as Osborne said, "Get a move on these two behind us are nutters."

"Insubordination, Osborne. You are on a fizzer!"

"I wasn't talking about you, Sarge!"

"Then shut up and run, you horrible excuse for a man."

By the time we reached the camp Osborne was a wreck as were his pals. John Marsden had told me of this ploy.

We gave them no time to rest. "Drop your Bergens. Number Two Section you will defend the hill. Number One, we will attack." I nodded to Captain Marsden and Sergeant Curtis. "If you two would like to act as umpires?"

"Righto."

It was a little unfair as we had done this for a week and were well practised however it would give the larger section of Captain Marsden the opportunity to see how it was done. His section had a K gun but only four Thompsons. We divided into four teams. Our secret weapon was Crowe. If we could have used Davis then we would have cleared the hill in minutes but it was unfair to use live ammunition with Captain Marsden's section.

We moved quickly and used every inch of cover. Each time the K gun stopped to reload we advanced further up the hill. Shepherd was one casualty but Captain Marsden's section lost four. When Crowe began to drop his adapted grenades into the heart of the defence the K gun and machine-guns were eliminated and we were declared the winners.

Whilst the majority of Captain Marsden's section were impressed by our assault Osborne, Harris and three of his friends were not. Sergeant Poulson and I became umpires as Number Two section attacked. When they tried to advance as Smith reloaded, half of the section were shot by the two Thompsons at the top. As one was the grenade launcher and a second Sergeant Curtis it soon became apparent that they were going to lose. I saw that Osborne and Harris, along with two other soldiers had hung back. When it was over they stood grinning as though they had outwitted us.

The Captain and Sergeant Curtis had not seen the act and, as we gathered for a brew, they were full of questions about how we had pulled it off. Sergeants Poulson and Barker explained. I watched Osborne and Harris. They were up to something. They were sidling back to their Bergens. I shouted, "You two! Stop there!"

They stood like guilty schoolboys. "Weren't doing nowt, sir. Just getting my Bergen."

I pointed to the others. "Those men were listening and learning how to survive. Unlike you and your cronies, they did their job. I would not like to advance towards Germans with you cowards behind me!"

"You can't call us cowards sir!"

I laughed as I walked up to him, "Of course I can you pathetic little man! You and the others made no attempt to attack the castle! What would you call it?"

"It is just a daft game, sir!"

Captain Marsden and Sergeant Fletcher followed me down the hill. I could see that John was angry. He fought to control it. "Captain Harsker is right Osborne. I don't want you behind me when we invade France. Nor you, Harris." He turned and glared at the other four who had wisely sat with the rest of the section. "As for you four, I will watch you." Osborne and Harris were both grinning. I confess I would have liked nothing better than to smash Osborne's face to a pulp but I knew he wanted that.

Captain Marsden was now grinning, "Funny is it, Osborne? Let's see how funny you find it when I transfer you out."

He stood defiantly, "Another Brigade will suit me, sir and Harris, here too!"

"Oh, it won't be another Commando unit. You will go back to a regular battalion with a full report about your conduct!"

His face infused with colour, "You can't do that sir! The money!"

"Commandos get the extra money, Osborne because they earn it. You do not. Now sit over there. I will have the transfer orders ready by tomorrow morning. We are shot of you."

The two of them glowered but they were now well outnumbered. The other four had been hangers-on and knew which side their bread was buttered. As the two ringleaders went to their bags I said, "Sergeant Barker and Sergeant Hay. Fetch me their Bergens! They looked rather well packed for an exercise at the mine."

"You can't do that! They are ours!"

Ken Curtis laughed as he strode over to help my two sergeants, "They are army property! What are you hiding, you horrible little man?"

With three of the toughest sergeants in the Brigade facing them the two backed down and their sagging shoulders told me that they were now resigned to their fate. Our men had equipment in their Bergens but it was just that which was necessary for the exercise. No one carried excess. I was an exception. When the two bags were opened and the contents dropped to the ground even I was surprised. A half dozen Colts and ammunition tumbled out as well as two pairs of binoculars.

I looked around at the other four. "Sergeant Poulson, empty their bags too!"

One of them, Private Jones shouted, "We have nowt like that sir. We didn't take owt! It was them two."

"Shut your mouth or..."

Osborne got no further as Ken Curtis put all of his pent up anger into a blow to his face. Osborne fell, as though poleaxed. Captain Marsden said, "Explain yourself, Jones, and make it good!"

"Sir, we knew they were up to something but not what. If anyone went near their bags they gave us a going over."

"If I thought for one moment that you four were involved in this scheme as well...."

"Honest sir."

Sergeant Poulson had emptied the bags. He shook his head, "They are clean, sir, but that doesn't mean that they didn't know about it."

"We suspected sir but..."

I nodded, "Let's get them back to camp. The Major and the Sergeant Major will be there. They can get the Military Police. As for you four, if you aren't telling the truth..."

"We are sir. Honest."

John said, "Thanks for that, Tom. Sergeant Curtis and I will deal with these." Osborne had come to and was wiping the blood from his face while glaring at Curtis. "Come on you pair. Wilson, Cartwright, you take charge of these Bergens." Ken Curtis picked up the two rifles and handed them to another two of the section.

This reminded me of Waller all over again. The difference was Waller had not been a thief, he was just a thug. "Right lads, double-time down the hill."

I led. Captain Marsden and Sergeant Curtis would bring up the rear with the two prisoners. We ran hard. It was less than a couple of miles to the camp and the hard run would burn off some of the anger we all felt. We were a mile from the camp when the sound of the hand grenade made us dive for the ground.

"What the..."

I had my Colt out in an instant and ran back up the hill. I saw Captain Marsden and Sergeant Curtis. They were lying in a pool of blood. Their Colts had been taken. "Hewitt!" Of Osborne and Harris, there was no sign. Hewitt knelt.

"They are alive sir!" He turned to Johnson who was the medic for the other section. "Here Johnno, give me a hand."

"Emerson, run down to the camp and get an ambulance. The rest of you, drop your Bergens. We have two killers to catch."

I took my new sniper rifle and held it across my chest. "Fletcher, find their trail."

It was not a hard trail to find. They had just run. They headed across the rough ground. The undulating land filled with dips, hollows and scrubby trees made spotting them hard. "Spread out in a long line. Keep Fletcher in sight."

We were approaching a wood and Scouse ran off to the right. Private Jones and another of their section, Private Delaney were the first to reach the path. They tripped the wire and bore the full brunt of the grenades. I was knocked to the ground by the concussion. This time there was no doubt that they were both dead. The fragments of grenade casing had torn through their faces and opened up their skulls. They were dead.

Gordy snarled, "Bastards! They were their mates!"

The time for recriminations would be later. I decided that I would not risk any more of my men. "Davis, fetch your rifle. You and I are going hunting! Scouse, here."

"Sir?"

"Where would you go if you were these two?"

"They have been leading us up hills sir. They are trying to lose us. Both are city lads they will hide in a town. They need a car." He waved a hand up the slopes. "They won't find one here."

"The camp!"

"That's right sir. A nice motor with army plates. I reckon they are there."

"Sergeant Poulson, take charge here. Leave a couple of men with the bodies and then check for more booby traps. Fletcher and Davis are coming with me. Bring the rest of the two sections back to the camp."

"Sir. Be careful!"

I patted the rifle. "I intend to be."

We knew the area better than the two killers. We were fitter than they were and we were angry. The three of us ran across country. I worked out that we could eat into their lead by running directly downhill taking the line of least resistance. The camp was not totally empty. There was a platoon of regulars who would be guarding it until the Brigade returned. They were armed and it was not those who worried me. The Major and Sergeant Major Dean rarely went armed around the camp. Neither did Private Larkin. I feared what Osborne and Harris would do. They were ruthless. I realised now that we had stumbled upon a lucrative black market. The two were stealing weapons and selling them. I had no doubt that some would end up in the hands of spivs. I had wondered why they had joined the Commandos and tried so hard to stay in. Now I knew.

I heard a shot. Our instincts kicked in and the three of us went to ground. I could see the camp. It was half a mile away. I saw a soldier lying on the ground. Even as I watched I saw Osborne shoot a second soldier. The others had their hands in the air. Harris suddenly struck one of the soldiers with his Colt. I saw that it was Reg Dean. He did not go down.

That decided me. "Davis, I want you to shoot Harris. I will shoot Osborne. We fire together."

Scouse said, "Are you sure sir?"

"There are four dead men and two wounded men already. I won't risk any more men's lives. When you have a mad dog there is only one answer, you shoot them." I realised that it might be hard for Davis to make a killing shot. They were Englishmen. "If you can wound him then fine but do not miss!"

He nodded, "Right sir. I won't."

I put the rifle to my shoulder. I peered through the sights. The two targets were suddenly bigger. I saw the car being driven around and a regular got out of the driver's side. Osborne pointed his Colt at him to move him out of the way. The soldier backed off towards Major Rose, his hands in the air. They were going to drive away. I had to shoot and shoot quickly. I had only used the rifle four or five times. I could not afford to miss and so I aimed at Osborne's chest. It was a big target. He climbed into the driver's seat.

"Now!"

I squeezed off one bullet and then loaded a second. The windscreen of the car shattered. Harris dropped to one knee. Davis had hit him in the leg. I saw Osborne look in my direction and then the car started to move. I fired the second round. This time there was no windscreen to weaken the shot and I saw Osborne's head explode like a ripe plum.

Fletcher needed no urging and as Davis and I put our rifles over our shoulders Fletcher hurtled down the slope to the camp. By the time we got there, he was applying a bandage to Reg's head. Major Rose was downing a beaker of something. From the smell, it had to be whisky.

Reg smiled, "I reckon we owe you two our lives, Captain." Two of the infantry had their rifles aimed at Harris. He was being bandaged by a third soldier. Reg pointed. There was a Mills bomb lying by his feet. "Osborne told Harris to throw the grenade at us. They were three fine shots."

Major Rose said, "What the hell happened, Tom?"

I told him what I knew. "We will have to question Harris here when the hospital has finished with him." I went over to him. He was crying. "Give me something for the pain! For the love of God!" He pointed an accusing finger at Davis. "You have crippled me you bastard! I'll have you!"

"He saved your life, Harris. I told him to kill you. It's still not too late." I pointed my Colt at him and pressed it between his eyes. "I am certain that no one here will say anything if I just shoot you now!"

Fear filled his face. "You wouldn't do that!"

"Wouldn't I? Forget waiting until the ambulance arrived! What happened up there? Talk!" The cocking of the Colt made him speak.

"We kept going slow so that there was a gap. I pretended to fall. When the Captain came to help me Osborne threw the grenade and we took cover. They are alive aren't they?"

I pointed to the dead soldiers whose bodies we had covered. "They aren't nor are two of your mates where you booby-trapped the trail. You are going to hang for murder!"

His face filled with terror as my words sank home. "It was all Osborne. It was Charlie! He has a contact in London for the guns! It was a nice little earner. I didn't shoot anyone. It was Charlie."

"And the booby trap?"

He looked down, "That was Charlie too. I kept watch!"

"You are a liar!"

The bell of the ambulance hurtling up the road ended the conversation. A police car pulled up behind it. As the ambulance men carried Harris into the ambulance I said to one of the policemen who emerged. "This man is responsible for the deaths of four soldiers. He needs watching."

The sympathy which had been in the policeman's eyes evaporated. "We'll watch him. If you gentlemen could come down to the station and make a statement." He turned to the young constable who had stepped from the car. "Wilkinson, you go in the ambulance and keep an eye on him."

"We will sort out the statements when the rest of our men arrive. We have two more injured men." I turned to the ambulance men. "There are two soldiers up the road a ways, towards the mine. They need help. I have left some medics with them. This piece of scum is not worth bothering with."

"Right sir." They closed the doors and drove out of the camp.

I looked up as Sergeant Poulson led the rest of my men into the camp. They had improvised stretchers for the two dead men. He said, "I see you got one of them, sir. Where is Harris?"

"In the ambulance."

Sergeant Poulson seemed to see the dead bodies of the regulars for the first time. "Bloody hell sir, what a mess!"

It was. The car was now covered in the blood and brains of the dead Osborne. I nodded, "The sooner we get to France the better. I have some anger and it needs to be taken out on Germans."

Chapter 14

Captain Marsden and Sergeant Curtis were both hospitalized for some weeks. I was given their section until they returned. When I visited them in the hospital I saw the determination written clearly on their faces. John Marsden shook his head. He had suffered many cuts to his face and been lucky not to have lost an eye. "It was my fault that they were allowed to do what they did. You were right, Tom, weeks ago. Men have died because of my mistake. The least I can do is get to France and atone for that."

Curtis felt the same and so I tried to get the rest of the section up to the standard of mine. The rest of the Osborne crew, the four of them were shipped off. There would be an enquiry. Major Rose would chair it and their stories would be investigated. One thing was certain; they were finished in the 1st Special Service Brigade. It was for their own good. My men would take matters into their own hands. What they had done had crossed an invisible line.

It was the middle of April when we eventually reached the camp in Devon. We had had to spend more time at Falmouth than I would have liked. Captain Marsden's section needed rebuilding. The rest of the brigade had finished their training already and Lord Lovat sought me out. "I want you to train with the Americans. It is important that we work with our American allies and both your sections needs the experience of landing from Landing Craft. The ones the Americans will be using are the same as ours."

"Yes sir."

The Americans, to be fair to them, were more than generous about the whole thing and my men appreciated the rations which were much better than ours. They were intrigued by such exotic items as corn and sweet potato. The steaks were seen as a luxury which most would not have eaten even in peacetime.

We made a few practice landings on the Devon beaches without any opposition just to ensure that everyone was comfortable with disembarking. Our experiences on 523 helped. Then the order came down that we were to practise a landing on the 27th of April with guns from the heavy cruiser **'H.M.S. Hawkins'** firing live shells on the beach. It was felt that we needed to simulate an actual attack on a beach. This would help for most of these soldiers had come directly from training in the States. The experienced soldiers were still in Italy.

We met the French Commandos. They were obviously pleased that I could speak fluent French. I got on with them well. To be fair to them they did not see the need for the practice but they participated. Unlike my section and Captain Marsden's, they took little interest in the proceedings. They were just desperate to get back to their homeland and liberate it. The old railwayman from the signal box came to mind.

As usual with such exercises, especially when there were different nationalities, forces and services involved, there was confusion. We seemed to bob about on the water for longer than we should. When the cruiser began to fire it was terrifying for the young American recruits. It was the signal for us to go in. My men would be the first ashore from our landing craft but there were four other landing craft ahead of us. It was the American's show and we did not mind. In truth, I was still concerned about Captain Marsden's section. There was only one sergeant and, to my mind, he showed too much deference to my sergeants. I wanted someone who was more decisive in action. Sergeant Ashcroft was a good Commando but he had been promoted too far. Perhaps I was worrying too much about them. After all, I would not be leading in on the real invasion. Captain Marsden would be returned by then.

As we headed in Sergeant Poulson said, "Those shells are remarkably close to the shore sir." He pointed out that they were striking the sand.

I pointed to some white tape halfway up the beach. "If you notice, Sergeant, there is white tape. I am guessing that the shells are landing on the other side of the tape."

Poulson watched and nodded, "You are right, sir. Then all we have to do is to stop at the tape."

That is right, Sergeant." I turned, "Get ready to land! No one goes past the white tape."

To my horror, I saw the first Americans to land had raced up the beach and they crossed the white tape. Surely the cruiser would stop firing. But it didn't. I felt sick as the cruiser's seven 7.5" shells began to toss the soldiers in the air as though they were rag dolls. As the ramp began to descend I raced along it and leapt into the water. I ran towards the nearest Americans who were already moving towards the white tape. "Stop! Don't go near the white tape!"

An American Major, with a cigar stuck in the side of his mouth shouted, "Who the hell are you to tell us what to do?"

Fortunately, he had halted, as had his men. The French Commandos stared from the ramp. I pointed at four men who were a hundred yards from us and over the white tape. They had not heard my shout. One shell hit them and they disappeared.

"Jesus!"

The exercise was stopped.

The Major said, "Thanks, buddy. How did you know about the tape? Have you done this before?"

I shook my head. "I just guessed that the white tape was there for a reason."

The exercise was stopped. The bodies were cleared and we embarked again. General Moon, who was in command, decided that we would try again in the afternoon. We sailed out into the Channel to make an approach much as we would on the actual day. We were led by a corvette, "*H.M.S. Azalea*". There were just nine landing craft in the column. The corvette led us out to sea to approach much as we would when we did attack France. My men and I were on the deck close to the ramps. As the third ship in the line, we had a fine view of the corvette and the other landing craft.

Gordy Barker was smoking a cigarette, "It will be a damned sight hotter when we do the real thing. The guns of the cruiser will seem like pop guns in comparison with the big boys."

John Hewitt nodded, "I just hope that they have got their act together this afternoon. We don't need more friendly fire casualties."

Sergeant Poulson said, "We just land and stay close to the water. We don't need to go any further do we sir?"

I never got to answer him as a line of nine E-boats suddenly opened fire as they raced towards us from the east. I knew what they were capable of. It seemed to take everyone by surprise. "Get the K-guns out. Crowe, grenade launcher!" I shouted in French, "Commandant Kieffer, fetch your men. Fire everything you have!"

As soon as the one hundred and seventy-six Frenchmen realised that there were Germans to kill their lassitude ended and they raced to every vantage point to fire at their hated enemies. The two Oerlikon gunners swung their guns around to bring them to bear at the rapidly moving E-Boats. This was, quite literally, a baptism of fire.

I took out my sniper rifle. I doubted that they would get close enough to use the Thompson. Before I could even aim the rifle I saw a pair of torpedoes race towards LST 531. The E-boats were so close that I knew they could not miss. I did not see the torpedoes strike as I was watching another E-boat coming directly for us. The bridge was armoured and the skipper protected but the men operating the torpedoes were not. "Fire at the E-boat! Every gun we have! Davis, shoot the crew!"

I fired at one of the men at the torpedo tube. He was bouncing around and he was three quarters of a mile away. I wounded him with a ricochet. Davis hit a second. I fired at another of the crew and he took shelter behind the tube with the rest of the crew. So long as they were sheltering they could not fire a torpedo. The range was decreasing and the two K guns sent bullet after bullet at the bridge. The E-boat captain turned; there were easier pickings than us. I switched targets to the next E-boat. This time he was approaching obliquely, coming down the line. The corvette was firing her small guns but she was seriously outgunned. I saw another landing ship hit by torpedoes. Every one of my two sections were firing The French were all firing. We were sending a wall of bullets at them. Crowe's grenade launcher sent a spout of water up just ten yards from the bows of the E-boat. There were other easier targets.

I saw a second landing craft set on fire. The scale of the disaster was brought home when I saw bodies of Americans drifting by. They were face down in the water despite having life vests. I saw another E-boat. It was over a mile away. I fired more in hope than expectation. I emptied the magazine. When it veered away I knew that I had hit something. I probably only hit the ship itself but it was a small victory on a day of huge losses.

After we disembarked we trudged back to the camp. It was one thing to lose men in battle but to lose them like this seemed wrong. I felt guilty. The Americans were our allies and it had been our job to protect them. The Navy had not done enough to protect the convoy. Where were the air force? I was made to feel even worse when the Americans praised us for our defence of the ship. We had done little enough. I am not even certain that we had killed any Germans. We certainly hadn't hurt their E-boats. Even our evening meal, pork chops- a real treat, tasted like sand. When our lorry arrived to take us to our camp at Southampton I was glad. This had been an episode of which I was not proud.

The driver was Private Larkin. As I climbed into the cab he handed me two letters. "Sergeant Major Dean was most insistent that I give you these straight away sir. He said how you might have been waiting for them."

I looked and saw that they were both from Susan. I had had no letters since Windsor. That had been almost three months ago. To be fair I had only had one from Mum. I had begun to think that things had moved on too quickly and she was having second thoughts about me. Larkin was concentrating on driving. Devon roads can be narrow and dangerous at the best of times. I was able to read in peace.

London
February 1944
Dear Tom,
Thank you for a wonderful day. Your mum is lovely! We chatted all the way back to London and she stayed overnight in a hotel. We went shopping the next day. I bet

your ears were burning for all we spoke of, was you. You are a hero! Your mum is right you need to be more careful.

Your mum and I agree on many things. We both think the war has almost run its course. She told me about your aunt and that pilot, Charlie. I cried when I heard. That really was tragic. I don't suit black. Look after yourself.

We had another air raid.

There was a section blued out by the censor. I guessed it was the Dragon. Susan was not used to others reading her letters.

I know you think this is all going a bit quickly. We are different that way. I think we were meant to meet. That means we are meant to be together. You might not know it yet but we are going to be married. It is forward of me to be the one to bring it up but your mum has told me that if I wait for you I will be an old maid. I have yet to meet your dad but from what your mum says you are just like him. I know that it will be some time before we can meet up again but I will write to you every week.

Keep your chin up my love and your head down!

All my love,

Always,

Susan xxx

I read and re-read the letter. Mum had told me about the shopping trip and how much she liked Susan. I wondered why the letter had taken so long to reach me. It was in Susan's hand. When I looked at the postmark I saw that it was April. I opened it.

Church Lawton
April 1944
Dear Tom,

Don't be cross! I know I have not written for some time. I am so sorry. It was not my fault. Mum was taken ill and I had to come home to look after Dad. He wasn't well. Mum had a stroke and they took her to Alsager. Dad insisted on going every day on the bus to visit. She wasn't awake but he wanted to be there. They are like your

parents; very close. What with travelling and looking after dad I had no time to write. I felt awful about that but I hope you will understand. I got all of your letters two weeks ago. They were a lovely surprise. The Dragon sent them all on with a note apologising for the delay.

I have read them so many times and cried so much that they are barely legible any more. I can remember every word. Thank you. Windsor seems such a long time ago now.

Mum died last week. It was a mercy. It broke dad's heart every time he saw her lying there. Since the funeral, he has hardly stirred. He does brighten when I tell him about you. I think the only thing which keeps him going now is the thought that one day he will meet you. He is looking forward to that. He keeps talking about the hero in the family. I hope you don't mind. I have told him that we have an understanding. We do, don't we?

I never thought I would say this but I miss Operations. I knew where you were. I know that the big day can't be far away. I suppose I will read about it in the newspapers.

I received a couple of letters from your mum. They were forwarded to me. I will write to her. She will think I am rude for not replying. This war!

I will have to go now. I still have a lot of mum's things to sort through. I also have to write to my brother and tell him. He has it hard enough on the convoys without this bad news.

Now that the weather is getting better I have taken to getting Dad out of the house and walking. It does us both good.

I promise I will write more frequently but you know you are always in my thoughts and my prayers.

All my love,
Always,
Your own,
truly,

Susan xxx

Our new camp was just ahead when I put the two letters away. Poor Susan. I don't know what I would do if anything happened to Mum. I knew that my first task after I had found my quarters was to write two letters; one to Mum and one to Susan.

Part 3
D-Day

Chapter 15

Captain Marsden and Sergeant Curtis were waiting for us as we descended from the lorry. The scars on their faces had healed but both looked thinner than before. I shook John's hand as my sergeants crowded around Ken Curtis commenting on his scars. They bantered, that was their way.

"Thanks for looking after my section, Tom."

"You would have done the same for me. Everything all right?"

"We both had to fight to get back into action but Major Rose came and said that the hospital was hindering the war effort by keeping us there. He is a brick."

I nodded, "He is no action man but he cares about the Commandos. He is a good adjutant." I told him about the disaster at Slapton Sands.

John spread his arm around the vast field of camouflaged tents, "That does not bode well for this then." I shrugged as he led me towards the officers' tents. "You have been over there, Tom. What will it be like?"

"In a word, bloody! You remember that last exercise before..." He nodded. "When I was umpiring I was being realistic. That is how many of your men would have died."

"But your lads did all right."

I had to be honest with him. "John, your men weren't the Germans. I would have lost half of my men too."

"God! I took heart from the fact that you and your section are so good. I thought we could follow you."

I leaned a little closer, "I think that you will be going in with the rest of the Brigade. Lord Lovat is using us as pathfinders.

You don't want to follow us. We will be the first off the boat and if the tanks haven't cleared the mines then you will see our bodies when you land."

"Surely there must be an easier way."

I shook my head as I laid my bags on the bed in the tent. "We have to go in by sea and Hitler has a solid barrier of concrete and steel all the way from Denmark down to Spain. If we are going to take it back we have to buy it back with the lives of our men."

It was now obvious to everyone that the Second Front, as the newspapers were calling it, was coming. All leave was stopped. My men understood that better than most. When we were not training with the rest of the Brigade we took to running down the country lanes of Hampshire. We were under no illusions. Davis and I practised constantly with our sniper rifles. The merits of the weapons had been shown in our manhunt and in the E-boat attack. Crowe became so adept with the grenade launcher that he could hit a target four times out of five. I assigned Hewitt to be both his minder and as a backup. My medic became almost as good with the precious weapon. The K gun proved to be a better weapon than we had thought. The only problem was the weight of the magazines. Gordy and his section would be going in heavily laden.

As May passed we were ordered to keep our Bergens ready for instant action. Every piece of equipment was scrutinised and only packed if we knew we would need it. The officers were now given a daily briefing. Sergeant Poulson took my men on another run each time I was absent. We were confined to camp and the target was known to all. Aerial photographs, constantly updated, were shared. I saw that the battery at Merville had been finished and guns were in place. The calibre could not be seen. Unlike the rest, the defences at Riva Bella were more obvious to me. I had seen them at close hand. Lord Lovat even used me once to go through them. I saw Commandant Kieffer smile and nod as I translated for the French.

Lord Lovat took me to one side. "You and the French will land first. Let them be the first to set foot on the beach eh? National pride and all that. But I want you and your boys to find us that way through. I don't want the Airborne leaving with their arses hanging out to dry." I nodded. "Tell me, what is the fastest that we could make it? From landing to boots on the bridge."

"If we could run all the way, then an hour or so, sir."

"Good."

"But I would quadruple that sir." He cocked an eye. "The roads are narrow. As soon as we land they will block them. It will be house to house fighting. Remember Dieppe and St. Nazaire sir. Our lads showed how hard it was to winkle us out. The Germans know these streets. Four hours sir, that is my estimate and that assumes the minefield is cleared!"

He laughed, "Not an optimist then Captain?"

"No sir, a realist."

"And that is just what we need. The Colonel Flemings of this world think it will be as easy as strolling around Hyde Park. We both know it won't be."

As May ended it became obvious that the invasion would not take place until June. Annoyingly the weather was perfect. As we sat in the tent which was the officer's mess, Captain Marsden said, "Typical! The sun is shining and the sea is flat calm. You can bet that the staff will not send us in until it is blowing a gale."

I was more phlegmatic. "As long as it is not too bad I think it might help us. Hobart's funnies might struggle but a bit of rain makes the enemy hunker down a little."

Major Rose had not seen the new tanks we would be using. "What do you think to these tanks then Tom; Hobart's funnies?"

"I think the Duplex tanks will help us. They don't need to disembark from a landing craft on the beach and as soon as they are in the sand they can fire. I just hope they aren't launched too far out. The Crabs with their flails and the Bullshorn Ploughs could, potentially, save lives. They will clear the mines. That is my biggest fear. If we have to rely on the Engineers to clear the minefield then it will be a bloodbath. The machine-guns and mortars on the beach will have a field day."

Captain Marsden had begun to smoke more heavily since his return from hospital. He nervously lit another. "I wish we could go right now."

I glanced at Major Rose. We had both been worried about John since he had been hit by the grenade. The Captain and

Sergeant Curtis felt more foolish than anything. They realised now that they should have searched Osborne. Then they would have discovered the grenade. I know that John had run through the incident in his mind over and over. He saw now, in hindsight, what went wrong. He had allowed a gap to develop between the prisoners and the rest of the section. He had not had his weapon out; it went on and on. As I told him *'hindsight is always twenty, twenty'*. Now he was eager to prove himself again. The person he was trying to impress was himself and that is always harder.

"We will soon be ready to go. My uncle, one who was killed in the Great War, told my dad that the hardest time was just before you went into action. When they began to advance you had no time to think and to worry. That's the trouble John, we are sitting and wondering. I think Dad had it the easiest. He took off and was in control of his own destiny."

Major Rose downed his whisky, "Suppose he was outnumbered? What then, Tom?"

"Dad is a superb pilot. Talking to the pilots who flew with him they reckon he had a sixth sense about flying. Did you know that he tangled with the Red Baron? Damaged his aeroplane once. Even when you are flying into flak there is always more chance that they will miss than hit. On the beach, they can create a killing zone. Even with smoke blinding them they know that a man will be on the ground or six feet in the air. That is a narrow window. A man on the beach does not have many places to hide."

John suddenly stood and went outside. I heard him vomiting. I shook my head, "That was stupid of me! I have just fuelled his fears."

"John has his own demons, Tom. He wasn't even listening." He shook his head, "Look after him, Tom."

"I'll try sir." Realistically I knew that it would take all my concentration to watch after me and my men.

I received a letter from Mum in the last week of May. I had written to her and told her about Susan. To my delight, Mum had taken it upon herself to visit with Susan and give her a hand. I could not have had a better mum. She was thoughtful and kind. As a nurse, she was able to give Susan solutions she had not thought of and being of an age with Susan's dad she was able to talk his language.

It was the last paragraph which touched me the most:

"Susan has told me a little bit about what you have been up to. I should have known you wouldn't tell me! I still worry about you, Tom. I imagine the worst. I know that soon you will be in danger once more. It is your lot in life. Know that Susan and I will be here for you when you return. Your Dad hasn't met her yet but, like me, he knows she is the girl for you. Don't wait for the end of the war! God knows when it will end!"

Mum was a realist. Perhaps she was right. Once we had finished with this invasion I would put my house in order. And then the thought struck me; for the first time, I was imagining surviving. That was always a mistake. I folded the letter and put it with the others. I would read them but not until I was safely back home. They were dangerous; they gave you hope. Hope was a luxury for others; not a Commando.

We moved down to Southampton on the 1st of June. The vast fleet which was being assembled was gathered there. I went down to LC(I)523. Bill Leslie was at the gangplank, smoking his pipe. There were two young seamen with him. He was obviously imparting some knowledge for they were nodding as he spoke and gesticulated with the stem of his pipe. He grinned when he saw me, "Good to see you, sir. Ready for a trip across the pond eh?"

"I am indeed. I thought I would see if you were still here."

"Can't get rid of me." He pointed at me with his pipe, "Now this is a real hero. He isn't wearing them but he has the Military Cross and the Victoria Cross. There's not many of them about! More than that he is a real gentleman."

I felt embarrassed by his comments. "Do they know about your medals Bill? Or that you have saved my life before now."

"Not the same sir. It's like comparing an ordinary horse with a Derby winner!" Bill liked his horseracing. "These two are my gunners. They are keen to get to grips with Jerry. This is

Ordinary Seaman Jack Higgins and Ordinary Seaman Walter Grant."

They saluted, "Pleased to meet you, sir."

I saluted back. Turning to Bill I said, "You know you will have Frenchmen on board. You will be able to practise your French."

He laughed, "I'll leave that to you, sir."

One of the gunners said, "Do you know where we are going, sir?"

Bill shook his head. I looked at the gunner and pointed east. Bill laughed, "Honestly Grant! You haven't got the sense of a flea! Captain Harsker knows, Lieutenant Redmire knows, I have a good idea but you have seen the posters, 'tittle-tattle lost the battle'. You will find out soon enough."

"And when you do, Seaman Grant, keep your head down," I advised.

"Is that what you do sir?"

Bill snapped, "Don't be cheeky! Just because I am familiar with Captain Harsker there is no need for you to be."

"That's alright, Bill. Let us just say that I have been fighting for five years and I am still here. I make sure I don't get shot! Bullets don't discriminate. They kill anybody!"

Lieutenant Redmire appeared. Bill snapped, "You two cut along!"

"Captain Harsker. I am just heading to the port office. I think we are about to get our orders."

I nodded, "It won't be long; that is for certain. I was just having a recce so that I knew where the boat was. Well, I'll be off. See you soon!"

We boarded on June 3rd. The rumour was that D-Day, as it was being called, would be June the 4th. It was a long way from Southampton to Normandy. I had done it by submarine and E-boat. The E-boats which had attacked the American convoy were still out there. I knew from *'Lucky Lady'* just how deadly they could be. We were packed like sardines on the landing ship. Even the ramps were covered. We were lucky: the French Commandos knew us as did the crew and we had more room than some of the other Commandos.

We organised ourselves so that we were comfortable. We could be on the ship for eighteen hours; it would depend upon the crossing. Everyone knew their job from the crew of 523 down to the last Commando. I was luckier than most. I knew exactly what faced us. I had given Herbert my Thompson. The K gun needed protection. Besides my Colt and my sniper rifle were all the weapons I needed. Our Bergens had never carried as much. We intended to drop them as soon as we could. It was hard enough fighting without being encumbered with a fifty-pound pack. The morning of June 3rd was glorious and promised a fine crossing; perhaps too fine. A clear day would afford the enemy more chance to see us. By the same token, the fine weather would make the job of the airborne easier. I did not envy the Horse pilots who had a narrow strip of boggy ground on which to land.

We had not left by the time darkness fell. I left my men sleeping and headed to the bridge. The Lieutenant and Petty Officer Leslie were on duty. Grant had just brought them some cocoa.

"Cocoa, sir?"

"That would be lovely, Grant."

"I'll go and get you a mug sir."

"Is there a problem?"

"The sea is getting up. They are delaying the attack. Some RAF meteorological type reckons the weather over there is too rough."

"Bloody daft sir, if you ask me. Flat as a millpond!"

Just then, as though the weather gods decided to punish us, the first drop of rain fell. A gust of wind made us rise a little too at our moorings. Grant arrived with my mug as the first drop of rain became a few. He poured my cocoa and the boat began to move in the wind which had sprung up from nowhere.

Lieutenant Redmire said, "Leslie! You and your big mouth!"

"Sorry, sir."

Then the heavens quite literally opened. The weather changed almost in an instant. The rain cooled my cocoa enough so that I downed it quickly. "I had better get back to my chaps." It was not my men I was worried about but Captain Marsden. Given his state of mind, a storm was the last thing we needed.

Sergeant Poulson was resourceful. He and the others had taken our rubber capes from our Bergens and rigged up shelters. "Here y'are sir. We've kept a little hole for you. Snug as a bug in a rug eh sir?"

"Thanks, Emerson. Well, it looks like we won't be going tonight."

My men nodded. Sergeant Poulson said, "We can do nowt about the weather. We will just have to grin and bear it." He nudged Beaumont. "It was a damn sight wetter when we paddled them canoes!"

They began talking about the missions we had taken and the night passed. Others found the experience less easy to handle. I heard men vomiting over the side. There were curses, some of them in French when men failed to reach the water. Soon an all-pervading smell of sea and vomit drifted across the boat. I realised then that the delay could hurt us. Trained to a peak we were not used to having to wait and bodies and minds were becoming weaker.

"Make sure you all have plenty of water."

"You mean drink from our canteens, sir?"

"No Fletcher, save that. You and Crowe go and fetch a dixie from the galley. Let's be the first. I reckon others will realise that they need it soon."

It was a long night. We slept but many others did not. We woke to grey skies and showers but the winds had abated slightly. It was still uncomfortable and the ship stank. During the morning word came that we would try again and that we would be leaving at dusk. We were lucky that we had Commandos, French and English. We were resourceful and we used the ship's hoses to clean the ship. We were damp but the smell had gone and it kept us busy. The galleys provided the used corned dog sandwiches which we ate as we knew we would need the sustenance and then, as dusk fell we heard the order to head out to sea. We edged slowly from our morning and join the huge fleet which was going to assault Fortress Europe. We were the largest number of ships ever assembled and it was humbling to be part of it.

In the blackness, all that we could see were the stern lights of the ship in front and the bow lights of the ship astern but we could make out shadows in the dark. We were not alone. Those who could, slept but I saw that John Marsden was nervously pacing and smoking. I joined him.

"You need to rest, John. Did you sleep last night?"

"What, in that storm? This is madness! How can we go ashore like this? My men are exhausted already!"

I said, quietly, "They are watching you, John. Try to relax. It helps the men."

He sat down, "I wish I could be like you, Tom. Even when you were just a sergeant I admired you. Leadership seemed to come easily to you."

"It didn't. I suppose I have been lucky. Listen, John, tomorrow try to keep your head down. It is not our job to attack those machine-guns. Hopefully, the tanks will clear the beach but when we get into Ouistreham make sure you keep looking up and to the side. Have your Colt ready and fire first. The odds are it will be a German that you see."

"You will be going ahead, won't you?"

"Yes, we have to clear a path for Lord Lovat. You will be supporting the French. They are going for the Casino. That will be a tough nut to crack."

He seemed to relax a little. "I suppose if you and the French are going ahead of us then it won't be so bad."

"That's the spirit."

I noticed that his men had laid down and were trying to sleep. As John lit another cigarette I knew that he would not.

We hove to at about two-thirty and I assumed we were off the French coast. I wondered why and then the big guns began to fire. *'Warspite'*, *'Ramillies'* and *'Roberts'* began firing their huge guns at the coast. The smaller cruisers and destroyers added their firepower and the horizon was lit by the flashes from naval artillery. No one slept then. We all prepared for war. Everyone had jobs to do. Fletcher checked his radio. Guns were readied and Bergens were checked. It passed the time but, more importantly, it made sure we were ready. We would literally hit the ground running.

We began to make our way towards the beach at about six. Smoke rose from the shore. Targets had been hit. Fighters kept an umbrella up above us and the guns kept firing. I saw Bill

Leslie at his wheel. They were wearing steel helmets on the bridge. None of the Commandos were. We had on our berets. The two gunners and their loaders were on their Oerlikons. I knew they were both eager to fire their weapons in anger. I knew that I had my first time. It seemed a lifetime ago now.

The German guns had not been knocked out. I saw one destroyer struck. In the distance, I could make out E-boats as they darted in to release torpedoes. The Germans were not giving in without a fight and we were still offshore. Our progress seemed painfully slow. The DD tanks were bobbing about in the water close by. They had been launched three miles from the shore. The sea was not as stormy as it had been but it was still rougher than I would have liked had I been a member of the crew. The waves made it hard to see them and despite lookouts, tragedies occurred. I saw LC(I) 527 catch a tank. It was a glancing blow but it was enough to send it and its crew to a watery grave.

The closer we came to the beach the more intense became the gunfire. We were on the extreme left flank of the attack. I saw the mole and the wire in the distance. I had the advantage that I had seen it and knew what to expect. However even I was in for a few surprises. They had mounted an 88mm on the roof of the control tower. It began to duel with the gunners on the landing craft. I saw a shell strike LC(I) 527. It did no damage but it was a warning.

Lieutenant Redmire shouted, "Open fire!"

The range was extreme but it would give heart to the crew. The tracer showed the trajectory of the shells. Seaman Grant was either lucky or good. His first burst struck the Command Centre and must have showered the gun crew with stone. Certainly, it stopped firing, briefly. That didn't matter as every German gun appeared to be targeting our ship. I knew it was an illusion. The two gunners shifted target. I wondered if Sergeant Eisner was firing back. Perhaps Captain Schwarz was bellowing out orders too.

I had just glanced back to check on the progress of the other landing ships when a shell took the head of Seaman Grant. The loader and Bill Leslie were showered with blood and brains. His dead fingers were on the triggers as his body fell backwards and the shells fired high into the sky. The loader started sobbing. I heard Bill Leslie shout, "Pull yourself together son. Get Grant out of the harness. It is your turn now!"

I turned back to look at the beach. The first tanks were edging ashore and we were less than four hundred yards away. We were arriving too fast or the tanks were too slow. They were supposed to have cleared the beach before we went ashore. Plans changed. "Are you ready Commandant?"

The French were using the starboard ramp and we would use the port ramp.

I saw him grin and shake a defiant fist at the shore, "I have waited five years for this! Of course, I am ready!"

The first Crab tank crept up the beach. Its flails exploded mines. I identified its path. That was where I would lead my men. Then the tank was struck by a shell. As the crew tumbled out they were machine-gunned. Still, we crept closer but more tanks were arriving. The problem was that there was less space than the planners had expected. I saw two landing ships grind together. A couple of Commandos were thrown from the ramps to their deaths. It was a waste.

Another ship lowered its ramp and I saw Commandos from Number Three race ashore. Our orders were to wait at the water line until the beach was cleared. I suppose they were enthusiastic or perhaps the joy of battle was upon them. A whole section ran forward across the minefield. machine-guns cut some of them down while two struck a mine. The rest dropped. To my horror, a Crab landed and began to approach them. The driver would not be able to see them. As his flails whipped forward the whole section, wounded and dead were blown up. I punched the side of the LC in frustration. Plans always looked wonderful on paper. Real-life was different.

I took out my Colt and went to the end of the ramp. Bullets zipped past my head. I focussed on the section of beach which had been cleared. It was just forty feet wide and twenty feet deep. It would have to do! The Crab which had accidentally slaughtered the Commandos kept moving up the beach. It reached the wire and then threw a track. The crew kept firing the machine-gun. The ramps hit the water and I raced straight down it. I saw Commandant Kieffer leap into the surf. I knew that the

French were supposed to be the first on the beach but the dead Commandos already had that honour. I landed in water up to my waist and I began to wade towards the three tanks I saw just beyond the waterline. They would give me cover. I was inordinately proud of my men that day. We hit the sand beyond the water as one group. We had made it. We were on Sword Beach in Normandy. Then the killing began!

Chapter 16

I saw that the cleared mines were closer to the part of the beach where I knew there were no mines. As I heard Lord Lovat's piper, Bill Millins, begin to play his bagpipes I shouted, "Follow me!"

We had thirty yards of protection from the damaged tanks. The smoke from one of the burning tanks also gave us some protection but bullets zipped over our heads and clanged off the tanks. I turned at the wire and ran up the sand. I know that those on the ships would have thought I was reckless and expected an explosion but we had walked this narrow strip of sand. Rifles and machine-guns turned their attention to us. Fred Emerson fell clutching his arm. John Hewitt dropped next to him his medical kit already out.

"Drop your Bergens! Take cover." I holstered my Colt and shrugged off my own Bergen. As I pushed sand in front of me I shouted, "Concentrate your fire over there!" I pointed to the two tobruks which stood next to the 75mm. "Crowe! Grenade!"

I could still hear the pipes from Bill Millins as the Brigade came ashore. The Free French dropped close to us followed by Captain Marsden and his section. We were a tightly packed group of Commandos on the beach. The tanks were clearing the beaches further down the beach but the mortars, machine-guns and rifles were causing too many casualties for them to make serious inroads.

I unslung my rifle and as Crowe began to lob grenades into the pits I fired at any flesh I could see. It only took Crowe four attempts to destroy the two machine-guns close to us. Commandant Kieffer saw the danger had diminished and shouting, "Viva La France", he leapt to his feet and ran up towards the town firing from the hip as he went.

"Cover them!" My men poured bullets, blindly into the enemy emplacements.

Captain Marsden thought that the way was clear and he raced up the beach after the hundred and seventy Frenchmen who followed the Commandant. I looked over to Emerson. He was grimacing but he was alive. "Are you okay to be left?"

He turned the grimace to a grin. "I'll be fine sir. John has done a good job. I'll be right as rain in no time." He nodded over to the Bergens. "I shall keep an eye on them, sir!"

"Right lads, smoke grenades and then after the others!"

Eight of my men hurled their grenades and after they had exploded over the German foxholes and as the smoke began to drift down the beach, we jumped up and ran. Bullets hit the sand we had just occupied but we made it safely to the anti-tank ditch. We sheltered there with the other Commandos. I saw that some of the French Commandos had been hit but they had taken out the last two tobruks at this end of the beach. Two of Captain Marsden's section lay dead.

The anti-tank ditch was filled with our men. There was no order. Fire from the unoccupied buildings kept up a withering fire at every head or hand which appeared. I shouted, "Captain Marsden, have you a grenade launcher?"

"No, Tom!"

"Right Crowe, it's up to you. Keep firing them at those buildings until you run out. Sergeant Barker, get the K gun set up. The rest of you keep your heads down."

This was the nightmare I had feared. The buildings afforded a good view of the beach and they could fire at us at will. The K Gun was set up so that the barrel pointed at the buildings. Smith kept his head down. He would have to fire blind and traverse the barrel. I counted on the fact that the prodigious rate of fire would make the German defenders fear for their lives and hang back. We needed respite from their bullets. One of Captain Marsden's men peered over the ditch. A single bullet struck him in the head. We were wearing berets. A helmet might have saved him. Two French Commandos tried to move and they were hit by the snipers. More Commandos followed up the beach behind us.

Eight died before the rest made the safety of the anti-tank ditch. That safety was an illusion as the snipers were able to fire at the concrete behind us and the ricochets sent sharp splinters of stone into our backs. The wounds they caused were slight but they were wounds, nonetheless. The K Gun worked but each time they withdrew it to change a magazine then the fusillade began again.

"Davis, bring your rifle and follow me. Sergeant Poulson, take charge!"

I didn't wait for the reply but zig-zagged back to the mole. Private Davis didn't say a word he obeyed orders. He was a good Commando. When we reached the end of the wall I slung my rifle and began to climb. If there were any guards at the top I relied on surprise to take them. There were sentries but all seven of them lay dead. Their defensive position had not saved them from the naval shells. Their bodies ringed a crater on the other side of the sandbags. I dropped behind the sandbags and unslung my rifle. Davis joined me. The buildings were only eight hundred yards away but, more importantly, they were on a level with us. I scanned the building until I saw the first sniper. He was aiming at the easy targets just three hundred yards from us. I was used to my weapon now and I squeezed slowly. The bullet took him in the side of the head. I moved my rifle right and saw a machine-gun poking from the window. The gunners were hidden. With no one able to fire at them they could depress the barrel and fire with impunity. I fired at the barrel. The heavy bullet smashed into the barrel. It did not hurt the gunners but the gun fell to the ground.

A bullet struck the sandbags as the defenders saw the danger we represented. I heard Davis say, "No you don't you bugger!" He squeezed the trigger and another sniper fell tumbling to the ground.

We had distracted the men in the buildings as they tried to eliminate our threat. The German sandbags and dead Germans made an effective barrier. I looked at the top of the building. I saw an officer. My bullet caught him in the chest and threw him from the top of the building. Suddenly I saw a tank shell strike the building and then another. Oerlikon shells began to pepper the building as those offshore saw the danger the building represented.

It was time to move. There were more sandbags at the end of the mole closer to the anti-tank ditch. "Right Davis, run!"

The tanks had distracted the gunners and snipers in the building. I had never covered three hundred yards as quickly. The rest of my men sheltered still in the ditch. Sergeant Poulson looked up and waved. I saw more dead Commandos. I hoped that none of them were my men.

We were now much closer to the building which the enemy had made into a strong point. The tanks had weakened it and made it less sound. Crowe sent a projectile sailing into a hole made by a tank shell and the building bulged alarmingly as the grenade went off. I fired three bullets in quick succession. A sergeant, an officer and a sniper fell. They were much closer to me now and I had the feel for the weapon. I was in a rhythm. I heard a cheer and looked down as John Marsden rose from the ditch and led a valiant but foolish charge with his men. The fire from the building had diminished as the defenders reorganized. The withering fire from a heavy machine-gun which was in the street, two hundred yards away and close to the command centre, cut them down to a man. Davis and I emptied our magazines into the gunners. They fell, pulling the gun with them. It was too late for Captain Marsden and Sergeant Curtis. Their bullet-riddled bodies lay with their men in the streets of Ouistreham.

I heard the pipes coming closer which told me that Lord Lovat and his men were approaching. I slung my rifle. "Cover me, Davis!

"Sir."

Drawing my Colt I burst from behind the sandbags. I ran down the mole which ended at the street. I did not fire blindly but aimed and squeezed at every German head I saw appear at a door or window. Davis did me proud. I saw four men fall to his bullets and I made the wall of the building. Just thirty yards from me lay, Sergeant Curtis, Captain Marsden and their men. I holstered my Colt. I had four grenades on my assault jerkin. I took out two of them. Keeping hold of the handles I pulled the pins. There was a window six feet above my head. The barrel of a heavy machine protruded. To my left was a door. One of

Crowe's grenades had damaged it. I threw one grenade through the window and then ran along the street. I hurled the grenade through the damaged door and fell flat on the roadway. My hand touched Sergeant Curtis' boot. The two explosions sounded simultaneously. I heard screams. I stood and drew my Colt. I ran into the damaged door. It was like a charnel house. I caught sight of a movement coming down the stairs. I dropped to one knee and fired three shots. Two Germans fell at my feet.

Bill Hay burst through the door, Thompson at the ready. Outside I heard a cheer as the Free French burst from the tank trap and into the village. The strongpoint had fallen. They ran for their target, the Casino! The rest of my men joined me. "Gordy take some men and clear the rest of this building."

"Sir!"

Davis burst through the doorway. "Well done Davis. Sergeant Poulson, any more casualties?"

"Just cuts from the stones. Nothing too bad."

We heard the crump of grenades and then the sound of Thompsons as Barker, Herbert and Shepherd cleared the building.

As I spoke I took German grenades from the dead close by me. "Right, it is time for us to do our job. Hewitt, you are tail-end Charlie. Take care of any who fall and keep in touch with the rest of the Brigade. We are the breadcrumbs they will follow." He nodded. I looked at my watch. It was eleven o'clock already and I knew that the Airborne troops were expecting us at one o'clock at the latest. We had the whole of Ouistreham to get through and then the canal.

Barker returned, "All the enemy are dead sir!" I didn't ask him how they had died; this was war.

"Right we have to move quickly. There are a hundred and fifty men holding out at the canal bridge. If we don't get to them and relieve them then the Germans will blow the bridge and all of this will be a waste. Shepherd and Fletcher you both have Thompsons, you come with me. Gordy, keep the K gun at the rear. Poulson and Hay, if we meet opposition you take them out. I intend to keep going until I reach the bridge." They nodded. The three men I had brought with me the first time knew the town as well as I did. "I intend to head down to the square and then cut across to the canal. Let's go!"

As we turned the corner to run down the narrow street I heard the sound of the guns of the French Commandos as they attacked the Casino. It now held the German Headquarters. As such it was heavily defended. The brave attack of the French would buy us enough time to burst out. My rifle was slung and I had reloaded my Colt. With a Luger and a full magazine, I had enough firepower. We ran down the narrow street. Some might have said recklessly but we did not run in a straight line. We kept dodging in the doorways and the experience of the last few years meant my men constantly scanned for danger. Fletcher's Thompson barked and two Germans who had burst from a doorway fell. Shepherd fired in the air and a German tumbled from a first-floor window. Behind me, I heard grenades as my men dealt with isolated groups of Germans who had been sheltering in the buildings.

Once we reached the square I halted. A German tank and a squad of grenadiers was approaching. "Crowe!"

Alan Crowe appeared. "Sir."

"How many projectile grenades do you have left?"

"Just three sir."

"Then use them well. I want them fired at the tank and the grenadiers. We need it to be disabled."

"Right, sir."

"Fletcher and Shepherd throw two smoke grenades, now!"

Crowe fired the first grenade as the pins on the smoke grenades were thrown. It was a good shot. It landed close to the right front track and exploded. I saw the tank slew around as the track came off. The smoke began to fill the air as a second grenade soared. "Move! Follow me!" The tank's machine gun and cannon fired. Next to that, the two crumps of the grenades sounded inconsequential. The fragments from the grenades would still be devastating to the infantry and the tank was held up. I hoped that Lord Lovat and his men had a rocket launcher with them.

The defences were geared to stop an attack from the beach. As we ran down the narrow side street it felt like a sudden place of calm. No one fired at us but I knew that wouldn't last. As we emerged from the side street a light machine-gun in a sandbagged emplacement across the road opened up. The canal was defended. I shouted, "Back!"

"Davis!" I said, "Shepherd, Fletcher, give them a burst from your Thompsons."

"Sir."

As they did so Davis appeared. "Take out the gunners!"

"Sir!" He unslung his rifle and slid forward as Shepherd and Fletcher took it in turns to poke their guns around the corner of the building and fire. The German machine-gun began to hack away at the corner of the building. Davis appeared to be taking too long but I knew that it was an illusion. His gun bucked and he worked the bolt. He fired again and then a third time. He shouted, "Go!"

I trusted my sniper and I ran from the safety of the side street with my Colt held before me. He had hit the gunners. Another two men were trying to move the bodies from the gun and began to fire. A Thompson from behind me stitched a line across the chest of one of them. I dropped to one knee and took aim. The second fell. I took out a German grenade. Twenty yards from the position I dropped again, smashed the porcelain top and, shouting, "Grenade!" hurled it.

I fell flat. There were screams from behind as the grenade went off and then I raced to leap over the top. The Germans were dead. The canal lay to our left and I could see the path. Bullets began to fire from the next position down the road.

"Gordy, set up the K gun here. Keep those Jerries down the road busy."

"Sir!"

"The rest with me!" Even as we ran and before Gordy could set up the gun Ken Shepherd was hit by a stray bullet. I did not know his fate. Hewitt would have to deal with him. Suddenly Beaumont was at my shoulder. He held a Thompson. He grinned, "Fred Emerson asked me to look after it, sir."

"Good lad!"

The trail was undefended but, as we burst out of the thin trees a barge moored in the middle of the canal began to fire. We had taken them by surprise and they fired high. We threw ourselves to the ground.

"Open fire!"

Fletcher and Beaumont sent round after round at the flat wooden boat. It was less than thirty yards from us. All that saved us was the fact that the canal was slightly higher than we were and we had shelter from the bank. Above us, the branches were shredded as the German machine guns traversed.

"Davis!" I holstered my Colt and managed to take my rifle from over my shoulder without exposing myself. I rolled to my left. I kept rolling and as I turned I saw that Davis was copying me. My men held their guns over the top of their cover and fired blindly. It was unlikely they would hit anything but it distracted the Germans. When we were twenty yards away I stopped rolling and carefully lifted my head. We were fifty yards from the boat. It looked to be an old barge they had converted. There were steel plates running along the side but I could see grey. If I could see grey then I could kill.

I did not wait for Davis. I raised my rifle slowly so as not to make too much disturbance and poked it through the long grass. I aimed at a gunner and I squeezed. His head exploded and I worked the bolt and fired at the next gunner who had been exposed. He too fell. Even as I worked the bolt Davis fired at the officer who turned to shout orders. They had no guns facing this way. They were there to guard the canal. I knew that the fire on the bank had diminished. I fired at another German who tried to turn his gun. He fell wounded. As I aimed for another shot I saw an explosion on the barge and then another. Suddenly the whole barge seemed to lift out of the water as more grenades were thrown. We were showered with pieces of debris. I risked rising. There were no more boats. We ran back to the others.

Alan Crowe lay there. He had been hit. Sergeant Poulson said, "Hewitt is on his way, sir! Crowe took out the barge with a grenade. The lad did well."

I looked at my watch. It had gone twelve noon. The bridge could now be seen. It was a mile away but who knew what dangers lay before us? I heard the K gun as Gordy and his men protected our flank. There were now just six of us left. We had lost three men and Hewitt would have his hands full. Had John Marsden not done a Light Brigade charge we would have had more chance. Of Lord Lovat, there was no sign. I knew that he and his men would be hurrying after us but who knew if they had managed to evade the tank or run the gauntlet of the canal road? I stirred myself. I still had my job to do. It seemed impossible but then Commandos did the impossible every day!

I slung my rifle and loaded a fresh magazine into my Colt. "Reload. We have a mile or so to go. I doubt that they have had time to booby-trap this path so we run. Sergeant Poulson, you come with me. Fletcher, send a message back to his lordship and tell him where we are then you follow."

"Sir!"

I made sure that the last German grenade I had could easily be reached and then I set off with Sergeant Poulson down the narrow track. We ran!

We surprised the first four Germans. They were heading towards the bridge. Emerging from another path to our right we saw them when they were less than twenty feet from us. As their weapons swung towards us Polly and I let rip. I emptied my magazine. As the cordite and smoke filled the air I saw that they were dead. Bullets ripped through the air. We had surprised these four but not the ones who were following. Poulson fell clutching his leg.

I dropped to the ground and as I reloaded Beaumont sprayed the hidden path. We were rewarded by the cries of those we hit. "Hewitt!"

I lifted my head and saw the Germans just thirty feet from us. They were trying to set up a machine gun. I emptied the Colt at them and then took out the grenade. I smashed the porcelain and threw it high. "Grenade!" It was fortunate that I yelled when I did. Beaumont threw himself across Poulson as pieces of shrapnel scythed through the air. As my ears rang I picked up Poulson's Thompson and ran down the path spraying all before me. The ten-man section lay dead or badly wounded and I returned to my men. Beaumont had applied a tourniquet to Sergeant Poulson's leg. Poulson shook his head, "All these years and I get this now!"

"You'll live." I looked ahead and saw that the enemy were fortifying their position by the canal. I could hear fighting up by the bridge. It was maddeningly close. With my K gun guarding the road and no grenade launcher, we were left with close weapons. "Until the Brigadier arrives we keep their heads down. Davis; it's up to you and me."

Bill Hay suddenly rolled on his side and began to take off his rubber-soled boots. Scouse Fletcher said, "What the hell are you doing Sarge?"

As he started to take his trousers off he said, "I am going to swim underwater and drop an egg in that nest."

Bill Hay was a good swimmer. He and I had used flippers and masks in the Mediterranean.

"Are you sure, Bill?"

He shrugged, "I'll give it a go!" He stripped to his shorts and vest. He placed the grenades in his beret and stuck his beret in his shorts.

"Wait until we get their heads down. On my command give them every weapon we have. Good luck, Bill!" I peered through my sights and saw the top of a helmet. As we all fired I aimed at the helmet and managed to hit it. We were close enough for the velocity to penetrate the steel. The others loosed so many bullets that a pall of smoke drifted before us. I saw the slight splash as Bill slipped into the canal. He could hold his breath for a long time. I heard a shout as Fletcher was hit in the hand by the return fire. We kept up the barrage until we all ran out of ammunition and had to reload.

A lieutenant burst from the shrubs and hurled himself to the ground when he saw us. "Sir, Lord Lovat is just half a mile behind me."

"Good. Join in Lieutenant, we need the firepower!"

He took out his revolver and began to fire. I could not see Bill but I did see the explosion from the grenades. As the smoke rose I shouted, "Up and at 'em lads!"

I knew not how many there were but I knew that they would be stunned. I carried my rifle in my left hand and ran forward screaming like a banshee and firing my Colt as fast as I could. The Lieutenant and the remains of my section hurtled after me. As I reached the German position an officer raised his pistol to fire at me. As my Colt clocked on empty I threw myself at him. My Colt caught him in the eye and I twisted his right hand as we fell to the ground. The gun bucked and the Major went limp beneath me.

Ahead of us more Germans were preparing to attack us. I stood and took out my Luger. With the gun held in two hands, I began to pick off the advancing Germans. Davis worked the bolt of his rifle as quickly as he could. Hewitt had joined us and his Thompson sprayed the enemy. Beaumont too was lying prone and firing as fast as he could. A half-naked Bill Hay threw himself to the ground and, grabbing a German rife, he too began to fire as quickly as he could work the bolt. We bore a charmed life or perhaps there were so few of us that they were a larger target than we were. They began to fall back to a position just a hundred yards from the bridge.

I heard a familiar voice behind me, "I think Captain Harsker that when you resort to having your men fight half-naked it is time for me to take over." He loaded a bullet into his .30-06 Winchester and said, "Millins, *'Blue Bonnets'* if you please! We are late and that will never do!"

As the pipes began to wail we made way for our comrades who marched past us towards the bridge. It proved too much for the men we had just seen off and their hands stretched into the air. The Lieutenant grinned as he said, "A pleasure to serve with your sir, however briefly! I shall dine off this story after the war!"

Chapter 17

It took some time for the Brigade to pass us. I saw that I had more wounded men than fit ones. "Come on Corporal Hewitt, let's get these men back to a dressing station."

"Right, sir."

"And Hay!"

"Sir?"

"Get some clothes on!"

"Yes sir! I do feel a bit exposed! I have had dreams like this!"

Fletcher could walk and we made a stretcher from a German greatcoat and a pair of rifles for Sergeant Poulson. My sergeant wanted to walk but Hewitt was having none of it. When we found Alan Crowe he was being tended to by two of the Brigade medics. He was pale but alive. They had a stretcher. Corporal Hewitt said, "If you leave the stretcher with us we'll take him back to the dressing station."

"Thanks!"

We had five men to carry the two stretchers. When we reached the road I was relieved to see Gordy Barker and my two K gunners still alive. I could not keep the smile from my face."I am pleased to see your ugly mug, Sergeant Barker."

"And you too sir. At least we haven't left anyone behind."

Sergeant Poulson grimaced as Beaumont slipped a little. "Sorry, Sarge."

"Can't be helped." He jerked a thumb at me, "We nearly had to have a body bag for this Captain Harsker though Gordy. He charged Germans like Errol Flynn!"

"What happened to Shepherd?"

"Medics took him to the dressing station in the town."

"Come on, let's find Emerson!"

If we thought that because we had reached the bridge over the canal it was over we were wrong. We still had not managed to clear the beach and the only part of the town we had taken was the part between the town square and the canal. I saw the Free French flag flying over the Casino and knew that Commandant Kieffer had achieved his objective. The dressing station was in the cafe we had first tried to get a drink. It was overflowing. A weary-looking doctor said, "Put them down where you can, Captain. We will get to them when we are able."

Corporal Hewitt said, "Can I give a hand sir?"

"Are you a medic?"

"I have training sir."

"God knows we need that. Wash up and give a hand."

Hewitt turned to me. "I will catch up with you later sir."

I led the last five men I had back to the beach. I had no idea what the orders were. I decided to head back to the beach. We would need our Bergens.

Emerson was still there with the Bergens. I saw a Military Policeman remonstrating with him. "Is there a problem Sergeant?" There were two stretcher-bearers hovering nearby.

"I am going to put this awkward bugger on a charge, sir! He refuses to leave the beach. These medics have tried to evacuate him four times."

As soon as he saw me his face lit into a grin, "I'll go now, sir. I just didn't want to leave the bags." I glared at the military policeman. "There's some thieving bastards around here." He suddenly saw how few men were with me. "The rest?"

"No one dead, Fred! Just wounds. Now hop on to that stretcher. That is an order."

"Yes sir." He rolled on to it. His leg and his arm were heavily bandaged. "Home my man and don't spare the horses!"

As he left the Sergeant chuckled, "You Commandos are as mad as a sack full of cats sir, if you don't mind me saying so."

"No, I would agree with you. Any food on the go, Sergeant?"

"You were with the first wave, sir?" I nodded. "Then you deserve it. Back on the beach just where the Frenchies came ashore."

"Right lads, pick up the Bergens. We'll have some food and then see what the orders are."

It was bizarre. Troops were still being landed; shells were still firing and yet there was hot food available. There was a field kitchen. The cooks were all wearing steel helmets but I could smell hot food. We were recognised by our shoulder flashes and berets. Without asking food was ladled on to metal plates and thrust into our hands. We sat on the rocks by the mole. As we ate I checked my watch. It was just mid-afternoon. Twelve hours ago we had been in the landing ship listening to the naval bombardment and now we were on the beach.

As we ate Gordy asked, "Do you reckon we are winning, sir?"

"What do you think, Barker?"

"I reckon we caught them on the hop, sir. Apart from that tank, we saw by the square we have only seen infantry. They have bloody big tanks, sir. I am guessing that they will hit us soon."

"And I agree. As soon as we have eaten let's see what we can pick up. A grenade launcher or rocket launcher would be ideal. Anything to attack a tank would do."

"A pity we have lost Fletcher eh sir? He could have a nun's knickers off before she knew he was there."

Roger Beaumont had finished quickly. "Davis, come with me. Let's have a look-see!"

As the two young privates headed off Gordy shook his head, "That Fletcher is a bad influence, sir. When those two joined us they were as pure as the driven snow!"

We finished the food. I felt guilty. We were on the beach and had full stomachs. The rest of the Brigade were still fighting. I decided to rejoin them. "Pick up the Bergens, lads. We will head back to the Brigade."

"What about Davis and Beaumont, sir?"

"They can catch us up."

Just then I saw the two of them running along the beach with a wooden crate. Gordy shook his head, "What the hell have you got there?"

Davis took out his bayonet and prised the lid open. "It's a PIAT sir! And we have twenty odd rockets too."

Barker snapped, "You didn't steal it off some other unit did you?"

Beaumont said, sadly, "The operators won't miss this sir. They are dead. We found their bodies covered with blankets and this was close by. The tide would have taken it soon."

I nodded, "Get it unpacked. Smith, you can be the loader. Beaumont, you get to fire it!"

Davis said, "Sir..."

"You are too valuable with the sniper rifle, Davis. Don't worry, this war is not going to end tomorrow!"

It took us an hour to get back to the bridge. The Airborne were still there. They told us that Lord Lovat and the rest of the Brigade were digging in between Hameau Oger to close to Bréville-les-Monts. They were between the Airlanding Brigade and the 3rd Parachute Brigade. It took us another hour to find them. The Brigade had occupied a ridge of high ground. We could see as far as Ranville. Below us lay Bréville-les-Monts. Lord Lovat had set up his headquarters at a forward position. He still carried his Winchester. He pointed to my sniper rifle. "We could have done with that when we crossed the bridge! Snipers killed twelve of my men. All headshots!"

I wasn't certain if he was criticising me. I suppose I could have left my men to be seen to later but that was not my way. "Sorry, sir. We are here now."

He gave me a quizzical look, "Not criticising old chap. You did exactly what I asked of you to the letter. If you had toddled off home I wouldn't have blamed you."

"Where would you like us, sir?"

He noticed the PIAT over Beaumont's shoulder and the K gun. "Dig in at the edge of the village. The Germans are holding Bréville and there are rumours of armour reinforcing them. We are on our own until reinforcements can be brought in. You have seen Ouistreham; we are behind schedule. Don't expect help in a hurry eh? You know what to do and communications are a bit haphazard at the moment."

"And our orders sir?"

"Stop the Germans!"

I heard Beaumont chuckling as we headed to the southern end of the village. "Something funny, Beaumont?"

"Just the Brigadier. Simple sort of orders eh sir? Precise and yet vague. Perfect orders for Commandos."

As the houses, now deserted, petered out I saw a small wood on a gentle slope. It would be perfect. We passed a deserted farmhouse which had already been hit by a shell. Number 3 Commando were to our left with the Airborne Division to our front. We couldn't see them but we knew roughly where they were. We had plenty of grenades and ammunition as we had brought all the Bergens. It also meant that we had plenty of Tommy guns.

I led the men down to the wood. It was not large but some of the trees were thick and ancient. They would stop rifle and machine-gun bullets. "Right, let's use the camouflage netting to disguise our position. Beaumont and Smith set up the PIAT. Sergeant Barker, sort out the K gun. The rest of you I want as much brush and branches gathering as you can manage. Find as many logs as you can. The house yonder will have a supply of firewood. Use it to make a wall and then cover the wall. Then pile soil on the inside and outside of the logs. It will stop bullets penetrating and disguise our position. It is what the Normans did when they built their wooden castles. This will be our castle! This is now Chateau Commando! I want us hidden from view. Let's give Jerry a nasty surprise."

After taking grenades from my Bergen and attaching them to my assault jerkin I began to walk down the slope towards the road. We were on the edge of Ampreville and the German-occupied village of Bréville was just a mile or so away on a ridge overlooking us. I wanted to check out the road. It was not wide and there were hedgerows running along either side. I took out my Colt as I hurried down the road towards the village, apparently held by the Germans. I saw a flag flying but I saw no grey uniforms. I had pushed my luck enough and I headed back towards the small wood. As I ascended I saw the paratroopers digging in further along the ridge. By comparison with us, they were very lightly armed. What we needed was anti-tank guns. I hoped that they had landed with enough.

As I approached the woods I spotted our emplacement. The barrel of the K gun could be seen and I could discern the faces of Herbert and Smith. "Lads, you need to black up and we need more foliage. I could see your faces and the machine-gun. Use some of the netting in the front and put leaves in it." I pointed.

"Look there is some ivy. That plant is as tough as old boots. Pull it up and put it in the net. If you put the roots in the ground it might last a few days longer."

Herbert asked, "A few days sir? We won't be here that long will we?"

"How many tanks can you see Herbert? Where are our big guns? We are the Commandos and the Airborne. We go in light. If Jerry throws anything big at us then we will be in trouble."

"What kind of heavy stuff do they have sir?"

"Hopefully they will just have the Panzer Mark IV. We met them in the desert." I saw Bill Hay nodding. "They have two machine-guns and a 75mm. The front armour is three inches thick. Don't even think about hitting that Beaumont."

He nodded, "The sides then sir?"

"Over an inch but a better target. The side skirts are the thinnest armour and the tracks are vulnerable." They began to realise the problem. "Davis, if you can, then a bullet through the driver's visor might upset them. But it is a hard shot and you need a perfect angle. The K gun will have to deal with the infantry. We will be outnumbered and we need to lay down a wall of fire which discourages them. Now get to it."

I dropped my own Bergen and took out more grenades. I would dearly have loved to put booby traps in front of our position but I did not know where the Airborne Division positions were. The slight slope worked to our advantage for we could throw grenades and make them explode in the air. I waved Gordy over. "There are just seven of us. I want three men on watch at all times. I will take the first one, as soon as it is dark. You take the second and Bill the third. The lads will have watch on and watch off. Give them four hours."

"What about reinforcements, sir?"

"Don't expect any help for a while. We are the flank. They will be flooding Ouistreham, Caen and all points south. We will just have to hold."

He nodded, "We have a reasonable amount of ammo but we only have dry rations."

"I will wander back up to HQ and see what they can do. You take charge here."

By the time I reached Lord Lovat's headquarters, there was some semblance of order. His lordship had been summoned to Airborne's headquarters to discuss the dispositions with a liaison officer, Colonel Parker, but a Captain Macready told me about food. "Use the rations you brought ashore first. We are having a drop of supplies tomorrow. Just grab whatever you see!"

"Thanks, I will. Do we know where the paratroopers are?"

"Not exactly but you are the tip of our southern lines. If you hear movement in the night it will be Number 3 Commando setting up their defences."

By the time I headed back, it was drawing on towards dusk. We could still hear sporadic firing while further down the coast, bigger naval guns were being fired. If we had had more men I have no doubt that we could have advanced and taken more land but we had been up for almost twenty-four hours and taken more casualties than the planners had expected. We would have to hold until relieved.

Beaumont hissed, "Sir! Movement! Someone is coming towards us!"

"Stand to!"

I cocked my Colt and peered into the darkening gloom. I saw two shadows approaching. I heard Herbert cock the K Gun. "Wait!" I said. Then louder I shouted, "Identify yourselves!"

"Hewitt and Fletcher sir! We've been looking for you for hours."

"I thought you were wounded, Fletcher!"

"Just a scratch Sarge! I couldn't let me mates face all these Jerries on their own now could I. Besides I still have the radio. Who else is gonna use it?"

I looked at Hewitt. "He's fine sir. Sergeant Poulson and Alan Crowe wanted to come too but they could barely walk. They were being shipped back to Blighty with Emerson."

"Shepherd?"

"Still with the doctors, sir! I reckon he should be all right but..."

"You did well today, John."

"Just doing my job, sir."

As the two settled into the camp Gordy said, "Well that means we just have four hours on and four hours off sir. A bit better that way!"

The hot food we had had back at the beach meant that we did not need to eke into our dry rations. We filled our canteens from the deserted house. Herbert brought back a bagful of apples he had found. "They would have gone to waste if I had left them, sir."

I was fairly certain that the French would not begrudge us a few apples and we munched contentedly. The flashes from guns lit up the skies. Sporadic fire came from the distance. There was an occasional shot from close by which put us on the alert but by and large all seemed to be quiet. While the rest slept I kept watch with my three sentries. Smith said, "What do you reckon sir? All over with tomorrow?"

Smith was a good Commando but unlike Beaumont and some of the others, he could not see further than a day or two ahead. "I doubt it, Jimmy." I pointed north. "We played a lot of tricks on Jerry to make him think that we were landing close to Calais. That helped us to get ashore. He now has his best Panzer divisions just to the north of us. They don't travel fast but you can bet your last shilling that they are trundling down the road right now. The troops in Le Havre will be ready to follow them south. They will hit us and hit us hard. We managed to get hold of a little bit of France today but it is a little bit. This part is the extreme north of our line. We have no armour here. They will try to winkle us and the paratroopers out and then push down to the beach. Unless we can hold out the invasion will be halted and it will be Dunkirk all over again."

"A bit gloomy sir."

"Oh, it's not all bad. The Americans were landing far more men on their two beaches. With any luck, they have pushed inland further than we have. Their Airborne weren't sent to hold bridges they were sent to cut off a whole Peninsula. We will see."

In truth, we were counting on the Americans at Utah and Omaha. Major Foster had not told me the whole plan but I had gleaned numbers. The British and the Canadians were sending in large numbers but the Americans were sending in more. The fact remained, however, that we had to hang on with our very fingertips. We were relieved at ten and I rolled up in a ball. It was not particularly warm for June and I snuggled down close to the empty Bergens for warmth.

Sergeant Hay shook me awake. "Sir, movement. I can hear something."

"Wake the lads." I went to the K gun which was the centre of our defences. Beaumont and Davis were there. They didn't say a word but pointed to the north-west. I couldn't see anything but I heard, in the distance, the rumble of armoured vehicles. Tanks! Germans never sent tanks on their own. There were always men before them and with them. I took out my Colt and made sure it had a full magazine. Everyone was awake and ready to fight. I glanced at my watch; it was gone four and dawn would be here soon. I suddenly realised that I could no longer hear the firing from the big guns. We had no idea what was going on elsewhere. Our battle would be fought here in this tiny wood. I had no doubt that there were other troops close by but we could not see them. It felt like we would be facing the might of the enemy alone.

"Drink some water and eat something. We have a long day ahead of us."

I swallowed some warm water but did not bother with the food. There was the crack of a bullet and a fusillade in reply but sound travels a long way at night. It could have been in Ouistreham or further south. It was a warning that the second day of the invasion was about to begin. I thought of the British soldiers who had done just this in times past. The hundred men at Rorke's Drift must have woken to face the four thousand Zulus and wondered if it would be their last. The Guards at Hougoumont had barred their farmhouse and prepared to face the might of a French Division. In France, the archers of King Henry the Fifth had buried their stakes knowing that they had to face the heaviest cavalry in Europe armed with a piece of wood and some twine. The fact that they had survived gave me hope that we would too. This was not Belgium. We had been unprepared and untrained then. We were not warriors. Now we were. I had a handful of men but they all knew how to fight. We had plenty of weapons and ammunition and our defences were better than I could have hoped. We would acquit ourselves well.

Fletcher said, "What's funny, sir, you are grinning?"

"Oh I was just remembering my Shakespeare; you now, *'Once more unto the breach dear friends'*. It sort of inspired me."

"We didn't do Shakespeare in my school, sir, but I can recite the *'Charge of the Light Brigade'* by Tennyson."

I laughed, "Well parts of that are appropriate. I would guess that there will be *'cannons to the left of us and cannons to the right'*."

"*Shot and thundered*!"

"And there will be that but just remember lads that we are doing what British soldiers have been doing for almost a thousand years. We are standing together and saying to our enemies, *'knock us off our perch if you think you can.'*"

Bill Hay said quietly, "I reckon compared with the poor sods in the trenches in the Great War we have it easy."

"Amen to that Sarge."

There was the loud crack of a German shell and this time it was within a few miles. "It won't be long now lads and if I might just quote another bit of Shakespeare: *'We few, we happy few, we band of brothers- for he that sheds his blood with me shall be my brother.'* Good luck lads and remember today there is no going back. We hold this line or we die. The Germans don't take Commandos prisoner!"

Beaumont said, "*I swear, but these my joints, which if they have, as I will leave 'em them shall yield them little!*"

"What's that Beau?"

"More Shakespeare Jimmy. The Captain is right this is our Agincourt and I for one am proud to be here with you lads. I know I am one of the newest but I feel like one of your brothers."

I heard the men all murmur, 'aye'.

"To your posts!"

Chapter 18

This did not start as the previous day had done. There was no huge barrage and we were not part of a vast armada. Guns began to pop along our flanks and tank shells began to crack. In fact, we didn't see any grey until almost eight o'clock. Davis and I had our rifles at the ready. We had a clear view of the road below. We saw German helmets moving along the other side of the hedgerow. They were heading towards Ouistreham. My men looked at me for orders to fire but I shook my head. We were less than ten men. Our job was to stop the Germans advancing on the brigade. They could move up and down the road all they liked. There were a few hundred paratroopers close to Ampreville. We would stop the Germans from turning their flank.

We had not seen exactly where the Red Berets were but when we heard the sound of machine-guns not far from our right then we knew that they were close to us. That was reassuring. There was a short sharp firefight and then we saw helmets running back down the road. "Davis, when they start to come through the hedge then you and I fire. The rest of you wait until they are in larger numbers and listen for my order."

I knew that when the scouts returned to their officers they would be told to flank the Airborne. That meant coming up our slope. I saw a German coming through the gate to my left. I hissed, "The first one is mine, Davis!" I tracked him as he walked along the hedgerow. He stopped and looked up towards us. I knew he could not see us. The end of my rifle was camouflaged and I had inspected our position. He would have no idea that we had fortified the position. He turned and waved. I heard him shout something. A line of soldiers came through.

As the scout headed across the field I squeezed the trigger and worked the bolt. Even as he fell the sergeant behind him was hit by Davis. I shot the corporal who followed. Davis hit one German in the back as they hurtled back out through the gate. It was strangely silent. Then I heard shouts in German. The hedgerow began to shake as they started to cut it down. The single gateway was a death trap. One hardy German, perhaps looking for glory, found that out when he tried to dart through. Davis' rifle threw him back like a rag doll.

I heard the whump of a heavy mortar as they began to fire blindly from behind the hedgerow. With no spotter and without knowing the range they were wasting their shells. Four hundred feet behind us was the deserted house. The Germans hit that. They managed to strike it with their fourth shell. One man peered through the hedge to see the effect. My bullet smashed into his head. They kept firing as the hedge was demolished.

"Wait until they begin to move across the field, Davis. Let them think they have got us." I was trying to think like the Germans. They knew we had two snipers. Was that all that we had? They suddenly burst forward in a long line of twenty men. I shot an officer, Davis, a Sergeant. Then I just fired and dropped any grey uniform I saw. When they were sixty yards away another twenty men joined them.

"Open fire!"

Everyone but Davis and I had automatic weapons. The K gun scythed through the grey uniforms. The Thompsons chattered death and the Germans fell. Herbert raised the end of the K gun and not only killed the mortar crews but the heavy bullets tore through the mortars. The survivors pulled back beyond the road into the next field. It was eight-thirty and we had beaten off our first attack.

"Fletcher, you and Hewitt take two Thompsons and cover the left flank." They nodded and crept along the floor to avoid detection.

"What about the right sir?"

"We know the Airborne and the Canadians are just down the road, Sergeant. The fact that Jerry came scurrying back so quickly means they got a hot reception. I am hoping that Lord

Lovat sends us some help having heard the sound of the gunfire."

A lull ensued. Davis and I kept our rifles pointed at the road. Any grey we saw we fired at. The yelps and shouts told us that he had hit what we had aimed at. We had plenty of .303 ammunition. In fact, we had plenty of everything so long as this battle did not last more than a day or so. We were assault troops; we travelled light.

At noon we heard the sound of a tank engine. "Get ready Beaumont. Now is the time for you to shine."

"Sir!"

"Davis we have a chance here. When the tank begins to come up the slope we will have a clear shot through the driver's visor. Hold your nerve. His machine-gun will be firing blind."

"Sir!"

"The rest of you don't waste bullets on the tank. That is the job of Beaumont!"

It soon became obvious that it was more than one tank. The three of them came with their turrets buttoned up. That meant that they had been warned about our rifles. There were enough trees in the hedgerow to make it hard for the turret to traverse. Consequently, the three of them headed for the gap that they had made in the hedge. The dead Germans were testament to the courage of the enemy.

"Beaumont you will have your best chance when he turns to come through the gap. You will have a clear shot at his side. Smith, have another rocket ready as soon as the first has been fired and keep out of the way of the back of that thing! It is lethal!"

The narrow lane made the task hard for the tank driver. The fact that we did not fire at them must have given them confidence. I knew that they would have a shell up the spout and the machine-gunner would be desperate to fire once the tank had turned. A great deal depended upon Beaumont. The hedge was two hundred yards away. It was a long range for a PIAT. A hundred and ten was effective range.

"Go for the tracks!"

"Sir!"

As the tank began to turn and the turret had free rein to traverse I saw the long barrel as it swung around. Beaumont disobeyed orders. He went for the gap between the turret and the tank. There were flames and an explosion. I don't know if he was naturally gifted or just lucky but the turret stopped turning. The tank, however, continued to turn. Smith did really well to reload. I saw him slap Beaumont on the shoulder and a second rocket hurtled towards the tank. This time he obeyed orders and we saw the ruined track. The rocket had penetrated the side armour and hit the driving wheel. Ominously the tank continued to turn. I heard a crack from my right as Davis took a chance. There was a ping and a cry. He had hit something. A third rocket hit the other track and the tank was stationary. It could not traverse. If fired its gun. The noise was terrifying for it was so close but the shell sailed to our right. I had no doubt the Airborne troops there would have had a shock.

The hatch began to open. Davis and I were ready. The first one to attempt to leave was hit by two bullets and that hatch was blocked.

"Herbert give a burst under the tank. There is an escape hatch there."

The K gun ripped across the front of the tank. There was another cry. Had we had a grenade launcher then we could have set it on fire. Effectively, however, we had blocked the route into the field and up to our emplacement. Unfortunately, we had also given the troops behind the tank some cover.

With typical German efficiency, the second panzer began to push the damaged tank out of the way. The broken vehicle complained and groaned. Suddenly I saw Beaumont burst from cover and run down the slope. What was the fool doing? "Give him some cover!"

The Germans did not see a man with a rocket launcher they saw a British soldier racing towards them. The PIAT could have been just a big rifle. I saw an officer turn to give orders. He did not look worried. My bullet hit him in the shoulder and threw him around. It brought a rattle of bullets up the slope at us. The logs in front of us absorbed the damage well. The broken tank was almost clear of the gap. The second panzer would need to reverse in order to make the turn. Beaumont was less than eighty yards from the tank. I watch him kneel and take careful aim. Herbert and the K gun chopped through the hedge and I heard shouts as the machine-gun hit flesh. Beaumont was no fool and he was not stupid. The minute he had fired at the second tank he turned and ran up the slope. This time the rocket struck the side armour of the tank. It was well within the optimum range. It penetrated the armour and managed to hit the ammunition. The whole turret was blown into the air.

Beaumont ran obliquely up the slope. We thought he had made it but he was hit. He pitched forward. My two sergeants ran forward to help him. While Gordy sprayed the hedge with his Tommy gun Hay picked up Beaumont, PIAT and all, and carried him back to our lines.

"Hewitt!"

I looked over my shoulder as Beaumont was laid down. His foot was bloody but he was smiling. "Daft as a brush as Sergeant Major Dean would have said!"

In answer, he held up the PIAT. "I saved this though sir and it will take some time to clear two tanks!"

Hewitt knelt next to him and took out his first aid kit. My two sergeants returned to their posts. As Hewitt was tending to Beaumont's wound he shouted, "Sir, we had a runner from HQ. We have Number 3 Commando to our left. They are on a line with the empty house. We can retreat back to the house whenever we like. We were told to expect armour!"

"At the moment I think we are safer here. How is Beaumont?"

"He can't walk but he is in no danger. The bullet took away part of his heel."

Beaumont's voice came back, "But I can still fire the PIAT."

I looked at my watch. We had five or six hours of daylight left. "We will pull back after dark. Hay, I want this area booby-trapping. No one goes down the hill any more. They will try with the last tank soon and then they will wait until dark." I was grateful for the high hedges

"Sir!"

"Have the Bergens taken up there. When we go we will have to fly!"

To the left and right of us, I heard firefights as the German infantry probed for weaknesses in our thin line. The smaller explosions of grenades and mortars were augmented by the louder bangs of tanks. We would have been overrun some time ago had it not been for the slope and the wood. Once the remaining tank could bring its turret and machine-gun to bear they would make short work of us. The log barricade could withstand grenades and bullets but a 75mm shell would make short work of it. Hewitt returned to the left flank and Beaumont, a little paler now, crawled back to his PIAT. He was not going to let anyone else fire his new weapon.

I caught sight of movement by the hedgerow. They were trying to cut down more of the hedgerow.

"Sergeant Barker, shred the hedge!" The machine-guns all fired blindly and brought a fusillade in reply. I heard something shouted and men ran from both flanks. They had called our bluff; they knew how few men we had. "Stand to! Davis, take the right, I'll take the left."

Our job was to kill the officers and sergeants. They were keeping low and working in pairs. Even as I peered through the telescopic sights I saw a submachine-gun aimed at me. It fired and I felt the bullets hit the log before me. I forced myself to concentrate. It was a sergeant firing and my bullet smacked him in the chest. The rifleman next to him dropped his rifle and picked up the submachine gun. I fired at him. My bullet struck his shoulder and he rolled, with the gun, down the slope. Our earth and wood defences were holding but the Germans were methodically clearing the hedge. Soon the tank would be upon us. The K gun finished off those on the right and the rest fell back.

A plume of smoke told me that they had started the Panzer. They would not waste fuel. This was not nineteen thirty-nine.

"Beaumont get ready with the PIAT. When it starts to come I want smoke grenades thrown in front of them. Let's upset their aim."

To our left, a furious fusillade began and then the sound of both mortars and heavier weapons. Bill Hay said, "Looks like a major attack, sir!"

"It does. Be ready to race back to the house."

The barrel of the Panzer Mark IV could be seen over the hedge. Then I saw its front as it passed the gap and it slowly began to turn. Beaumont shouted, "I'll try a shot before the smoke sir!"

"Go ahead!"

He fired and he hit the tank but this time he only damaged one of the sprockets. One side would not be as efficient as the other but it would still progress towards us. The machine-gun fired as the front turned. The bullets smashed into the logs and earth. Beaumont fired again. It was a hopeful shot. He aimed at the front. Sometimes luck favours the brave. It did not penetrate the armour but it hit the gun. I could only hope that the gunner had been hit too. The 75mm could now fire and it belched smoke and flame as its shell shredded the trees above our head. It then smashed into the roof of the house. We were all deafened. It began to climb the hill. It had not built up speed and it was going slowly. Smith was loading as fast as he could. Like Davis, I was firing into the driver's visor in the hope of hitting something. The rest of my men were firing at the advancing grenadiers and infantry. They paid a heavy price for every foot of ground they climbed.

Beaumont was an engineer and a clever one at that. He knew that the armour on the front was too thick for one rocket and so he kept firing at the same spot. It took skill and it took courage for the leviathan was drawing ever closer. The second shell came so low that, had we been standing, it would have cut us in two. As it was our cover was disappearing rapidly and the house behind was becoming a ruin! Even I could see the spot Beaumont had hit twice was glowing. The third one was slightly off target but as it struck at eighty yards it spread the red. His fourth one penetrated the armour and the tank exploded before our eyes. Perhaps the gunner had a shell in hand I do not know but the tank erupted in a sheet of flame. The soldiers who were close by were set on fire. I saw two running down the slope screaming; they were one huge flame. The attack ended.

I looked at my watch. It was now six o'clock. Although the tank would stop burning it would not be for some time. It also gave the enemy cover. When it stopped burning it would prevent us from firing across the whole of the slope. They would come. I said, "Quietly, move out. Smith, help Beaumont. Tell Hewitt and Fletcher. Back to the house. Take the netting from over our heads. We can use it again. Davis, you stay with me. Let's pick off a few more."

"Right sir!"

The Germans had lost three tanks. They would not be happy. The smoke from the burning tank drifted across our front and I knew that they would be heading back up in the hope that they might catch us unawares. The real attack would come after dark but they would probe until then. Davis and I were firing at shadows but the telescopic sight magnified the shadows and we could tell that they were men. We shot four before they went to ground and began to fire through the smoke. Our wood and soil wall had held up well but there were weak parts now.

I heard a whistle from above me. "You go back."

As Davis scurried up the hill I took a German grenade from my tunic. After smashing the porcelain I threw it as high as I could. Then I turned and ran up the slope to the house. I did not run in a straight line. That proved a wise move. After the grenade exploded two machine-guns began a crossfire. The smoke meant that they couldn't see me but a lucky bullet could still hit me! I threw myself over the rubble from the damaged roof of the deserted house. My men were already setting their weapons up. Gordy was rigging the camouflage netting across the front of our positions. The damaged roof made a secure place to anchor it. The Germans had aided us by building a defensive wall of rubble in front of the house. We used the shattered windows and doors.

Bill Hay raced in followed by Hewitt and Fletcher. Hewitt gestured behind him with his thumb. "The rest of the Brigade are getting some stick, sir. Mortars made a right mess of one whole section."

I nodded, "Then we are on our own. Barker, get some water sorted. See if there is any food left in the kitchen, Davis. How is the heel, Beaumont?"

"Painful sir but I will live with it."

I nodded and peered down the slope. "Don't fire yet. Let them trip the booby traps. We have good cover here."

We were still preparing for our defence when Fletcher shouted, "Ey up sir! A runner!" He had his Tommy gun up in an instant.

I saw that it was a Lieutenant from our Brigade. "He is one of us."

The Lieutenant threw himself inside our walls. "Message from Major Styles, sir. The brigade is going to attack Bréville at dawn tomorrow morning."

"Attack?" I could not keep the incredulity from my voice.

He grinned, "Yes sir. It appears they have just reinforced the enemy. Lord Lovat wants us to attack Bréville. Give them a bloody nose and then withdraw to our positions here."

"Dawn?"

"Eight o'clock sir. We go in kill as many as we can and then return back to the ridge." He looked at me expectantly.

"We'll be there."

After he had gone I gathered my men around me. "Patently we can't take Beaumont in the attack and I am not leaving him here on his own. Fletcher you and Beaumont will watch our position; use the K gun. Give your Thompsons to Herbert and Smith."

Although they nodded I could see the doubt on their faces. That doubt was voiced by Gordy Barker. "Sir is this right? It seems daft to me. We should be digging in."

"Lord Lovat doesn't make many mistakes. If they have been reinforced then an attack by us should damage that confidence. We have destroyed three tanks here. Do you honestly think they believe that this house is held by just a handful of men? If we attack then they will think it is a company, at least." I took out my map. "Bréville is a mile and a half from here. It isn't as though we have a long march is it?" I was trying to convince myself as much as I was trying to convince them.

Hay asked, "Do we take the PIAT, sir?"

"No, and Davis and I will leave our rifles here. We need firepower. Thompsons, Colts and grenades. However, I believe that we will have to repel boarders soon enough."

Fletcher said, "That is easy sir!"

"Easy?"

He grinned and gave me the old music hall reply, "Stop changing the sheets!"

The groans from the others broke the tension. They were still confident and that was worth everything. We ate and drank before night fell and then we stood to. The first booby trap went off at ten o'clock at night. There was a flurry of shots and shouts and then an officer demanded silence. Had we had Crowe and the grenade launcher then we could have decimated the Germans. As it was we waited. I had my Luger and Colt ready to hand as well as four Mills bombs. I wondered if they had found and disarmed the traps when I heard a second one triggered, a little further to the right. I wished I had had a flare gun but I did not. We would have to wait.

The third bomb helped us dramatically for it was behind our former defensive position and it lit them up. They were a hundred yards away. A line of infantry was advancing up the slope.

"Fire!"

At that range, even ordinary soldiers could not miss and these were Commandos. Our bullets tore into them. I chose my shots. The flashes from their guns showed where they were and I shot the Captain who was leading them. They fell back down the hill when they had lost ten men.

I hissed, "Hay, Fletcher, come with me."

We slipped down the hill. I had my Commando knife in my hand as well as my Colt. "Find any weapons and grenades. Make booby traps amongst these dead Germans." It was a gruesome task but it was necessary. I found a German submachine gun and two magazines. I took them. The six grenades I found I tied in pairs to make a series of booby traps. We all carried old parachute cords in our tunics. I heard movement below and I hissed, "Get back now!" As I turned and ran I took a Mills bomb from my tunic and rolled it down the hill. I doubted that I would hit anyone but I wanted them to think that some of their men were alive and had set off a booby trap. It went off with a sharp crack halfway from our former emplacement.

We had barely made it back inside the rubble when the Germans attacked. They fired blindly up the hill at our position. We heard them shouting encouragement to each other as they ran up the hill to find their wounded comrades. We were safely hunkered behind the rubble. I waited until the booby traps were triggered and then I shouted, "Let them have it!"

The air was thick with the sound of gunfire and cordite. We too were firing blind but we put up a wall of steel. I used the captured submachinegun. I fired until the magazine was empty and then changed it. They were determined this time. They reached the rubble. The submachine gun jammed and I took my Luger and fired point-blank at the German Corporal who was trying to bayonet Fletcher. I just fired until I had no bullets left and then drew my Colt and did the same.

They fell back.

"Anyone hurt?"

Bill Hay groaned, "Bastard stabbed me in the arm with a bayonet sir."

"Hewitt!"

"Sir!"

The bodies lay like a wall before us. "Sergeant Barker. Make sure they are all dead and bring any weapons you can."

At midnight I decided that they were not coming again and we set sentries. One team would watch until four and the other from four. This time we all really needed our sleep! I took the first watch. I found it helped to keep busy and so I cleaned both my pistols and loaded fresh magazines. The dead Germans had yielded more grenades and more ammunition for my gun. I decided to use the silencer on my Colt. It might give us some surprise the next day. When that was done I looked towards the Orne River. Since dark, it had been quiet. The battle to the south of us had moved. Had they taken their objectives? I doubted that. I knew that we were supposed to have been relieved already. We were the assault troops. Having taken our objectives it was up to more mobile troops to exploit the land we had bought.

Something had gone wrong.

Chapter 19

I woke Hay and Barker at four. It was getting close to the equinox and the sky was becoming a shade lighter already. I curled up in a ball and fell asleep. Barker woke me at a quarter to eight. We drank and we ate. It was somewhat mechanical. We tasted nothing. Everything tasted of cordite. The bodies of the Germans had all set in stiff poses of death. They were macabre. The burned-out German tank stood halfway down the hill. Behind it, I could see nothing. The Germans were there and this time we would be attacking.

"Right Hay, you are in command. Use the radio today to find out what the hell is going on. The rest of you; we are not going in charging. There is little to be gained. We sneak down. Use the captured German grenades first. Once we cross the road then we cut across the field. Bréville is due south of us. I intend to wait until we hear the attack from our left before we attack. Stay close. This band of brothers is getting much smaller!"

"Sir!"

I looked at my watch. It was almost eight. It would take a minute or two to get to the tank. "Let's go. We will go to the tank and then try to get across the field unseen." Having been the attackers for a whole day I doubted that the Germans would be expecting us to attack them. We made the tank. It had a rank smell. The burned bodies and the charred tank were pungent. I led my men towards the hedgerow. The Germans had cleared their dead from that side. I moved towards the other two tanks. They were not as badly burned and they would provide cover. I had my Colt before me.

There was a gap between the tanks and, while my men formed a skirmish line, I wriggled through the gap. I saw two sentries across the road lounging against the gate which led into the field. I raised my silenced Colt and fired. As one slid to the floor the other looked up as though the bullet had come from the skies. I fired and he grew a third eye. Just then there was the sound of British mortars and Thompsons to our left as the attack began.

"Let's go!"

The German infantry, it looked to be a company, had camped in the field. They just lay on the ground. I hurled a grenade and took cover behind the wall. As it exploded we burst into the field. I fired my Luger. It was drowned by the machine-guns of my men. Herbert had a prodigious arm and he threw his grenade a long way. Even so, he shouted, "Grenade!" and we took cover! It scythed through half-dazed men.

I saw an officer trying to rally his disorientated and shocked troops. I levelled my pistol and shot him and the NCO next to him. The rest of Number 4 Commando were firing to our left and the remnants of the company took flight. They did not see a handful of men; they saw a major attack with machine-guns. There were just six of us but we were Commandos; we did not know when to say, 'enough'!

The wounded lay where they fell and we ran after the Germans. One brave fellow turned and raised his rifle. He was less than twenty feet from me and my pistol shot knocked him to the ground. We had ammunition enough. Smith was firing a German weapon and he sprayed the hedge at the other side of the field before we burst through the gate. The road now led directly to Bréville. There were houses on either side of the road. Some were burned out and few looked occupied. We just ran down the road. Other Commandos joined us from the left and ahead I could see another group of Commandos as they fired at an unseen enemy. As we ran a Sergeant from our Brigade, Sergeant Thompson, said, "Can we join you Captain Harsker? Our officer, Lieutenant Wilson, was hit in the leg!"

"Feel free, Sergeant Thompson! The more the merrier!" His ten men now gave me more men to command than I had had so far in France. I saw a sign to our right, 'Bréville-les-Monts'. We had reached our objective. That was confirmed when a German machine-gun tore through the Red Berets ahead of us. Four fell and the rest took cover.

I saw a side road to the right, "Follow me." We darted between the houses. I knew that speed was of the essence. The Brigade had too few men to be held up by a machine-gun. Once they stabilised their defences we would be in trouble. We had to hit them before they could organize. As we burst out into an open space we happened upon a German squad. They were carrying a machine-gun and obviously intent upon setting up a defensive point. We fired first. One of the Germans managed to fire his weapon and one of Sergeant Thompson's men died.

"Herbert, Smith, bring that German machine-gun!"

"Sir!"

I did not pause but ran down the road. There were fields to our right. I heard firing ahead of us. Our rubber-soled shoes made no noise on the road. We burst out and found ourselves behind a company of Germans who had built a crude barricade and were firing their machine-gun. Six grenades hurtled through the air as I emptied my Luger. Sergeant Barker shouted, "Grenade!" and we fell to the ground.

As soon as the wave of concussion had passed I stood and started firing my Colt. I still had the silencer on and I saw the look of surprise on the German officer's face as my bullet smashed into his middle. It was a vicious fight. The Germans had enemies on two sides and they fought hard. What won the day was the fact that we had been fighting for three days. These Germans had been in a barracks in Le Havre until the previous day. They hesitated where we did not.

Major Styles strode over. "Well done, Harsker. Take your men and clear the west side of the village. When I fire a red flare pull back to your original positions." He pointed to the men with him. "We have just what you see. Forty men to clear this village. We get in, destroy their weapons and then high tail it out of here."

"Sir!" I turned to Herbert and Smith. "Set the German machine-gun up here in case any Jerries try to flank us."

"Sir!"

I took the silencer from my Colt and holstered it. I picked up a German submachine-gun and waved my new section forward. This was not a large village but the Germans had filled it. Our sudden attack, however, had not allowed them to build defences.

We came across another group of Germans who were trying to build a barricade across the road. They fled as the first bullets hit them. We kept running. It was the German Kubelwagen which almost did for us. It burst from a road leading into the village. It came so fast that two of its wheels left the ground as it raced around the corner. That speed saved us for the machine-gunner was too busy trying to hold on to fire his weapon. As it raced towards us fourteen guns opened fire. The driver was hit and as he died his dying hand jerked the wheel around and the vehicle rolled over. We had to race out of its way. It lay at an unnatural angle, its crew dead. And then we reached the edge of the village. We heard gunfire from our left.

"Back to back lads. We form a barrier here. We stop anyone from leaving and any reinforcements arriving."

I checked my magazine. I still had half left. That would do. Sergeant Barker suddenly shouted, "Sir, troops from the south!" Then a heartbeat later he said, "It is all right sir. It is the Red Berets."

A lieutenant, Sten gun in hand, strode towards me. He had a grin on his face. "Dyson, 9th parachute Battalion. We heard the shooting and our Major told us to investigate. Jolly glad to see it is you chaps."

I gestured behind me with my thumb. "Lord Lovat decided to clear this little lot. We only have forty men with us."

"Things aren't much better with us, sir. We are holed up in the woods up yonder." He pointed to the area close to our ridge. "Any idea how the main battle is going?"

"Not a clue."

"Well sir, we will toddle back to our woods. I have no doubt that Jerry will occupy this again."

He was to be proved right but I also knew that we did not have enough men to hold it. The ridge upon which we had built our defences would have to be the barrier.

"Sir, the flare!"

I looked in the sky and saw the red flare descending. "Right lads, back up the road."

As we passed the Kubelwagen my men took ammunition and grenades. Suddenly Sergeant Barker shouted, "Davis, with me! I'll catch you up sir!" He ran up a narrow passage between two houses towards the centre of the village. With anyone else, I might have worried but Gordy knew what he was doing.

We reached Herbert and Smith. "Pack up the machine-gun. That will be useful on the ridge."

Sergeant Thompson said, "We might as well follow you, sir. I am not certain what the Lieutenant intended after the attack."

"Where were you?"

"Hameau sir. We were with Headquarters."

"You might as well. As far as I can see there is a gap between the 9th and us. If I can see it then you can bet your bottom dollar that Jerry will too."

Sergeant Barker ran up. He and Davis were carrying a large metal box between them. It was the kind used by German field canteens. It smelled good. "Chickens sir! I could smell 'em. They are a bit scrawny but they are hot food!"

"Good man!"

It was early afternoon when we reached the German tank. We had gathered as many grenades from the dead Germans as we could. "Sergeant Barker and Sergeant Thompson. We will make the tank part of our defences. Build another log and soil barrier around the side and lay booby traps in the ground between the road and here."

"What about the chickens, sir?"

"Build the barrier and lay the traps. Then we eat!"

I saw the disappointment on his face. The smell had made me salivate too. "Right sir. Come on you shower! The sooner we get this built the sooner we eat!"

I went up to the house. Bill Hay rose. "Everything all right sir?"

"Yes. We have reinforcements now. Carry this stuff back to the castle! We are rebuilding it."

As they left I decided to explore the house. The upper floors had been demolished and the ground floors badly damaged. I sought food but it was all destroyed. Then I spied the door to the cellar. It was locked and I kicked it in. There was no power and it was dark. Holding the rail I descended. With the door open there was enough light to make out what was there. I found a small wine cellar. Some of the bottles had been destroyed but I found six that were not. I found an old bread basket and put them in. I was about to go back when I spied, hanging from a hook, a cured ham. I took that.

By the time I had made my way back to the rest of the men the barrier had been built and the men were carefully laying and disguising booby traps. I took a bottle out and waved it and the ham. "We eat and drink well tonight lads!"

That was all the encouragement they needed and, even though they were exhausted, they worked like Trojans. It was late afternoon when they had finished. The two sergeants divided the food evenly and I doled out the wine. There was only enough for a couple of mugfuls each but it would seem like bounty from heaven after water for four days. I noticed the smiles on all their faces as they tucked into chicken which was still warm and sliced ham washed down with rough red wine. These were warriors for the working day and they had earned their food.

I took my mug of wine and inspected our defences. The K gun and the heavy German machine-gun would both enfilade the ground on either side of the tank. The new barrier was the first line of defence and the men would fall back from there to our old position. After they had eaten I would have them bring some of the rubble from the house and pile it in front of the soil and timber palisade. From what the Major and the Lieutenant had said we were a thin line. The red berets of the Paras were mixed with the green of the Commando. It would have to hold. I glanced at the sky. We had been lucky that the Germans had not attacked us from the air. We had no defence against that.

I saw that Beaumont had finished and was checking his PIAT. "How is the wound?"

"Hewitt checked it when he came back sir and changed the dressing. It aches like mad sir but there is no infection. That is good. I wouldn't fancy losing a leg!"

I nodded, "You should know that I am putting you in for a promotion when we get back. You deserve it."

He shrugged, "Rank doesn't seem to mean much here sir." He laughed at the irony of his words. "You apart that is. We all just get on but thank you, sir. I appreciate it." He waved a hand at the rest of our men. "They all deserve something, sir."

"They do indeed, Beaumont."

With more men to perform sentry duty, we all got more sleep than hitherto. I had the men stand to at dawn. One of Sergeant Thompson's men had gathered up the bones of the chicken and the ham and we had collected some young vegetables from the garden to the house behind us. We made a soup to keep us going and we kept watch. To the south of us, we heard the crack of mortars and then the heavier sound of tank guns. We prepared to be attacked. The woods that the 9th occupied were just a mile away. The skirmish lasted an hour and then we saw German uniforms in the woods. It was too far away for us to intervene but we watched in case the attack turned towards us. By mid-afternoon, the firing had stopped and the grey disappeared from the woods.

"Is it over sir? We haven't been attacked all day!"

I looked at the sky. There was still time, "I doubt it, Sergeant Thompson. Let's just stay alert. We will all live longer that way."

At five o'clock I heard the sound of German engines. They were fighters. I could not see them and so I went up the hill towards the house. I took out my binoculars. They were FW-109s and they were dive-bombing and strafing the bridge over the Orne. That was ominous. It was our only retreat across the river. Were the Germans planning a major attack? I watched their bombs drop but the bridges remained intact and they headed east up the valley. As I made my way back to the house I heard more engines. This time it was Stirling bombers. Were they coming to bomb the Germans? Then I saw the mushrooms of parachutes. It was either reinforcements or supplies. I followed them down with my binoculars. They landed close to the woods where the 9th were sheltering. It was not men, it was anti-tank guns and ammunition. It gave me hope.

The next morning I was up at six. I checked our lines. "Anything, Sergeant Barker?"

"No sir."

Just then Fletcher shouted, "Sir! I just picked up on the radio, a patrol from the 13th say that there are Germans massing in Bréville-les-Monts."

"Everyone, stand to!"

The previous day had seen an attack to the south of us. The Germans must have known of the gap. It would be our turn next. We had not been idle the previous day and we now had substantial defences in front of us. The men had dug trenches and used debris from the half-demolished house to give more protection. We had even taken the burned side skirts from the tank and made a roof for the machine-guns.

We heard the artillery and the mortar before we saw the shells. They pounded the house. The Germans had last seen us retreat there when they had last attacked. The camouflage netting hid us from their view. "Fletcher! Get on the radio and tell Head Quarters that we are under attack!"

"Sir!"

When the shells began to fall behind the house I knew that it was a creeping barrage. They had no spotters, The woods, although they had taken some punishment hid the house from view.

"Sir, Headquarters said that the attack is along the line. We are on our own!"

Sergeant Barker snorted, "So what's new?"

The barrage lasted thirty minutes. "Hold your fire until I give the order!"

Davis and I, along with Hooley, Sergeant Thompson's sniper, were spread out across the line. Our job would be to decimate the officers as the enemy advanced. It would not stop the Germans attacking; they were brave soldiers but in taking away the leadership it might encourage the men to make the wrong decisions.

We spied the first Germans at nine o'clock. It was a couple of companies and they came up in extended skirmish order. I estimated that there were two hundred men. I tracked a Major who appeared to be leading. Halfway up he stopped and I saw him speak to a radio operator. He and his men lay down.

I hissed, "Take cover. Keep your heads down." Mortar shells began to crash down behind us hitting and shredding the woods and our castle. I heard fragments strike the metal we had incorporated into our defences. After ten minutes it stopped and I heard a whistle. "Stand to!"

I had no idea if any of my men had been hurt but the whistle meant they were attacking. They began to march up the hill. I aimed my rifle at the Major. The first booby trap which was tripped was to my left. Then there was another to my right. The Major made a mistake. He ordered a charge. As he shouted and took a step I dropped him and shouted, "Open fire!"

The K gun and the German heavy machine-gun chattered through the Germans. Some dived to the ground and set off another booby trap. Light machine-guns were deployed and began to fire back at us. I aimed at the gunner of one. He appeared to be looking directly at me. The sight made it appear as though I could touch him. My bullet went through his eye. His head dropped. I switched to the loader and my bullet hit him in the side of the head.

Davis and Hooley were equally effective and it became too much for the leaderless Germans. Three ran towards our lines screaming insults and they were cut down. The rest retreated beyond the road.

"Anyone hit?"

"Two of my men bought it, sir. Direct hit from a mortar shell. They knew nothing about it."

"Well, they know where we are, now so expect more mortar shells. Take whatever steps you need to get some cover." The men now had trenches and a mortar hit would be unlucky. This was when I wished we had helmets. Whizzing shrapnel was deadly. Ten minutes later the mortars began. It was horrific. Mortars exploded all around us but the Germans would have been better to use fewer of them and have a spotter watch their fall. Some hit the tank others hit the same place. I heard a scream and knew that someone had bought it. They must have shifted the artillery for it was only mortars we heard. When it stopped I could barely hear anything. I stood and shouted, "Stand to!"

I saw a bloody mess where one of Sergeant Thompson's men had been. It was his sniper, Hooley! The sergeant's decision to join my band had cost him, three men, already! He just had seven left from those who had joined us. This time the Germans knew where we were and knew about the booby traps. They threw their own grenades to detonate ours. It worked but it meant they attacked with just their guns. They were also less reckless.

They worked up the slope in twos. They had sufficient numbers to keep our heads down. Davis and I worked our bolts as fast we could and each bullet found a mark. The sights were very effective.

As Herbert and Smith cleared a section of attackers I looked to the gate where three officers conversed. It was a good half a mile away. "Davis! The gate!"

I took aim at the chest of one and fired my rifle. A second bark told me that Davis had fired too. Two officers fell. Once clutched his back. The third took cover. A whistle sounded and the Germans began to fall back. My men took potshots, wounding four more before they reached the safety of their field. I glanced at my watch. It was ten-thirty and we had beaten off two attacks already at the cost of three dead. The field before us was littered with bodies. When would the Germans decide they had had enough?

To the right, I heard six pounders duelling with German tanks. "Fletcher tell Headquarters that we have repelled another attack and that the 9th are being attacked by armour."

"Sir!"

I went around the men to make sure they were all unwounded. Hewitt was dealing with the cuts from flying shrapnel and splinters of wood. I found Sergeant Thompson smoking and wrapping bandage around his hand. "Regret joining us, Sergeant?"

He laughed, "No sir. No matter how bad it is here I know it will be just as bad everywhere else besides everyone says that you bring luck to those who serve you."

"Who says that?"

"Oh everyone sir. The Lieutenant was always desperate to serve with you. He reckoned he would get a going if he did. Sergeant Major Dean and Daddy Grant spoke highly of you too. No sir, I don't regret this. Mind I thought that once we took the bridge that would be it and we would be back off to Blighty!"

Fletcher came running over, "Sir, HQ says they are being attacked from the north and to watch out for armour!"

Sergeant Thomson shook his head, "That is all we need! German armour!"

Chapter 20

"Beaumont!"

Beaumont had made himself a crutch and he hobbled over. "Get a layer from Sergeant Thompson's section. We have German armour coming!"

He was unfazed by the news, "Righto sir. Will do." He looked at a young lad who was smoking next to Sergeant Thompson ."What's your name?"

"Hart."

"Well, Hart the Captain here has just said you can be my layer. Let's see how fast you can load a rocket eh?"

I saw immediately why Beaumont had picked the young lad. He was enthusiastic. "Great!" As soon as he said it I knew that he was a compatriot of Scouse Fletcher. He was a Liverpudlian!

I went around the men. "We will have another attack soon. This time it is armour. Don't waste bullets on the tanks. Concentrate on the infantry."

Gordy said, quietly, "We can't hold out much longer sir. We had plenty of ammo but at the rate, we are using it we will be out by the morning."

I nodded. "Then tonight we see what we can get from our German friends!"

I made sure I took plenty of water. Although the house had been destroyed there was still a well. So long as we had water we would survive. I had had the men add salt and the last of our porridge to it. We needed all the sustenance we could get.

When naval guns began to fire from behind us and hit the German lines in front of the Airborne we knew the attack was imminent. "Get ready lads!"

The mortars began to crack and then I heard the sound of engines. This time it was not tanks but armoured cars. They were faster. "Beaumont, armoured cars!"

"They only have half-inch armour at best sir! I just hope I have enough rockets!"

"Davis, they have tyres and not tracks. Try to get their tyres when they come through the gaps."

The gap in the hedgerow had been widened and was now over forty yards across but it was still a pinch point. I saw that three of the first to come through were the lighter Leichter Panzerspähwagen. These had just quarter-inch armour, four wheels, a 20mm cannon and a machine-gun but the fourth was a Schwerer Panzerspähwagen. They had six wheels and half-inch armour. The pennant on the turret told me that it was the commander.

"Beaumont, take the six-wheeled one!"

"Sir!"

The four of them would begin to fire their cannon as soon as they were within range. That would be half a mile. Beaumont would have to wait until they were a hundred yards away. The only weapons which could reach them were our two sniper rifles. I aimed at the first of the four-wheeled Leichter Panzerspähwagen. I missed the tyre with my first shot as the driver swerved to avoid a dead German. The second hit the tyre. I saw the hatch open as a crew member clambered out to change the tyre. My bullet hit him in the back and he drooped over the hatch. I could not see the others because of the angle of the Schwerer Panzerspähwagen. It was grinding up the hill its cannon now firing. The uneven ground made it inaccurate. Some shells hit the wooden barricade while others hit the trees above our head.

I aimed at the front tyre and fired. This time I hit it. With five others it did not need to stop. It kept coming. I fired a second shot and missed but my third hit the middle tyre and the car slewed around. It still climbed but it was now crablike and I could not bring my rifle to bear on any of its other tyres. It was still only a third of the way up the long slope. I could see the grenadiers as they ran after the three vehicles which were still advancing and firing at us. The K gun bore the brunt of their fire.

Herbert and Smith were chopped up by the combined fire of two of the cannon.

Beaumont had been a close friend of Smith and I saw him raise the PIAT. I wondered if he was wasting a shell. Then I saw that the crab-like approach had given him a shot at the side. The armour there was just over a quarter of an inch. The armoured cars used petrol and the whole of the car lifted bodily in the air as it exploded. The other two armoured cars could now be seen and I fired at the front tyre of one of them. I hit it but it kept coming towards us. Beaumont now fired at the one I had just hit and it too exploded in a fireball. The armoured car was designed to take punishment from small arms fire and not a rocket launcher!

The last one was the furthest back. The smoke from the two burning vehicles prevented me from getting a good sight of its tyres. I would have to leave that for Beaumont. The infantry were now within range and I shouted, "Fire!" We were a K gun down. This would be desperate. Ignoring the cannon and machine-gun shells whizzing above our heads we fought. Had we run we would have died and so we fought. I methodically worked my way through the officers and NCOs who advanced. I missed some. They dived to the ground or were obscured by the smoke. They then began to fire their own weapons in reply. When Beaumont finally penetrated the armour of the last Leichter Panzerspähwagen the infantry were less than a hundred yards from us.

"Use grenades." Although the range was long we had the advantage of height and the Mills bombs would roll. I hurled all four of mine and then dropped. A line of grenades all exploding together causes many wounds. I saw the grey-uniformed Germans fall to the ground. As we had thrown our grenades the fire had diminished and the grenadiers thought we were out of ammunition and they rose to charge us. The ripple of grenades rolled along the line and they were beaten. The survivors ran back down the hill leaving the burning vehicles.

Hewitt was already with the dead. He shook his head. "There is barely enough to bury sir. And the K gun is buggered."

Beaumont went to the bloodied battle dress of Jimmy Smith and took out a letter. It was holed and bloody. "It was to his mum sir. She was all that he had. I'll copy it out and then write a letter of my own."

I knew how he felt. Losing a good friend in war was hard.

We laid the dead together and then began to clear our lines of debris. "Think they will come again, sir?"

"I don't know, Gordy." I could hear gunfire to the north and south of us. "Someone is still fighting. Take charge, Gordy. I am going to the house to have a look-see."

When I reached the top I could see smoke everywhere. My binoculars showed me where vehicles burned. Then I saw a sight which gave me hope, it was a line of tanks and they were coming from our lines. Someone had summoned armour. Now we had a chance. When I returned to the castle I saw that the men were ready for the next attack. "I think we might have a lull for a while. One man in two go and get some food and bring it back for the others."

One of Sergeant Thompson's men said, "Where from sir?"

Sergeant Thompson growled, "Are you a Commando or not Ridley?"

"Sorry, Sarge!"

The rest of the day passed without an attack and we rested. A spotter aeroplane, one of ours lazily circled for an hour during the afternoon. Some anti-aircraft guns tried to discourage it but they failed. Then it flew west. At dusk a runner from headquarters found us. He looked relieved when he found us. "Major Styles said you would still be here sir but from the smoke, we saw I had my doubts."

"Any orders Private?"

"The Major did not want to write this down but he said there will be an attack on the Germans tomorrow. The Jocks are coming in, sir. They are going to attack Bréville-les-Monts, sir."

"And?"

"And what sir?" He looked confused.

"What are we to do?"

"Oh, he said that we were to hold. If he needs you to do anything sir he will use the radio."

"Thank you. Then tell him we are down to ten men who are fit to fight. We are a little restricted in what we can achieve."

Gordy said, "Aye, tell him Berlin is out of the question!"

He saluted and left us. "Well, gentlemen it seems we have a chance."

"Unless they come again in the morning sir. We are down to less than forty rounds each!"

"Right, after dark we will see what we can get from the dead!"

We were undisturbed as, like grave robbers of old, we took the guns and ammunition from the dead Germans. By dawn, we had enough to hold them off if they attacked. In the event, they did not for we had a front-row seat to the attack of the Highland Division on Bréville-les-Monts. The Scottish Division had Bren carriers and were supported by the Hussars. We saw the battle unfold in pieces as the fighting came back and forth before us moving in and out of sight behind hedges, woods and buildings. They lost most of their vehicles but the Scots managed to take the outskirts before being forced back to the 9th Airborne sheltering in the woods. Things looked grim and, as night fell the Germans still held Bréville-les-Monts. Scouse came running over. "Sir, it's Major Styles. He wants to speak with you."

"Yes, Major."

"We have had a bad day today, Harsker. Not us personally but the Highland Division has been badly knocked about. Brigadier Hill is going to use everything we have to attack at twenty-two hundred tonight." He paused. "Lord Lovat intends to use whatever spare men we have to support them."

I shook my head. The words blood and stone came into my head. "Sir I have ten men who are fit to fight."

"And that is ten more men who can help, Harsker. I know you have done more than enough but just one more push. Lord Lovat is going in too. When you hear the pipes then you know where he will be."

I sighed. I knew when I was beaten, "Right sir, and our objective?"

"Support the 12th Paras; Lieutenant Colonel Johnson. They are attacking the crossroads. You know it. That is where you were the other day."

"Right, sir. We go in at twenty-two hundred?"

"There will be an artillery barrage first then you go in. Your start line is the road close to your position."

"Aren't there Germans there, sir?"

"Aerial reconnaissance reckon they have consolidated in Bréville-les-Monts."

That made sense. "Right, sir. We could do with some medical attention for our wounded sir."

"As could we all. Do your best eh Tom. We are counting on you."

"Are you coming along too sir?"

"We will be approaching from the other side. Hopefully, we will meet in the middle eh?"

"Yes sir."

I gathered my men around them. I owed it to them all to give them the news at the same time. "We are going to help the 13th tonight." They took it stoically enough. "I will only take the men who are fit. That means just ten of us. Lance Sergeant Hay, I am leaving you in command. Hopefully, this will be the last battle for us. I have told the Major that we need pulling out. Be ready at twenty-one hundred. Get some rest and get some food!"

I handed my sniper rifle to Bill Hay. He nodded. "I'll look after it, sir. Just until you get back."

I began to fill my battle dress pockets with ammunition and hung grenades from my assault jerkin. I made sure that my guns were both loaded. I fitted the silencer. Attacking in the dark that might just give me the edge. I blacked up. It was a habit but it worked. I made sure that the backs and palms of my hands were also camouflaged.

I drank my water bottle and had Scouse refill it for me. When he handed it to me he said, "I can come with you, sir. I have one good hand!"

"I need you here on the radio and we need men who have two good hands. Thanks for the offer, Fletcher. One of these days you will make sergeant. If I make it back then I will recommend you."

"Don't be daft sir, of course, you will make it back!"

I saw Bill Hay watching me. "Sergeant Barker, Private Davis and Corporal Hewitt are the only three left from our section who are still alive and don't have wounds. The odds are not looking good."

"Forget the odds, sir. We are the best section in the Brigade and that's no lie. We have been in worse positions than this.

We'll see yer in the morning, sir, when you and the lads walk back here. We'll have a brew on."

I brightened, "You have tea?"

"Not yet sir but that runner from headquarters reckon they have some there. When it gets nice and dark..."

"I don't need to know the details, Fletcher."

Nine o'clock soon came. The ten of us gathered by the tank, "Well chaps if I don't make it back I want you all to know that is has been an honour to serve with you. I could not ask for better comrades. You have truly been as close to me as any brother I might have had."

Bill Hay said, quietly, "Keep that story for after the war eh sir? We'll sit in a pub and talk about these times." The ones who were remaining behind all stood, even Beaumont, and saluted. I returned the salute and then I turned and led the men down the hill.

We halted at the road. This was our jump-off point and I did not want to advance any further. I believed Air Reconnaissance but I did not wish to stray into the maelstrom of an artillery barrage. We waited in silence. It was a deathly quiet night and sound travelled a long way. I looked at my watch. It was suddenly illuminated as the first shells were fired. Naval guns added their firepower to the Royal Artillery. Then the Germans fired their own in reply. It was an aerial duel. The field before me was suddenly filled with craters as the Germans shelled it. We dived into the ditch. It was confirmation that they had pulled back.

The barrage had diminished enough by ten so that we could risk the field. Knowing that the land was empty between us and the village we ran. I heard small arms fire ahead. I took out my silenced Colt. I avoided the roads and ran, instead, across the rough ground which bordered the outlying houses. As we ran I was aware that the German bombardment had stopped but mortars were still being fired. I saw ahead a knot of paratroopers. Thankfully they wore their berets. Their helmets looked very similar to the German ones. Even as we hurried towards them a shell fell amongst them and killed them all.

I knew that the crossroads was not far ahead. A furious firefight was going on. As we approached a shell exploded in a building and I saw, by its light, German soldiers setting up a machine-gun. A hundred yards away I saw British soldiers. If the machine-gun fired they would be slaughtered. I waved my men forward. Flames began to flare up from burning buildings and the fire caught hold. Soon it was like daylight to our left. I fired my silenced weapon. There were enough men ahead that I did not need to aim. One fell and the others looked at his body wondering how he had died. I fired again and this time my men fired too. The delay saved us for we were upon them before they could bring their weapons to bear. I emptied the Colt at point-blank range and then used it like a club.

"Get the machine-gun turned!"

As the last of the gunners was slain I spied more Germans coming from the east. Then a stick of paratroopers ran up to us. "Sergeant White of 3rd Platoon, A company 12th Airborne Battalion. Thanks, sir, you saved our bacon."

"Harsker of Number 4 Commando. Spread your men out, Sergeant. How many do you have?"

"There are just nine of us."

"And I have ten. We have double the numbers eh? Spread your men out and take cover. We will hold. Lord Lovat is supposed to be coming down that road."

"Right, sir."

I quickly reloaded my gun as Barker and Davis swung the machine-gun around. My men had placed the German bodies in front of the gun to afford some protection. machine-gun fire and grenades ahead told us that the battle was raging on the other side. We had our crossroads but it was tenuously held.

The Sergeant came back to me. "The men are in their positions, sir. But we are short of ammo. "

"Some of your lads were ambushed up the road aways. I know it is gruesome but..."

"Don't worry sir the dead don't mind and we are getting used to it." He hesitated, "Any survivors?"

I shook my head, "A 75mm shell. They knew nothing about it."

"Best way, sir. I'll go and get their ammo." He gestured back to his men. "No point in upsetting the lads." Sergeant White was a real leader. He looked after his men like a mother hen. He ran down the lane we had used for our approach.

We had been spied by the Germans. Bullets came our way. "Hold your fire until I say." I took out a grenade and placed it on the garden wall next to me. I was a little exposed but I had to have a good view. I wanted to inflict the maximum casualties with the small number of men under my command. Sergeant White ran back. His face was grim. He just shook his head and then began to distribute the ammunition.

My beret was suddenly plucked from my head. Gordy grabbed my arm and jerked me down, "Use some sense, sir! You are the only officer left!"

The advancing line was now a hundred yards away. "Fire!"

The MG 42 is a good weapon and it chopped its way across the ground to hit the Germans now lit up by the burning village. They were veterans. I could see that. They threw themselves to the ground and returned our fire. Some rolled to the side and took cover in the buildings along the side. My hope was the fire. If it drew close enough it might make them break cover and then we could shoot them. I had emptied my Colt and I now began to fire my Luger. I husbanded my bullets. I regretted now not bringing the rifle. The fire had made it easier to see the enemy. I saw a gun rise from behind a wall and I took aim on the gun itself. Sure enough, a head began to appear and I fired three shots. The head jerked back.

A German voice shouted, "Quick, Reckow, take five men around the back and flank them!"

I said to Gordy, "You and Davis come with me. They are trying to flank us. Sergeant White take command!"

"Sir!"

Picking up my grenade we turned and went back to the end of the village. I led them through the garden of the house. A shell had opened one room. When we got to the back garden there was a gate leading to a narrow path. We stepped on to it. As we did so the six Germans appeared. We saw each other simultaneously. I dropped to one knee and emptied the Luger. Davis sprayed with his Thompson and then fell behind me. I pulled the pin and threw it. "Grenade!"

Gordy dropped to the ground as I did but cried out. He had been hit. The concussion deafened me. I stood and drew my Colt. They were all dead. Gordy had been hit in the left arm. I looked around and saw that Davis had been hit in the side. His wound was more serious. I reached in to my assault jerkin and took out a field dressing. I opened his battle dress and pressed it next to the wound.

Gordy had fashioned a crude tourniquet around his arm. "I am fine sir. Let's get the lad back to Hewitt!"

Between us, we managed to get Davis on his feet. We carried him through the narrow path to the front of the house. The firefight was still going on and they needed me. "Hewitt!"

Corporal Hewitt ran towards us. "Two for you. Give me your Thompson!"

He thrust his gun into my hand and, cocking it, I ran to the line. The Germans had encroached further. I emptied the magazine in their direction oblivious to the bullets screaming past my head. I saw that two of the Airborne were down. We were losing. We had to hold! I fired a long burst from my Thompson then I took another grenade from my assault jerkin and hurled it high in the air. "Grenade! Down!" It exploded in the air. Although we were showered with small pieces of shrapnel the force was borne by the advancing Germans.

Suddenly the air was filled with the sound of shells being dropped. They were 25 pounder shells! We were being shelled by our own side! Luckily for us, we were on the ground and it was the Germans who took the full force of the barrage. When it stopped I could hear nothing. I stood, dazed. The Germans were dead or fled. We held the crossroads. I looked at Sergeant White, he was grinning and he held his thumb up. I nodded and pointed towards the village. He nodded. I went to Hewitt. Gordy was smoking, his arm in a sling. "Sir, Davis needs a doctor. I have stopped the bleeding but God knows what damage has been done."

I put my arm around him, "You have worked miracles, John. We will get a doctor."

I was not sure if I was telling him what I hoped or I believed. I had lost the ability to think.

Sergeant White shouted, "Sir! Someone coming!"

"Stand to!"

I put another magazine in the Thompson, "Stand to!"

We watched and waited. We had sent one company packing. We could not withstand an attack from a second! I saw the uniform of the paratroopers. It was the 12th. Colonel Parker, heavily bandaged, walked resolutely towards us. Sergeant White saluted, as did I.

Colonel Parker shook the Sergeant's hand and then mine. "Well done chaps. The village is ours. We have won." I grinned from ear to ear. He looked at me. "Well done Captain. Sorry about Lord Lovat."

"What sir?"

"Didn't you know? A shell hit the command post. I got this and Lord Lovat was wounded. We have no idea how he is. But he would be proud of you."

It seemed that the gods of war were indifferent in their games. You could be a lord and still suffer the same fate as a Cockney whose mother would grieve for the rest of her days. I slumped to the ground. We had won and yet, was it worth the price.

Epilogue

On the 13th of June, the Royal Ulster Rifles relieved us. We were sent on foot back to Ouistreham. It was filled now with lorries and men. We had our fingers in Normandy and we would hold on to it. Davis had been taken to a hospital. The Irish doctor who tended to him was confident that he would survive. Gordy left too. It was just Corporal John Hewitt and myself who waited at the quayside of the Orne Canal waiting for our ride back to England. He looked drawn. My corporal had worked wonders. He had fought as hard as any and he had saved so many lives that I could not even begin to count them.

"I shall put you in for sergeant, John."

He shook his head, "No sir. That would mean I would leave the section and I don't want that. The lads are too important. I have put them all back together, save yourself, sir. Part of me is in each of them. This can't go on much longer. I will stay with this section and see it through, if it is all the same to you, sir."

"I think you know me well enough to know the answer to that one, John. I could not be happier."

"Ey up sir! You made it!"

I looked up and saw Fletcher, Hay and the rest of my walking wounded limping down the quay.

Bill Hay grinned, "I knew you would make it." Then he frowned, "Gordy and Davis, sir?"

"They are alive. They have both got wounds. They will survive. All thanks to Corporal Hewitt here."

Fletcher put his arm around Hewitt. "I reckon I owe you a pint my Geordie friend!"

"That is Middlesbrough you Scouse ignoramus! I am not a Geordie! We live on the Tees and not the Tyne."

"Same thing!"

Hewitt shook his head and I smiled. We would win the war. Men like this told me that they would. They did not give in and no matter what the problem they dealt with it. I was proud to be their leader. Churchill had once said the 'beginning of the end' now I could see the end. We would push the enemy back to Germany and then we could go home. I now had a future. I had Susan!

The End

Glossary

Abwehr- German Intelligence
ATS- Auxiliary Territorial Service- Women's Branch of the British Army during WW2
Bisht- Arab cloak
Butchers- Look (Cockney slang Butcher's Hook- Look)
Butties- sandwiches (slang)
Chah- tea (slang)
Comforter- the lining for the helmet; a sort of woollen hat
Corned dog- Corned Beef (slang)
Ercs- aircraftsman (slang- from Cockney)
Fruit salad- medal ribbons (slang)
Gash- spare (slang)
Gauloise- French cigarette
Gib- Gibraltar (slang)
Glasshouse- Military prison
Goon- Guard in a POW camp (slang)- comes from a 19thirtys Popeye cartoon
Jankers- field punishment
Jimmy the One- First Lieutenant on a warship
Killick- leading hand (Navy) (slang)
LRDG- Long Range Desert Group (Commandos operating from the desert behind enemy lines.)
Marge- Margarine (butter substitute- slang)
MGB- Motor Gun Boat
Mickey- *'taking the mickey'*, making fun of (slang)
Micks- Irishmen (slang)
MTB- Motor Torpedo Boat
ML- Motor Launch
Narked- annoyed (slang)
Neaters- undiluted naval rum (slang)
Oik- worthless person (slang)
Oppo/oppos- pals/comrades (slang)
Pom-pom- Quick Firing 2lb (40mm) Maxim cannon
Pongo (es)- soldier (slang)
Potato mashers- German Hand Grenades (slang)
PTI- Physical Training Instructor

QM- Quarter Master (stores)
Recce- Reconnoitre (slang)
SBA- Sick Bay Attendant
Schnellboote -German for E-boat (literally translated as fast boat)
Schtum -keep quiet (German)
Scragging - roughing someone up (slang)
Scrumpy- farm cider
Shooting brake- an estate car
SOE- Special Operations Executive (agents sent behind enemy lines)
SP- Starting price (slang)- what's going on
Snug- a small lounge in a pub (slang)
Spiv- A black marketeer/criminal (slang)
Sprogs- children or young soldiers (slang)
Squaddy- ordinary soldier (slang)
Stag- sentry duty (slang)
Stand your corner- get a round of drinks in (slang)
Subbie- Sub-lieutenant (slang)
Tatties- potatoes (slang)
Thobe- Arab garment
Tommy (Atkins)- Ordinary British soldier
Two penn'orth- two pennies worth (slang for opinion)
Wavy Navy- Royal Naval Reserve (slang)
WVS- Women's Voluntary Service

Maps

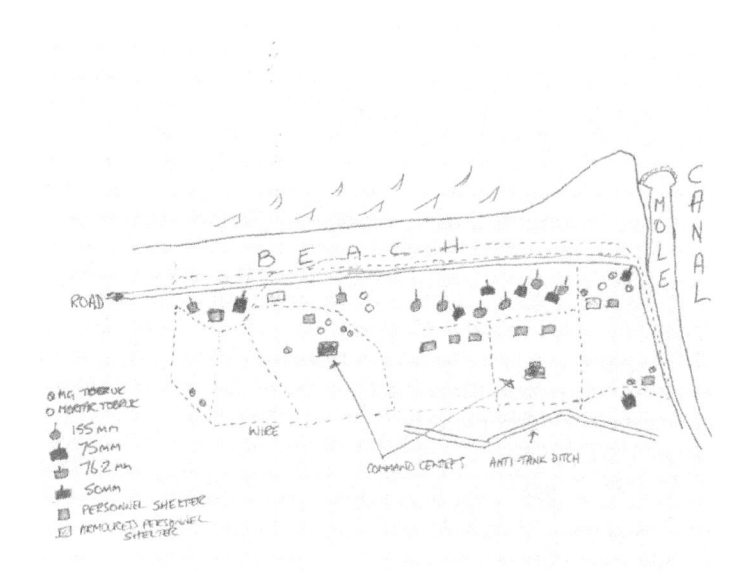

Riva-Bella/Ouistreham defences
Author's collection after Stephen Chicken

Historical note

The first person I would like to thank for this particular book and series is my Dad. He was in the Royal Navy but served in Combined Operations. He was at Dieppe, D-Day and Walcheren. His boat: LCA 523 was the one which took in the French Commandos on D-Day. He was proud that his ships had taken in Bill Millens and Lord Lovat. I wish that, before he died I had learned more in detail about life in Combined Operations but like many heroes, he was reluctant to speak of the war. He is the character in the book called Bill Leslie. Dad ended the war as Leading Seaman- I promoted him! I reckon he deserved it.

'Bill Leslie' **1941**
Author's collection

I went to Normandy in 1994, with my Dad, to Sword beach and he took me through that day on June 6th 1944. He also told me about the raid on Dieppe. He had taken the Canadians in. We even found the grave of his cousin George Hogan who died on D-Day. As far as I know, we were the only members of the family ever to do so. Sadly that was Dad's only visit but we planted forget-me-nots on the grave of George. Wally Friedmann is a real Canadian who served in WW2 with my Uncle Ted. The description is perfect- I lived with Wally and his family for three months in 1972. He was a real gentleman. As far as I know, he did not serve with the Saskatchewan regiment, he came from Ontario. As I keep saying, it is my story and my imagination. God bless, Wally.

The Hitler order

Top Secret
Fuhrer H.Q. 18. 10 1942

1. For a long time now our opponents have been employing in their conduct of the war, methods which contravene the International Convention of Geneva. The members of the so-called Commandos behave in a particularly brutal and underhanded manner; and it has been established that those units recruit criminals not only from their own country but even former convicts set free in enemy territories. From captured orders it emerges that they are instructed not only to tie up prisoners, but also to kill out-of-hand unarmed captives who they think might prove an encumbrance to them, or hinder them in successfully carrying out their aims. Orders have indeed been found in which the killing of prisoners has positively been demanded of them.

2. In this connection it has already been notified in an Appendix to Army Orders of 7.10.1942. that in future, Germany will adopt the same methods against these Sabotage units of the British and their Allies; i.e. that, whenever they appear, they shall be ruthlessly destroyed by the German troops.

3. I order, therefore:— From now on all men operating against German troops in so-called Commando raids in Europe or in Africa, are to be annihilated to the last man. This is to be carried out whether they be soldiers in uniform, or saboteurs, with or without arms; and whether fighting or seeking to escape; and it is equally immaterial whether they come into action from Ships and Aircraft, or whether they land by parachute. Even if these individuals on discovery make obvious their intention of giving themselves up as prisoners, no pardon is on any account to be given. On this matter a report is to be made on each case to Headquarters for the information of Higher Command.

4. Should individual members of these Commandos, such as agents, saboteurs etc., fall into the hands of the Armed Forces through any means – as, for example, through the Police in one of the Occupied Territories – they are to be instantly handed over to the SD

To hold them in military custody – for example in P.O.W. Camps, etc., – even if only as a temporary measure, is strictly forbidden.

5. This order does not apply to the treatment of those enemy soldiers who are taken prisoner or give themselves up in open battle, in the course of normal operations, large-scale attacks; or in major assault landings or airborne operations. Neither does it apply to those who fall into our hands after a sea fight, nor to those enemy soldiers who, after air battle, seek to save their lives by parachute.

6. I will hold all Commanders and Officers responsible under Military Law for any omission to carry out this order, whether by failure in their duty to instruct their units accordingly, or if they themselves act contrary to it.

The order was accompanied by this letter from Field Marshal Jodl

The enclosed Order from the Fuhrer is forwarded in connection with destruction of enemy Terror and sabotage troops.

This order is intended for Commanders only and is in no circumstances to fall into Enemy hands.

Further distribution by receiving Headquarters is to be most strictly limited.

The Headquarters mentioned in the Distribution list are responsible that all parts of the Order, or extracts taken from it, which are issued are again withdrawn and, together with this copy, destroyed.

Chief of Staff of the Army
Jodl

LC(I)523 leaving Southampton taken (I think) from LC(I)527 the Flotilla leader.
From my Dad's Collection

Operation Tiger was the name given to the practice attacks on the south coast. German E-boats did attack the convoy and almost a thousand Americans lost their lives. There were problems with signals as well as with training on life vests. Many Americans died because of incorrectly fitted jackets.

The Battle of Bréville was called one of the major battles of World War II. The Commandos and the Airborne Division had to fight off two infantry divisions and the 21st Panzer Division. The 21st had been part of the Afrika Korps. As such they were veterans. Until the 6-pounder anti-tank guns were dropped by parachute on the 90th of June they had to fight them off with PIATs and grenades. The counter-attack of Bréville did take place. It was stormed and then the Commandos were withdrawn back to the ridge. Theirs was a holding action until the main attack could break out of Caen. The battle was won on June 12th. Had they not held then I wonder if the main attack might have been halted.

Reference Books used
- The Commando Pocket Manual 1949-45- Christopher Westhorp
- The Second World War Miscellany- Norman Ferguson
- Army Commandos 1940-45- Mike Chappell
- Military Slang- Lee Pemberton

- World War II- Donald Sommerville
- St Nazaire 1942-Ken Ford
- Dieppe 1942- Ken Ford
- The Historical Atlas of World War II-Swanston and Swanston
- The Battle of Britain- Hough and Richards
- The Hardest Day- Price
- Overlord Coastline- Stephen Chicken
- Disaster at D-Day- Peter Tsouras
- Michelin Map #102 Battle of Normandy.

Griff Hosker June 2016

Other books by Griff Hosker

If you enjoyed reading this book, then why not read another one by the author?

Ancient History

The Sword of Cartimandua Series
(Germania and Britannia 50 A.D. – 128 A.D.)
Ulpius Felix- Roman Warrior (prequel)
The Sword of Cartimandua
The Horse Warriors
Invasion Caledonia
Roman Retreat
Revolt of the Red Witch
Druid's Gold
Trajan's Hunters
The Last Frontier
Hero of Rome
Roman Hawk
Roman Treachery
Roman Wall
Roman Courage

The Wolf Warrior series
(Britain in the late 6th Century)
Saxon Dawn
Saxon Revenge
Saxon England
Saxon Blood
Saxon Slayer
Saxon Slaughter
Saxon Bane
Saxon Fall: Rise of the Warlord
Saxon Throne

Saxon Sword

Medieval History

The Dragon Heart Series
Viking Slave *
Viking Warrior *
Viking Jarl *
Viking Kingdom *
Viking Wolf *
Viking War*
Viking Sword
Viking Wrath
Viking Raid
Viking Legend
Viking Vengeance
Viking Dragon
Viking Treasure
Viking Enemy
Viking Witch
Viking Blood
Viking Weregeld
Viking Storm
Viking Warband
Viking Shadow
Viking Legacy
Viking Clan
Viking Bravery
The Vengeance Trail

The Norman Genesis Series
Hrolf the Viking *
Horseman *
The Battle for a Home *
Revenge of the Franks *
The Land of the Northmen

Ragnvald Hrolfsson
Brothers in Blood
Lord of Rouen
Drekar in the Seine
Duke of Normandy
The Duke and the King

Danelaw
(England and Denmark in the 11th Century)
Dragon Sword *
Oathsword *
Bloodsword *
Danish Sword*
The Sword of Cnut

New World Series
Blood on the Blade *
Across the Seas *
The Savage Wilderness *
The Bear and the Wolf *
Erik The Navigator *
Erik's Clan *
The Last Viking*

The Vengeance Trail *

The Conquest Series
(Normandy and England 1050-1100)
Hastings
Conquest

The Aelfraed Series
(Britain and Byzantium 1050 A.D. - 1085 A.D.)
Housecarl *
Outlaw *
Varangian *

The Reconquista Chronicles
Castilian Knight *
El Campeador *
The Lord of Valencia *

The Anarchy Series England
1120-1180
English Knight *
Knight of the Empress *
Northern Knight *
Baron of the North *
Earl *
King Henry's Champion *
The King is Dead *
Warlord of the North*
Enemy at the Gate*
The Fallen Crown
Warlord's War
Kingmaker
Henry II
Crusader
The Welsh Marches
Irish War
Poisonous Plots
The Princes' Revolt
Earl Marshal
The Perfect Knight

Border Knight
1182-1300
Sword for Hire *
Return of the Knight *
Baron's War *
Magna Carta *
Welsh Wars *

Henry III *
The Bloody Border *
Baron's Crusade*
Sentinel of the North*
War in the West*
Debt of Honour
The Blood of the Warlord
The Fettered King
de Montfort's Crown
Ripples of Rebellion

Sir John Hawkwood Series
France and Italy 1339- 1394
Crécy: The Age of the Archer *
Man At Arms *
The White Company *
Leader of Men *
Tuscan Warlord *
Condottiere*
Legacy

Lord Edward's Archer
Lord Edward's Archer *
King in Waiting *
An Archer's Crusade *
Targets of Treachery *
The Great Cause *
Wallace's War *
The Hunt

Struggle for a Crown
1360- 1485
Blood on the Crown *
To Murder a King *
The Throne *
King Henry IV *

The Road to Agincourt *
St Crispin's Day *
The Battle for France *
The Last Knight *
Queen's Knight *
The Knight's Tale

Tales from the Sword I
(Short stories from the Medieval period)

Tudor Warrior series
England and Scotland in the late 15th and early 16th century
Tudor Warrior *
Tudor Spy *
Flodden*

Conquistador
England and America in the 16th Century
Conquistador *
The English Adventurer *

English Mercenary
The 30 Years War and the English Civil War
Horse and Pistol

Modern History

The Napoleonic Horseman Series
Chasseur à Cheval
Napoleon's Guard
British Light Dragoon
Soldier Spy
1808: The Road to Coruña
Talavera
The Lines of Torres Vedras
Bloody Badajoz

The Road to France
Waterloo

The Lucky Jack American Civil War series
Rebel Raiders
Confederate Rangers
The Road to Gettysburg

Soldier of the Queen series
Soldier of the Queen*
Redcoat's Rifle*
Omdurman*
Desert War

The British Ace Series
1914
1915 Fokker Scourge
1916 Angels over the Somme
1917 Eagles Fall
1918 We will remember them
From Arctic Snow to Desert Sand
Wings over Persia

Combined Operations series
1940-1951
Commando *
Raider *
Behind Enemy Lines
Dieppe
Toehold in Europe
Sword Beach
Breakout
The Battle for Antwerp
King Tiger
Beyond the Rhine
Korea

Korean Winter

Tales from the Sword II
(Short stories from the Modern period)

Books marked thus *, are also available in the audio format.
For more information on all of the books then please visit the author's website at www.griffhosker.com where there is a link to contact him or visit his Facebook page: GriffHosker at Sword Books or follow him on Twitter: @HoskerGriff or Sword (@swordbooksltd)
If you wish to be on the mailing list then contact the author through his website.

Printed in Great Britain
by Amazon